My Uncle the King
The Aliens Book Two

Sherry Derr-Wille

Dedication

I dedicate this book to my friends and loyal readers who enjoy whatever I write.

Prologue

My story begins many years ago when my father, Prince Nicos of Nalo, had a falling out with his twin brother, Prince Miro. Even in the womb they had been bitter enemies, each trying to get the most nourishment and fighting to be the first to be brought into the world by their mother, Queen Liona.

Miro, being the first born, was the heir to the throne. With this knowledge, he lorded his superiority over his two-minutes' younger brother throughout the time they were growing up.

Nicos, although not the heir apparent, soon learned to ignore his older brother and dedicate his life to education as well as military service.

While away on a diplomatic mission to Earth to become Nalo's Ambassador to Earth, he met my mother and fell in love.

Of course, I'm way ahead of my story, so I will let you read that which came before, so you can better understand my background.

Chapter One

Grato prepared to leave his home planet, Plantas. In a matter of days, Plantas would be destroyed and all of the old and infirm people who were staying behind would be no more.

Over the past few weeks, everyone had been planning for this journey. In the distant past, his people had gone to the planet Nalo to help the ancient people settle the land. In addition, they taught the same people to use written language, medicine and mathematics. Likewise, his best friend Ragnar's family went to Seros. Therefore, these were the worlds to which they would return.

Grato and his family were going to be on the first ship to lift off from Plantas while the woman he loved, Tarena, would be in the last ship. He hated the thought of being separated from her for the duration of the journey, but they were going to be mated once they both landed safely. With that knowledge, he decided he could stand the separation.

A week earlier, his family left to go to the first launch site on the other side of the planet. He protested going with his parents because it meant being separated from Tarena for longer than necessary, but it was important for his father, as for his family, to be on the first ship.

He settled into his seat and prepared for lift-off. As their ship soared into the air, he was able to watch the other ships destined for Nalo do likewise. They flew in a perfect formation for several months.

As an engineering expert, he spent many hours every day on the bridge. During those long hours, he was often in contact with the other ships, including the one carrying Tarena and her family.

The first medical officer, Wasla, made a daily trip to the bridge to not only check on those who were flying the ship but also to contact her soon-to-be-mate, Paren, who was on the third ship in the formation.

"Have you been in contact with Tarena today, Grato?" Wasla asked, when she approached him.

"Yes. Everything on their ship is going well. With luck we should reach Nalo without any difficulty within the next month."

"I'll be happy to be on solid land again. Many of our people have developed Time Warp Fever. I pray they will all be well by the time we land."

Grato agreed. He'd heard about the spread of Time Warp Fever and was even starting to feel some of the symptoms of it. He'd experienced a problem with vertigo and developed a nagging headache, but said nothing.

Wasla went about her daily routine, checking everyone on the bridge. By the time she got to Grato, she had a worried expression on her face.

"You don't look so well, my friend. Let me take your temperature."

As much as Grato protested, she soon used her wand thermometer to check his temperature. "I'm afraid I must send you to the sick bay. Your temperature is elevated and I can tell by looking at you, you are experiencing some of the symptoms of Time Warp Fever."

"That's nonsense. You know I'm one of the healthiest people on this ship. I have duties to perform. I don't have time for something like this."

"You do have time for it, son," his father interrupted. "I've noticed several signs of the disease making their presence known in you. It's best if you do as Wasla says. She's our top medical officer."

Reluctantly, Grato gave up his place at the helm of the ship and followed Wasla to the area designated as the sick bay. Even walking those few steps was difficult for him as his balance was now completely off. He was surprised at how much he had to depend on Wasla to support his weight as he made his way through the ship.

Passing through the other populated areas of the craft, he saw the worried expressions on the faces of his friends and family.

Is it possible I show more of the symptoms of this debilitating disease than I first thought?

Once at the sick bay, two nurses insisted on helping him out of his clothes and into a gown. He hated having to disrobe in front of these women, but knew it was necessary. When the fever broke, he was told, he would break out into a sweat and he certainly didn't want to ruin his robes.

The IV had been successfully inserted into his body when the ship began to shudder. IV poles toppled over, people were thrown from their beds, and medical personnel hung onto whatever they could to avoid falling to the floor.

"What was that?"

The question resonated throughout the ship without an answer for many minutes. They remained in an eerie silence until at last the shaking stopped and people were able to return to their seats or beds.

After what seemed like endless hours, Grato's father left the bridge and walked through the ship.

"We have been hit by a meteor shower. I was able to watch what was happening. I am afraid ours is the only ship to have survived. We will be able to make it to Nalo, but our communications with our sister ships as well as the missions to Seros and Earth have been completely destroyed. We will be traveling under diminished power so the remainder of the trip will take longer than anticipated. That being the case, we will also be rationing our food supplies."

Grato didn't know much about medicine but he did know patients suffering from Time Warp Fever needed added nourishment. He thought about his ability to heal. He was in the early stages of the disease and could probably survive until they reached Nalo, but what about the others in their party, who were in more advanced stages?

Once he finally evaluated their status, he thought of the other ships in their fleet. How could they all be lost? Was it even possible Tarena and Paren were dead, taken away from them in the blink of an eye?

Beside him Wasla grieved for the loss of her promised life mate. Shedding tears seemed too unmanly for him, but he couldn't stop the flow of them at the thought of his loss. Tarena was to have been his mate. Now he knew how his friend Ragnar felt when he'd been told Nina was going to Earth while he would be sent to Seros.

Even with the short rations, they managed to reach Nalo only a few days later than they expected. It took several days and a lot of work for the communications officers to be able to communicate with the inhabitants of the planet. It was amazing how advanced these people were. They were able to send out a tractor beam to bring their craft safely to a predestined landing area. Once they safely landed, they were greeted by members of the medical and scientific contingency.

At Wasla's insistence, the medical community of Nalo was told of the Time Warp Fever that affected many of their population.

Grato looked forward to being one of the first of their kind to contact the people with whom they would be living and working, but that was not to be. Instead of meeting with the leaders, medical personnel entered the ship and brought with them stretchers in order to transport those who had Time Warp Fever to waiting air ambulances for transportation to hospitals.

He began to protest but as soon as he left the ship, his father was at his side. "Go with them, son. We have informed them of what you are experiencing, and they are equipped to bring you back to good health."

"Your father is right," Wasla agreed. "I will be going with you and conferring with their healers. You will see, the future for us will be a bright one. Once you are past this illness…"

He knew she left the remainder of what she was saying unsaid. *Our lives were going to be here on Nalo but the lives of our loved ones are gone forever.* He would never be mated with Tarena just as Wasla and Paren would not be together again.

The next few days passed in a blur. At the hospital, he was able to see the broadcasts of the arrival of his people on Nalo. Thankfully, they had been accepted and had begun assimilating themselves into Nalo's society.

It was days later before he was finally well enough to leave the hospital and reunite with the other survivors of his party. While in the hospital, Wasla hadn't left his side. As much as they both grieved the loss of the ones they loved, he knew a relationship was beginning to form.

Chapter Two

Although Grato's passion had been farming, he was grateful to his parents for insisting he pursue a degree in engineering.

Nalo had been through a world war. The results of the war had left their city structures decimated. Added to that was the fact most of the farmland was destroyed, making it impossible to farm in the ways they had for many thousands of years. To stave off starvation, the farmers turned to hot-house farming. While there were several good farmers among their party, they spent their time learning the new advances the people of Nalo were putting to use.

As much as Grato wanted to be out working the land, his engineering degree was in greater demand. There were cities that needed to be rebuilt and a worldwide government to be established. Working with his father and the others, Grato oversaw the building of the cities. He also listened to all the news reports of the new government that was being put in place.

The countries who had democratic governments thought theirs was the best way, while the countries with monarchies argued for a king and queen to rule over the people. In the end a democracy was put in place.

~ * ~

After two years on Nalo, Grato had become an important member of the ruling party of the government. The president, who had been elected, did not seem to have the respect or confidence of all the people.

There were many who were calling for a coup to put a king in place.

Even though he didn't understand the need for a king, he decided if it made the people happy, why not? Besides, the only difference between a king and a president was the pomp that went along with the monarchy. Perhaps someday, the people looking for a king would be satisfied. In the meantime, a president had been elected. He could see no reason for change at this point, considering another election would be held within the next three years.

It was at an official ball when he saw Wasla across the room. He'd heard she'd been appointed to the Ministry of Medicine. Unfortunately, once he became involved in the government, he had no occasion to see her. If it was possible, she was more beautiful than she'd been on the ship during the journey from Plantas to Nalo.

"Wasla," he said, after crossing the room to be by her side. "It's good to see you. I hear there are congratulations in store. How do you like your new position with the Ministry of Medicine?"

"It's been very interesting. I am amazed at how easily the people of Nalo accepted some of the medical breakthroughs we have made. We are also learning many new procedures. It's an exciting time. Enough about me. I hear you are doing well in government as well."

"Everything has turned out well. Considering the Time Warp Fever left me weakened, I am better suited for a desk job than for one of activity in rebuilding this world. I am stationed here in Capitol City, near the hub of all the activities of the government. If I'm not mistaken, you will be transferred here with your new position."

Wasla batted her eyes seductively. "Are you suggesting we should be seeing each other socially?"

Grato wanted to chuckle, but suppressed the urge. "I had a little more than that in mind. I haven't found anyone who piques my interest the way you have."

"We are virtual strangers. We've both been living very different lives since we arrived on Nalo. I must admit I considered the fact you lived in Capitol City when I was approached about the position with the Ministry of Medicine. I've followed your rise in the government and prayed we would meet once I transferred here. I have observed the required mourning period for Paren and am ready to begin a life with someone of the opposite sex. To be truthful, I was hoping we could be a good match."

Grato allowed a smile to cross his lips. He too had observed the allotted period of mourning for Tarena. She wasn't coming back and he needed a woman in his life. What better life mate was there than Wasla? They'd been friends during the flight, as well as while she cared for him both before and after landing on Nalo.

Thus, began their courtship. As much as Grato once loved Tarena, he realized he'd found true love with Wasla. She was a very special woman and he knew they would complement each other not only as mates but also as life partners.

Two weeks later, with the blessing from both of their families, they were joined together for the rest of their natural lives. There were many parties to congratulate the young couple from both of their families as well as ones hosted by the women who were in the highest level of government.

After a honeymoon on the resort island of Permia, they returned to Capitol City and the new home they'd purchased together. With them both having important government jobs, their lives were complete.

~ * ~

Wasla returned home early one evening for a planned night out with her husband. The arrangements were made for the nursemaid to stay longer than usual to care for their daughter. To her surprise, Grato was there ahead of her. From the expression on his face, she knew something unsettling had happened.

"What's wrong?" she asked as soon as she entered their home.

"Nothing is wrong. As you know, our communication system was knocked out during the meteor shower. Even though we were eventually able to communicate with this planet, we were unable to regain communication with the parties who left our planet with us."

9

"That's nothing new."

"I know that. Our technicians have been working day and night trying to establish a connection with our counterparts on Earth as well as Seros. This morning they made contact. Believe it or not, the ship carrying Tarena wasn't hit with the meteors and made it safely to Earth."

Wasla felt her heart fall to the pit of her stomach. The woman Grato loved above all others was alive and well. Would her husband abandon her and their daughter to try to reconnect with Tarena on Earth?

"Isn't that fantastic news?" Grato asked.

"Y-yes, it is. What does that mean for us?"

"I don't understand what you're saying. It means we can have communications with the people, who like us, took to the stars to save our race."

"Can I be assured you aren't going to be leaving to go to Earth?"

Grato pulled her into a tight embrace. "Why would I go there? Everything I have ever wanted is on Nalo. It is possible Tarena and I would have grown apart once we landed here. You are the woman for me. No one else. All of our friends from Plantas have gone on and married people from their new planets. You and are I are not the only couples of our people who have married and perpetuate our race."

"What do you mean?"

"From what the communications officer has told me, Tarena married a man from Earth, and has children with him. Nina is also married to a government official from Earth and they have children. It's the same with Ragnar. Our communications department has learned he married a scientist from Seros. He is not only a doctor but also a college professor. In a few days, our communications specialists are going to be setting up a tele-conference between the three planets. It is so exciting. I can hardly wait to hear about all of their adventures as I'm sure they are anxious to hear about our journey as well."

Wasla relaxed. "I think it's a good thing we were planning to go out tonight. We have something to celebrate."

"Why is it I don't believe you? Are you jealous of Tarena?"

"Not jealous, really. I'm excited to learn the ship carrying Tarena and her party was spared but sad when I think about Paren. He was a good man and for many years I thought we would be mated. Like you, I wonder if our attraction would have survived here on Nalo. We are lucky to have found each other and learned what real love is."

Grato kissed her tenderly. "I'm pleased to know you feel the same way about me as I do about you. None of us who left Plantas on that day are living the lives we thought we would live. I never expected to be a government official. To be truthful I wanted to be a farmer, but with Tarena as my mate, between my engineering degree and hers in mathematics we would have been a good team. The same can be said for you and Paren. He was a great healer and the two of you were well matched. Of course, we cannot dwell on what would have been. The One God had other plans for all of us. From what I've been told the others have made great matches on their respective planets."

"In that case, I think we should be looking at the positive things in our lives. It won't take me long to get ready to go out for the evening. I just want to check on our daughter and change my clothes."

They did enjoy a wonderful evening alone, even though Wasla worried about the scheduled tele-conference with those they'd known on Plantas and who were now scattered throughout the solar system.

~ * ~

Grato made his way to the communication center from his office. He was glad he'd arrived before Wasla. It was hard telling which connection would be made first, but he wanted to be alone with his thoughts when it happened.

He no more than sat down in front of the communications console than Ragnar's face appeared on the screen.

"Grato, is that you?"

"It most certainly is. It's good to see you, Ragnar. From what the communications officer has told me, you've done well for yourself on Seros. I hear you are not only a healer but also a college professor."

"That's true and this is my life mate, Geni. What do you do on

Nalo?"

"You know my expertise was farming. Of course, my parents insisted I study engineering. The farming here is very different from on Plantas. I am glad I have been able to put my engineering degree to use. I have been helping with many building projects but I've been unable to do the heavy lifting I once did. Now I work for the government. The trip to Nalo was harrowing to say the least. Even before we were trapped in the meteor shower, I suffered from Time Warp Fever. Of all the ships in our contingency, ours was the only one to make it to Nalo. I've recently been told about the ship carrying Tarena, along with her father's party, and how they were able to land on Earth."

"You do know she has taken a husband from among the Earthlings?"

"Yes, and for that I am pleased. I, too, have found a mate to share my life. She will be joining me soon. Her name is Wasla. She lost the man she was promised to in the meteor shower. He was on the third ship in our party. The storm hit right after we cleared the area, meaning our ship was safe, but the others were lost. At least we thought they were. I can hardly believe in a short amount of time I will once again see Tarena and know she is happy. We did receive some damage from the meteor storm and our communication system was knocked out, but we made it to Nalo."

The other side of the screen came to life. Grato was immediately looking into the faces of both Nina and Tarena, along with the men they'd married.

"I can't believe you actually survived the meteor shower, Grato," Tarena greeted him. "I've also been told you have taken Wasla as your mate."

"Yes, she will be here soon. Her man was on one of the ships that was lost. As you know, she was trained as a healer and took care of me while I was sick with Time Warp Fever. She is now a member of the Ministry of Medicine. Together we are building a new order for the planet."

The expression on Tarena's face was one of great concern. "It saddens me to think you had to suffer from Time Warp Fever. The disease leaves so many people weakened. My mother was a victim of it and it shortened her life. I am so happy for both of you. You must know I married, also. Here we are called husband and wife. My husband's name is Paul. As for Wasla, I remember her fondly. I am so pleased the two of you were able to find love together."

A commotion behind Grato made him turn away from the screen to see Wasla enter the room.

"Am I too late?" she asked.

"You're right on time. Tarena and I were just talking about you. She is pleased to know we are happy together."

Wasla took the second seat in front of the console. "Tarena, it is wonderful to see you again. We rejoiced to know at least one ship in our party made it to safety. Do you like Earth?"

"It's different, but I do enjoy living here. How about you, Ragnar, was it hard to adjust to life on Seros?"

Grato sat back and listened to the banter between his friends. It was good to see Tarena as well as Nina. They both looked very happy with their lives.

The fantastic stories his friends told were a relief to hear. After suffering Time Warp Fever, and landing on a planet in complete chaos because of the planet-wide war these people had engaged in before their arrival, it was good to hear of the positive survivals of his friends.

The communication between the old friends was disrupted by several solar storms that happened with great regularity.

"I wish we would have had more time to talk," Wasla said, wiping the tears from her eyes when the screen went black.

"You know how these interplanetary connections are. Between the solar storms and the meteor showers it's a wonder we were able to connect with them at all."

"I know you're right, but it was so good to see the friends who left Plantas at the same time as we did."

Grato agreed with his life mate. It was good to see them, but seeing

Tarena with her husband brought a lump to his throat. As much as he loved Wasla, he still harbored feelings for Tarena. It was one thing he would never admit to Wasla. Their love was far different from the young love he had for Tarena. Finding love in a more mature way was something he couldn't begin to explain even to himself.

Chapter Three

Several days later, Grato wondered if he should have been so positive about living and working on Nalo.

For months there had been rumblings of people within the government who wanted to overthrow the current regime. The 'President' the people wanted so badly was nothing more than an idiot whose only agenda was for his own gratification. The good of the people wasn't being considered. In fact, it seemed as though he didn't care about or understand what the people of Nalo needed to rebuild their planet.

In the past week, Grato had been asked to join a secret society. It was this group of men, all using code names, who met by media-com to discuss the situation of the new world-wide president. The election had been a sham and the man they'd elected turned out to be little more than a pompous ass.

"Something has to be done," Agent 232 stated. "This man is a laughing stock to the people and is draining the resources of this planet faster than they can be restored."

"I know this has to happen, but what will become of the government?" Agent 333 questioned.

"Before the war, we talked of having a king. You know, like we did in ancient times after the Gods left us. It seems to me things worked quite well then," Agent 434 replied.

Grato didn't join in the conversation. The Gods they spoke of were the ancestors of his people. They were mere mortals and came from Plantas to do good, not to be worshiped.

"Where would we find this king?" Agent 333 asked.

For the first time, Grato thought he knew the answer. "There is one among the newcomers who has come to Nalo. I have heard he was the grandson of the last ruler of their planet. His name is Hedro."

His suggestion prompted much discussion among the anonymous conspirators. Knowing he'd put the name out there, he could now sit back and let others consider his suggestion.

~ * ~

"Have you heard the rumblings?" Grato asked Wasla that evening when they returned to their home.

She shot him a glance that said it was best if they didn't discuss this until after the nursemaid, they'd hired for their daughter, left for the evening. It was possible she'd heard what the secret society was doing and knew it was best not to speak of it in front of the woman who watched their daughter, Felda. It was hard to tell where anyone's loyalties were assigned.

Since their daughter ate her evening meal before they arrived home and was ready for bed, they took the little time they had to play with her before beginning to prepare their evening meal.

"The older she gets, all of this will change," Wasla commented. "I hate the fact we get home so late. I'll be happy when she is old enough to eat her evening meal with us."

"You know we'll still get home late every evening. By that time, she will be in school. Maybe we should think about another child. According to the laws here, we are allowed to have two children." He gave her a sly wink.

"I know what you're thinking and I agree with you, completely. Perhaps we can start working on this when the nonsense of rebellion has passed."

Wasla's comment took Grato by surprise. "What have you heard of this rebellion?"

"I heard one of the top members of our agency say the President has gotten wind of what is going on and has said he will have anyone involved in the conspiracy killed. I'm afraid if the conspirators don't act soon, there will be a bloodbath. I agree our President is completely incompetent. He only speaks to hear his own voice. He has no idea what the consequences of what he says or does will be."

Grato heard the same things but prayed they weren't true. Thank goodness his government job wasn't a high-profile one. He knew, no matter what his personal thoughts of the administration, his life wasn't in danger. It wasn't, unless his participation in the secret society were to be revealed.

Outside, sirens suddenly rent the air and it was as if the entire world was ending.

"What's happening?" Wasla shrieked. "Have we left one dying planet for another?"

Before Grato could answer, the in-home communicator began to broadcast. "The President has been assassinated. Stay in your homes. There has been a coup and it is dangerous for anyone to be on the streets."

"I can't believe it's happened so soon." Grato hardly realized he'd voiced his thoughts aloud.

"What do you mean?"

"I've been hearing the rumors for several days now, but I didn't think anything would come of it."

"You knew? Why didn't you tell me?"

Grato shook his head in dismay. "I thought it was just talk. Like before we left Plantas. You know there were always rumors of people wanting to overthrow the government, but nothing ever came of it because of the impending death of our planet. I thought it would be the same here. I never thought I would witness a coup. I've heard people calling it a coup. That's what came over the communicator. I have to tell you, some of the people behind this are those who came with us. They have no confidence in the President. I pray there will not be another war. Hopefully this will be as peaceful as everyone has said it would be."

"How could any of our people be behind this horrible thing? We have always been a peace-loving people."

Grato debated about how much he should share with Wasla about his involvement in this coup that was now taking place.

"I've been part of a secret society who has been meeting to plan for this minute in our history. It is what is best for this planet we now call home. The plan was to quietly poison the President sometime in the near future. I just didn't think it would happen today."

"Are you in danger of being arrested for your part in this terrible plan?"

"We have communicated in secret. No one knows the names of the other conspirators. We communicated by Media-com so no one would know our true names by seeing our faces on the telecom. None of us are in danger. This has to be something we never speak of again. If our names get out, it could be a death sentence for not only me but also for you and our daughter. We are only known by code names. I am Agent 636."

Grato realized he shouldn't have worried for his safety. He was but a minor player and no one knew his name. Over the next few days, everyone saw the reality of the coup.

Among the residents of Nalo there had been an audible sigh of relief. After the last planetary war, the idea of a planetary president passed, with few of the citizens realizing what the consequences of that type of government could be.

Dissuaded by the events of the days of the President's rule, many of them looked to the visitors from the stars to set up a monarchy. In the distant past, they were lauded as Gods and their coming was now seen as the realization of the prophecy.

~ * ~

Hedro was surprised when it was suggested he become king of Nalo and establish the monarchy.

"I am honored," he told the committee, who came to tell him of the suggestion made to the citizens of Nalo. "I have not been on this planet very long. How do you know if I am qualified to rule?"

"We have consulted with many people who came with you from the stars. They have told us you are trained in the ways of governing people. Your father, as his father before him, has been a fair and compassionate leader. We are certain you will do the same for the people of Nalo."

For a moment Hedro could find no words. "Like I said, this is an honor. I have been trained in the ways of governing people and I pray to the One God I will be able live up to your expectations."

"Are you saying you will accept our suggestion you become our king?"

"On one condition. I want to be able to pick my advisors. I have made many friends within the current government with people of both Nalo and the people who came with me when we left Plantas."

"We trust your choices. I see no problem with the people accepting anyone you would appoint to these people from both communities."

~ * ~

In the days that followed, the friend Grato suggested, Hedro, was crowned the first king of Nalo. The people worshiped him and his family as they had the ancients who first came to Nalo with the knowledge of language, mathematics, medicine, and the written word.

For Grato, Hedro was the perfect man to bring the planet under control. He'd been the grandson of the King of Plantas, as well as his namesake. Had it not been for the destruction of their home planet, he would have been a very important man in the government.

Wasla and Grato were relaxing after a long day of work for both of them, when there was a knock at their door.

"Hedro," Grato greeted him. "To what do we owe the pleasure of having you visit our home?"

"I have come on official business, my friend. I have been given free rein to choose the people who I want to be my advisors. I can think of no one better for the head of the department for rebuilding our planet than you. Not only because of the job you have been doing in the rebuilding of Capitol City, but also for your expertise in farming. It isn't just buildings that need to be restored, but also the farmland around the city. The hot-house farming is working but it's only a stop-gap solution. With your knowledge you will be able to restore the farmland around the city to what it once was."

Grato couldn't believe what he was hearing. Not only would his engineering degree be of use on this planet, but he could also indulge in his passion for farming the land.

Against Wasla's better judgement, Grato took the high-ranking job Hedro offered. It didn't take long for him to become one of the chief advisors to King Hedro. His position within the administration also brought Wasla into the inner circle of the ruling family. Their daughter, Felda, along with their son, Valen, were raised with the royal children as members of the court.

~ * ~

Felda loved being the playmate of King Hedro's son, Palen. They were both the same age, and with her father being a member of the king's inner circle, they received the same education.

"What do you plan to do with your education?" Felda asked, as they enjoyed eating their lunch in the outside park area of the palace grounds.

"Father says I will succeed him as king, but I plan to do something else before anything like that can happen. My father and I were speaking of the future just the other day. Once our secondary education is finished, he has secured my position at the university to study military tactics."

"Why military?" Felda asked, the panic she felt echoing in her voice.

"Certainly, you have been hearing the news. There has been an intergalactic war. So far, we have not been affected by it, but there is reason for us to be ready should something happen. Father said he trained for the military and said it was the best thing he ever did. He learned discipline and how to take orders. It has helped him in his position as king. Even if the war never comes to us, we will be ready. What about you,

Felda? What will you do when you finish with your schooling?"

"Mother and I both agree I should pursue something other than medicine. It has taken a toll on her life, as she has to work so many long hours. She totally regretted not being the one to raise Valen and me. Don't get me wrong, she is very proud of all her accomplishments. I plan to study to become an educator. I want to teach not only the history of Nalo but also that of Plantas. I am afraid the present will someday overrule the past, and the past should never be forgotten."

"Are you talking about the coup that overthrew the president?"

"Oh, Palen, you are so short-sighted. I'm talking about how the people from Plantas came to Nalo in the long-ago past to help shape the people of this planet. Also, how they returned when Plantas was destined to be destroyed. There is also the history of Nalo, how the people came out of the dark ages and became technical geniuses. Along with that is how they awaited the coming of the sky gods, in other words, the people from Plantas. We also cannot forget the planet-wide war that was waged prior to our parents' landing here. The history of both planets is so interesting it should never be lost to the ignorance of people who don't want to study it."

Before Palen could reply, the buzzer denoting the lunch break was over and classes were to once again begin sounded. Felda picked up the remnants of their lunch before hurrying back into the classroom.

After the school day ended, Felda contemplated their conversation. She thought of the rumors she'd heard about people who doubted much of the history of their planet. If that were the case, the truth of the past could be lost forever within the span of a single generation.

~ * ~

Palen returned from his recent deployment for the military. Although he was anxious to see his father, his heart longed to see Felda. After making the obligatory visit to his father in the throne room, he made his way to the school where he knew Felda would be teaching on the secondary level.

Classes were in session so Palen lingered outside the door to watch through the window and see her teaching these eager minds. Just listening to her talk about the ancient history of Plantas excited him. Over the months he'd been away from Capitol City, he'd thought of nothing but being with Felda. They'd both grown up since that day in the park when they first talked of what the future would bring for each of them.

He loved leading his men as much as Felda loved teaching these children who would be tomorrow's adults and leaders of the planet. Back when she first told him of her desire, he could see no point in it because of her intelligence. With her mind she would have been an ideal candidate for medical school or for scientific research. Watching her now, he knew she made the right choice for her future.

Almost before he was aware of what was happening, a buzzer sounded and the young men and women burst from the classroom hurrying to get to their next class.

"Palen, I didn't know you were back. How long have you been watching me?"

"Long enough to realize whatever you were teaching you had the entire class enraptured. I don't ever remember any teacher being able to mesmerize a class the way you do."

"Perhaps you never had a dedicated teacher. When did you get back?"

"Our ship landed earlier this week, but we had to go through debriefing as well as complete physical and mental examinations. We were dismissed this morning and I will be on leave for the next month. Father wants me to give up the military and join him in the throne room, but the mission we were on is crucial to the peace treaty between our planet and the confederation. They have set up an outpost on Bankos. It has been amazing working with them."

"Are there beautiful women there?" she asked with a sly wink.

"They are all scientists and devoted to their work. None of them are as beautiful as you are. When will you be free to join me for the evening?"

"I have only one more class for today. After that time, I will be able to meet you."

"Good. I'll be here waiting for you to be done. I wouldn't want you to get lost on your way to the palace. While you are teaching, I will be contacting the cook and arrange for a private dinner for the two of us. I certainly don't want anyone else to intrude on our reunion."

A curious look crossed Felda's face. "Is something wrong?" he asked.

"Of course not. I will just have to get word to my parents that I won't be joining them for the evening meal tonight. It shouldn't be a problem, but they do worry when I'm late. You would think I was still a child. I have my own apartment but they still insist I take the evening meal with them as often as possible."

"Are you certain it is your parents who will worry or is there another man who has caught your eye?"

The students were beginning to return to Felda's classroom. Playfully, she pushed him away from her. "Don't be silly. Where would I meet another young man? Many of them have joined the military. Those who haven't are either promised to others or dedicated to their careers. On that note, I'll see you at the palace once my class is ended."

As much as he wanted to take her in his arms, he refrained. He knew it would be improper, even for a prince, to kiss a young teacher in front of her students.

He'd thought he could stay at the school and just send a message to the palace. Since she said she would meet him there, he decided to go back to his quarters and dress for the evening.

~ * ~

"Was that Prince Palen you were talking to?" one of her female students asked.

Felda could feel a blush begin to creep into her face. She did nothing scandalous. It was not because she wasn't tempted but only because she felt the time and place was not right to act on all the dreams she'd had ever since Palen was deployed to Bankos. She'd prayed he would return safely. Even though he hadn't disclosed the destination of his deployment until today, she saw various news reports of the outlying planets where troops were being sent to show the strength of Nalo.

"Yes, it was Prince Palen. He is home from his deployment. It's no secret that we are childhood friends. My brother and I grew up with the prince and princess. The king and queen, along with my parents, came here from Plantas. We have always been close to the royal family. Now, enough about Prince Palen. We need to get back to our study of the ancients and the prehistoric inhabitants of Nalo."

Over the next hour, she outlined how the 'sky gods' came to Nalo and how they were, in fact, space travelers from Plantas. Speaking about how her people came here to teach the local peoples the mysteries of language, mathematics, medicine and the written word, transported her to the planet as it had once been so many eons ago.

The buzzer indicating the school day was ending came as almost a shock. Felda and her students were so engrossed in the lesson, they'd lost all track of time.

When the last of the students were finally out of the school, she took a moment to straighten up her classroom before she went home to change her clothes for her evening with Palen.

"I saw you had a visitor," her best friend and fellow teacher, Dana, said from the doorway.

"Yes, it was quite the surprise. I didn't know Palen was home on leave."

"What's it like to be on a first-name basis with the royal family? You seemed so comfortable in his company."

"It's not hard. Once King Hedro was crowned, he insisted my parents be moved onto the palace grounds. Palen and I grew up together and even had the same nursemaid. It wasn't until we both went to university that we were separated. We are very fond of each other. It's no wonder we are comfortable in each other's company."

"You're not fooling anyone. I saw the look on your face when you were 'talking' to him. You're in love with him."

"Unfortunately, he's in love with his command in the military. We will enjoy being together while he's home on leave. Once his leave time is over, he will be returning, if not to the post he just left, but perhaps another one on another planet in the galaxy."

Saying the words, she knew to be true saddened her and tempered her anticipation of her evening with Palen at the palace. In her dreams she would seduce him and get him to make love to her. With luck, when he left, she would be carrying his child. She knew it was only a dream because it was against the law for sex to be engaged in prior to mating. It was here the same as it had been on Plantas, or so her mother told her.

In the retelling of the trip from Plantas to Nalo, her parents told her how their promised life mates were killed in the meteor shower, only to learn Tarena, the woman her father planned to mate with, had been saved and was now living on Earth. What if her mother had broken with tradition and became pregnant with the child of her promised mate prior to leaving for Nalo? Would she have been shunned? Would she have given birth on the ship heading for Nalo? Would she have been arrested as soon as they landed?

The disturbing possibilities drove all thoughts of seduction of Palen from her mind. She could no more break the law than she could stop breathing.

~ * ~

Palen paced the floor of his apartment in the palace. He knew he should have stayed at the school and waited for Felda. To waste a moment of this evening was something he didn't want to do. Every dream he'd experienced during his deployment revolved around Felda. He wanted her, not as a conquest but as his life mate for the entire length of their lives. Tonight, he planned to ask her to mate with him when he returned from his next deployment. His enlistment would be up and he could join his father in ruling the planet.

His father saw him returning to the palace and insisted on a private audience. Even though he tried to explain about getting ready for his evening with Felda, King Hedro said what he had to say would only take a short amount of his time.

"I have been speaking with your commanding officer. He assures me you are needed back on Bankos, but that your enlistment will be up after this next deployment. While you are on this leave, I pray you will confer with me on the management of the planet."

"I would be honored. I thought, perhaps, you would insist I leave the military before my enlistment is up."

Hedro laughed heartily. "That was my intention until I spoke with your commanding officer. I had no idea how important you are to our military outpost on Bankos. With all of my duties, I neglected the most important duty of all and that is keeping up with what you have been doing during your deployment. I have done you a vast injustice. I am proud of your accomplishments as a father should be. With your military knowledge, you will be a much better king than I will ever be, when the time comes."

"Please do not talk this way, Father. You will live forever. I will be an old man when the time comes for me to take over your throne."

"Ah, the beauty of being young. You must know there has never been anyone on any planet in the galaxy who has escaped death. When the One God deems it is your time to join Him in the afterlife, there is nothing any one of us can do to change it."

They spoke for several more minutes, before his father reminded him of his evening engagement with Felda.

A light knock at the door interrupted his musings about the meeting with his father earlier in the afternoon. Pushing the memory to the back of the mind he opened the door to allow Felda admission to his apartment.

He expected to see her dressed as she had been at the school when he watched her in her classroom. Instead of the casual dress of a teacher, she wore an elaborate robe, a replica of the robes worn by the people from Plantas. Over the years, most of the people had adapted the dress of the people of Nalo, but for special occasions, there were stores specializing in the dress of those who came from the heavens as had been predicted for thousands of years.

"You look beautiful," he greeted her. "If I didn't know better, I would swear you just stepped off the ship that brought our parents to Nalo."

"Why thank you, kind sir."

She looked him up and down, apparently pleased with the regal uniform he'd changed into after arriving at his apartment.

"Won't you come in and make yourself comfortable? I have ordered a special meal for the two of us."

"Do I have to guess what you ordered?"

"I doubt it. I remembered all your favorites. We'll be starting with a green salad, followed by a gazlo steak, baked tuber, and finally that gooey dessert we used to beg for when we were children."

Felda's delicate tongue licked her perfect lips as if in anticipation of the meal Palen just described. "It sounds perfect. As I recall, that was the meal we shared with our parents the night before you were deployed. I haven't had it since."

Without further ado, Palen took Felda in his arms and kissed her in the way he'd wanted to do while at the school. Tonight, there would be no prying eyes and he could ask her the question that burned on his mind ever since their last meal together.

When they broke apart, Felda seemed to be breathless.

"I pray my kiss was not too brazen."

Felda laughed. It sounded like a tinkling bell. "Don't be silly. I have had dreams of seducing you. I know it's against the law, but I want all of you. What if something were to happen to you while you're deployed? I want your baby."

"In due time," Palen said, again taking her in his arms. "I have one year left in my enlistment and I will again be deployed. There is no danger in this mission. As an officer and the Prince of Nalo, I am well guarded. When I return, I want you to be my life mate. That is when we will work on making a baby to carry on our lineage. Will you agree to becoming my partner for the rest of our lives?"

Tears flowed from her violet eyes. "There is nothing I want more in this world."

Before they could say anything more, a knock at the door signaled the delivery of their special dinner.

~ * ~

Felda could feel a blush creeping into her cheeks as the servers brought in the first course of their special meal. Could the servants guess what happened just moments before they knocked? What she wanted to do was shout to the world how Palen just asked her to become his partner for all time. Her dream of a lifetime would be coming true within the span of the next two years.

Once the servants left, they gave thanks to the One God before they began eating.

"When do you think we can announce our engagement?" she asked.

Palen smiled at this question and remained silent for a long moment. "First we will have to tell our parents. I know my father will insist on a royal mating service. It will be the same with your parents. They like all the pomp and circumstance when it comes to something like this. It will be the first royal mating on Nalo and will be very important to everyone. If I had my way, we would run away and be mated privately. Unfortunately, being who we are, it would not be permitted."

"What if your sister decides to become mated before you return from your deployment? Won't her mating be the first royal mating service?"

"Not in the same way as ours. She is a princess and her chosen mate will be royal, but when we are mated, you will become a princess who is destined to become the queen of Nalo. I do not mean to brag. I am only stating a true fact. Once my deployment is over, I will be in training with my father for the time when I will rule. He was trained on Plantas just as I will be trained on Nalo."

Felda thought of the ramifications of the words Palen just spoke. All during their lives they'd been carefree children, raised together. Adulthood changed everything She'd trained as a teacher and Palen trained as a soldier and was soon to be trained as a monarch. Was she ready to become a princess, to say nothing of being a queen?

"I-I never thought about it that way. One day you will be king and I will be your queen. Do you think I am worthy of such an honor?"

Palen reached across the table that separated them and took her hand in his. "Worthy? I know of no one more worthy of being a queen than you are. Even though you aren't a princess, you have been raised within the royal household. Thus, you have an understanding of how the monarchy works. Even if you were nothing more than a commoner, you would be my choice. I have loved you ever since we were children and have longed for the day when I could ask you to become my life mate."

She watched as he reached into the inside pocket of his uniform to bring out the exquisite purple plush jewelry box. Everything seemed to move in slow motion as he flipped open the box to reveal a beautiful ring. The stone was a large clear diammoniate set in a band of golden mineralite intertwined with silver braid.

"I want you to have this ring as a symbol of the love I have for you, until I can add to it the matching mating band."

Tears of joy filled Felda's eyes. "I-I don't know what to say. I will wear this ring with the pride of being your life mate for as long as we both shall live. Like you, I have loved you since childhood and fantasized about mating with you. You have made me the happiest woman on Nalo and I know I can wait for our mating day."

The light from the solar-powered chandelier sparkled off the ring, sending prisms of light radiating onto the walls. Before either of them could say more, the light rap on the door announced the server was coming into the apartment with the main course for the evening's meal.

From the expression on her face, Felda knew the girl noticed the ring on her finger. "Oh, Your Highness, the ring is beautiful."

Palen winked at her broadly. "You must not utter a word about it until we have time to tell our parents. Once that is done, I will personally give you permission to tell the rest of the servants."

"Oh, no, Your Highness. I realize this is a private moment and I shall not mention this to anyone. I am so happy for you and Lady Felda."

As soon as the girl left the room, both Felda and Palen broke out laughing. "How long before you think she will have spread the word to the remainder of the staff?" Felda asked.

"She has been with our family for many years. I think we will be able to trust her with our secret. Just in case her lips are loose with gossip too good not to spread, I think we should make it a point to tell our parents as soon as we finish our dinner."

Felda agreed. If it were up to her, she would throw open the windows and shout the news of her upcoming mating to everyone in the kingdom.

~ * ~

Grato and Wasla made their way to the palace. They'd just finished the evening meal when Grato received a telepathic message from Hedro to meet him in the throne room.

"What could be so urgent for the king to demand our presence at this time of night?" Wasla questioned.

"I have a feeling I know what it could be. Didn't you tell me Felda was dining with Palen tonight?"

"Yes, but what would that have to do a royal summons?"

"Think about it, Wasla: Those two have been close friends ever since they played together as children. The natural progression of things could be the two of them agreeing to a mating ceremony. It is entirely possible tonight was the time when Palen made his intensions a reality. He has been deployed for two years and we both know how much our daughter has missed him."

"I hope that's what it is and not bad news. Remember when Hedro called us to the palace to tell us of Queen Leora's death. Those were dark days for the monarchy."

Grato pulled his wife into a tight embrace. "Let's expect good news. We mustn't let Hedro wait too long for us to arrive."

~ * ~

Felda thought she would burst with the news of her engagement to Palen before they were able to tell their families.

By the time they arrived at the private apartment of Hedro, both of her parents were already there.

"As you requested, my son, we are all assembled. What is this important announcement you have to make?"

Palen shifted from one foot to the other as though he was nervous about making their engagement public knowledge.

"You know I entertained Felda tonight for the evening meal. When we finished, I asked her to mate with me when my enlistment is up next year and she said yes. We hope that will give all of you time to prepare for the royal mating service."

Felda smiled to think Palen was nervous about making the announcement to their parents. Before anyone could say anything, her mother came to her side and gave her a hug. After their embrace, she looked at the ring that now graced Felda's finger.

"Oh, Grato, come and see the beautiful ring Palen has given our daughter."

Felda knew her father wasn't as interested in the ring as he was about seeing her so happy. "You've made a wise choice, Palen. I know you and my daughter have been close friends ever since childhood. I can think of no one I would rather see her mated with. Congratulations and welcome to our family."

"Thank you, Papa. The hardest part of this will be the two of us being separated for another year while Palen finishes his enlistment."

"If you want this wedding to happen sooner, we can make certain you will be released from this obligation," Hedro said.

"I ask for no special treatment. By finishing my military obligation, I will be better prepared for the day when I will be called upon to rule. There is nothing I would like more than to marry Felda as soon as possible, but I know I would forever regret shirking my duty to the planet."

Felda could feel tears threatening to fall, but willed them to stay away. Palen's sense of duty was admirable. Even though she knew she would miss seeing him for the next year, she was so proud of him, she would be willing to wait.

"I agree with Palen," she said. "His deployment will give us time to plan for our mating ceremony. I'm certain both you, King Hedro, and my parents will enjoy having that amount of time to plan for our special day."

Chapter Four

"Do you remember the night when the President was assassinated?" Wasla asked, as they prepared for their daughter's royal wedding.

"It is something I will never forget. You know I was against the President for a long time before his death. Hedro has done fantastic things for Nalo. All of the people have prospered and everyone loves him."

"I'm sorry I was so fearful about your involvement in the coup. I now see it was the best thing that could have happened. That man was pure evil. I expected terrible repercussions over it. Thank goodness, everyone has accepted Hedro. I think he is one of the best-loved rulers this planet has ever seen. I am so pleased to think Felda will someday be queen when she marries Palen. It will be a beautiful mating ceremony."

Grato agreed. He was happy for his daughter, but prayed she was up to the challenge of becoming a queen when the day came for Palen to take his father's place. Of course, that day was far in the future. Hedro was still a young man and in the best of health. He should be, with Wasla as his personal physician.

~ * ~

The next morning the three suns of Nalo were shining brightly, promising the perfect day for a mating. Felda was as nervous as any young woman could be. Even with her mother at her side, it wasn't until Grato came into the room where she was preparing to become Palen's life mate, she finally calmed down.

"Oh, Daddy, I'm so worried about becoming a Royal. I understand I've grown up with all of the same nannies and education as Palen, but I still worry. Palen tells me I shouldn't be concerned, but what if I do or say something wrong?"

"Listen to the man who is to become your life mate, daughter. He has lived a royal life and knows of the pitfalls. He will never allow any of them to capture you. Besides, you have grown up in the shadow of the palace. You are more prepared to begin the life of a Royal than any other young woman I know. Your background as a history teacher has also prepared you for this new role in your life. Now, are you ready to join with him for eternity?"

Felda nodded and allowed him to take her hand in his. As soon as their fingers touched, he remembered her as a small child, so trusting and content to play with the royal children. Now she was going to become one with them. He was losing his little girl as she became a beloved member of the ruling family.

~ * ~

The royal cathedral sparkled with the light of the three suns coming in through the stained-glass windows. Every pew was filled with the loyal subjects of King Hedro as well as family and friends who had made the journey from Plantas to Nalo.

At the front of the sanctuary stood the royal priest, ready to perform the ceremony to join Felda and Palen as life mates for eternity in the name of the One God.

Grato swallowed the lump that formed in his throat. From this day forward his daughter would be Princess Felda. As a member of the royal family she would forever belong to the people.

Forcing himself to remain calm, he walked confidently beside his beautiful daughter. At the altar he saw Palen waiting for the woman who would become his life mate. Grato wished he could turn back time and once again be the most important person in his daughter's life.

Once they stood at the altar, he gave his daughter to Palen, with a kiss on her cheek and a clasp of Palen's forearm.

Reluctantly, he backed away from the couple and took his seat beside Wasla.

"Isn't she beautiful?" Wasla whispered, wiping away a tear with a lace-edged handkerchief.

"She's as beautiful as her mother was on the day we were mated. From that moment forward I have never been able to see another woman but you."

Wasla squeezed his hand reassuringly. Inside he couldn't help but think of Tarena, the woman he'd loved and lost because of the meteor storm. Over the years they enjoyed several conversations between Nalo, Earth and Seros. It was good to see his old friends, but each time he saw Tarena and the man she called her husband, he felt a twinge of jealousy he never dared to tell anyone about. He did love Wasla, but he always wondered what his life would have been like with his first love.

"I now pronounce you mated for life. What the One God has joined, let no one tear apart for any reason."

Grato watched as Palen took Felda in his arms and kissed her for the first time as a mated couple.

As was the tradition, all of the mated couples stood, embraced and exchanged a loving kiss. His wayward mind told him he was kissing Tarena rather than Wasla. For a moment, he engaged in the fantasy of what could never be.

~ * ~

Felda and Palen wasted no time in starting their family. While on their mating trip to a vacation island on the other side of the planet, she conceived her first child.

By the time they returned to Capitol City, they were anxious to have their assumptions confirmed. Their first stop before moving into the home King Hedro had given them as a mating gift was to Wasla's office.

"I'm thrilled to see both of you," Wasla said. "Is there a reason you have stopped by my office? You haven't become ill while you were away, have you?"

"Nothing like that," Palen assured her. "We have come to see if you can confirm my lovely wife is carrying the next generation of the Royal Family of Nalo."

Felda and Palen watched as her mother broke into a wide grin.

"That should be a simple request to grant."

Wasla took her daughter and son-under-the-law into the examination room. After taking blood to be tested in the lab, she produced a diagnostic wand and ran it over Felda's body. Once the electronic diagnosis was completed, she plugged the device into her computer in order to read the results of the examination.

Palen held Felda's hand, knowing they were both excited about the results.

"I do believe your two-month mating trip has produced the heir that the kingdom is waiting for. It looks like in about eight months we will be welcoming a new prince or princess to the family.

"Oh, don't tease us, Mother," Felda said. "You know what the baby will be, I know you do. Aren't you going to tell us?"

"No, I am not going to give you that information. I have heard too many stories about couples who had learned the gender of their unborn child and were disappointed. I know one couple on Plantas before the evacuation, who tried very hard to rid the woman of the child only to have her lose her life. It is best for couples to not know the gender of their unborn child and be surprised once the baby is born."

"You know that wouldn't be us," Felda pressed. "Be the child a boy or a girl it will be warmly welcomed."

"I know it would, but I refuse to do for you what I will not do my other patients. Sometimes the old ways are the best ways."

~ * ~

Becoming a royal princess was more of an adjustment than Felda thought it would be. As soon as news of her pregnancy became common knowledge, her father-under-the-law insisted she should no longer be working as a teacher. He said she could possibly come in to contact with a student who was carrying a disease that could, unwittingly, put her unborn child's life in danger.

Even though her mother contended there was no danger, Palen decided to err on the side of caution and agreed with his father.

At first, she enjoyed staying home, but since the household staff took over all the duties that she had thought would be hers when she married, she soon became bored.

Felda was shocked when King Hedro made plans to send Palen to the other side of the planet on a diplomatic mission when she was in the last days of her pregnancy.

"Doesn't your father know you should be here, as the birth of our child could be at any time?" she pleaded.

"You know my father. He thinks nothing is more important than the ruling of the planet. Women have been having babies since the beginning of time without their mates being with them. Unfortunately, the unrest in the far eastern provinces needs attention and I am the best person to send. Besides, by the time the child is born, I will be back in your arms."

"Why not send one of the diplomats? Are you not too important to risk anything happening to you? As the prince who is destined to become king, I worry for your safety."

"It is no different than when I was in the military. My identity was known by everyone and I was well guarded. Nothing happened to me then and nothing will happen to me now. I will be home before you even have time to miss me."

Eventually, Felda agreed with her life mate and bid him good-bye at the space port. His sky skimmer had no more than lifted off when she felt the first pains of labor take over her body. Telepathically, she contacted her mother, before advising her hover car pilot to take her to the hospital where she would give birth to the next royal prince or princess.

~ * ~

Palen boarded the sky skimmer and watched as Felda waved farewell to him. He understood her concern about him being sent to the other side of the planet. He argued with his father about it when the mission was first mentioned. The excuse his father gave him was that with his military background, he could more easily assess the situation than a diplomat without an understanding of such things.

It didn't take long for his craft to reach cruising altitude and be too far away for him to see his life mate get into the hover car with her pilot to return to their home. With the pilot of his craft at the controls, he was able to relax and enjoy the flight.

He closed his eyes and reviewed the conversation with Felda prior to his flight. She was being overly dramatic. According to his mother-under-the-law, the child was still two weeks away from making its appearance into the world. As he told her, he would be home before anything would happen.

Chapter Five

Palen's craft landed at the space port on the other side of the planet. To his dismay, things were not what he expected. Instead of being met with the highest-ranking officials, militants who were heavily armed were engaging with the royal military.

"What is going on here?" he asked of the major who boarded his ship.

"There has been an uprising. The fighting started only this morning, Your Highness. I am afraid I cannot allow you to disembark. If it weren't for the fact your craft needs to be refueled and out of service for at least a day, I would have you leave immediately."

Palen's anger got the best of him. "Why weren't we told of these hostilities? We could have returned to Capitol City rather than continuing on here. We could have sent additional troops to assist you."

"We know, your highness. Everything happened so quickly. none of us were thinking about anything than handling the uprising to the best of our ability. It wasn't until your pilot requested permission to land that we realized this was the day of your arrival. Things have been a bit out of hand here."

"A bit out of hand? There is an all-out war going on out there. I've served two tours in the military and I know a war when I see one. What is the reason for the uprising?"

"The militants are from those who inhabited Nalo before the refugees from Plantas arrived. They say King Hedro knows nothing of life on this Nalo and they don't feel he is fit to rule. They are young and…"

"And nothing. Arrange for a meeting between me and their leaders. I will contact my father and let him know of the situation here. I doubt anyone has contacted him."

"We haven't, Your Highness, but I don't think it is wise for you to talk to the militants. That should be the job of the diplomats."

Palen took a deep breath before answering the man. "Major Domus, I am trying my best to hold my temper. I cannot see what the diplomats could do in this situation. Contact the leaders of this group and tell them I want to meet within them within the hour. I've had a long flight, I'm tired and hungry. That said, I am the only one here who can handle this situation. I still hold my rank of General in the military and I am ordering you to follow my orders. Do you understand?"

"Yes, Your Majesty."

The major saluted sharply and turned to leave.

"What are you going to do, Your Highness?" his pilot asked.

"I'm afraid we are too far away from Capitol City for me to telepathically communicate with my father. Can you make contact with the palace?"

"I'm trying to get an open channel, but so far am running into interference. I will try to contact the space station and see if they can relay a message from our position to the palace. It shouldn't take much more than a few minutes. I agree with Major Domus, I am concerned about your safety."

"I thank you for your concern. Once you contact my father, let me know."

Palen contemplated his upcoming meeting with the militants. If he couldn't speak to his father before the leaders arrived, he would have to make the decisions on his own.

Major Domus returned to the ship and told Palen he'd made arrangements for a meeting to take place inside the space port. An armed guard waited to take Palen to the meeting room.

"Have your made contact with my father?" he asked.

"Not yet, Your Highness."

"As soon as you make contact patch the call through to my

telecom unit. I will be going with Major Domus to the meeting."

Palen's heart threatened to burst out of his chest in fear. He would be going into this meeting totally unarmed. Anything could happen, in reality he could lose his life before he had a chance to hold his first child. He'd been foolish to take this mission when Felda was so close to delivering the baby.

Once he left the sky skimmer, the sounds of battle seemed to have dissipated completely. It was odd, to not hear anything, when he could see the war being fought as he and his pilot landed at the space port.

The security guard that awaited him made him think of the condemned prisoners being walked to their executions he read about in the numerous history books Felda kept in their library.

The walk from his craft to the headquarters of the space port took only a matter of minutes, but to Palen it felt like an eternity. If these militants were willing to do battle against the superior forces of the royal military, would he be safe meeting with their leaders?

He walked between the two lines of military guards across the building from the access to the sky skimmers awaiting take off or preparing for landing. He was surprised to see there was a pile of weapons on a table outside the door. Seeing them gave him hope. At least these men were honorable enough to abide by the rules of negotiation governing the leaving of weapons outside the meeting chambers. The door opened and he motioned for his guard to remain in the open reception area.

"You shouldn't go in there alone, Your Highness," General Domus advised him.

"I don't plan to go in with a show of force. Being unarmed and alone will speak louder to these people than to have a military escort when they have abided by the rules of negotiation."

"I would like to accompany you, without being armed. If anything were to happen to you…"

"Nothing will happen. Please remain out here with your men. If I need you, I can summon you."

Dear One God, please keep me safe and give me the wisdom to bring about peace with these people. Let me end this conflict and return to the arms of my wife in time to be the first one to hold my first child – Amen.

After sending his silent prayer heavenward, he entered the meeting room.

"Your Highness," an older man addressed him, getting to his feet. "I am Matos, father and grandfather of many of these men. We are honored with your presence."

"Thank you, but I would like to hear the grievance that has prompted the battle I witnessed as I approached the space port."

"I think you should be addressing me," a younger man said as he stood defiantly on the opposite side of the table.

"May I have your name, since I am sure you know who I am?"

"I am called Alden. My family is of pure descent of the planet Nalo."

"I am pleased to make your acquaintance, Alden. May I ask a question of you?"

Alden looked perplexed. "I don't know what question you would have for me, but if that is your wish, what do you want to know?"

"Are you left-handed?"

"What kind of a questions is that? I, like most of my friends, am left-handed."

"Are you not aware that being left-handed is a sign you are 'of the gods'? If I am not mistaken there are many archaeological discoveries in this area of the planet attributed to the early explorers from Plantas who tutored your ancestors in language, written language, mathematics, as well as the knowledge of medicine. Those early explorers came without female companionship. While they were on planet, they mated with many of the women, whom they found to be very beautiful. To this day, descendants of those relationships are left-handed. When you say you are one of the pure descendants of Nalo, you should think again. Perhaps you have not been taught the history, not only of Nalo but also of Plantas."

The color drained from Alden's face. "It can't be. I can trace my family back many generations and…"

"And what? Do you not think such a thing could have happened in the long-forgotten past?"

"Prince Palen is speaking the truth," Matos said, confirming the history Palen read in the books Felda had in their library.

"Stay out of this, grey beard. You are only saying the words the so-called prince is expecting you to say."

"I am your grandfather and if you would have stayed in school rather than being around the hotheads you call friends; you would have learned the history of our planet along with that of Plantas. I have long heard the rumor of left-handed people being descended from the sky gods we worshiped so long ago. When the refugees from Plantas landed on our planet, those rumors were confirmed. I was one of the first to pledge my allegiance to King Hedro. It wasn't a rash decision. I did my research well and know he was the leader we needed."

Alden stood facing the man Palen now knew was his grandfather, his mouth hanging open.

"Why don't we sit down and talk this out?" Palen suggested. "I've had a long flight, I'm tired and hungry, but understanding what is going on here is of the upmost importance to not only me but also to my father, your king."

Everyone took seats around the table and, almost immediately, food was brought. Palen assessed the young men who sat flanking Matos, sitting across the table from him. He felt alone and wished he'd allowed Major Domus to accompany him to this meeting.

"I can understand your resentment from those of us who came to Nalo when our planet was destroyed. Had such a thing occurred the other way round, I have a feeling many of our young men might have felt the same way as you do. We came here as refugees seeking nothing more than a place to relocate and prosper. I doubt many of you are old enough to remember our coming here. I know I don't remember it."

"We've been told you came to take over our planet," another of the young men declared.

"Nothing could be further from the truth. If you read the history of our arrival, you would realize there were several ships that came here from Plantas. They were scheduled to land in various locations throughout Nalo. In reality, only one ship survived the journey. The others were lost in a meteor storm. Those of our party who did arrive were weakened by Time Warp fever. Our medical officers were met with the healers of your planet and we were accepted as the friends we hoped we would be."

"Then, how did your father get to be king over all of Nalo?"

The question was posed by another of the young militants.

"When we arrived, there had been a great civil war and the people were determined to elect a president to preside over the planet. The longer the man was in office, the other leaders were learning not only was he a self-centered buffoon, he was also corrupt. When he was assassinated, people looked for a leader who was just. My father was the son of the last king of Plantas and had been trained to lead the planet. Of course, when the demise of Plantas became known, his father stayed behind with his people and my father came here, knowing he would have to learn a trade for which he wasn't trained. He was the choice of the people."

The faces of the young men across the table from him showed bewilderment. "That is not what we were told."

"Unfortunately, you were given falsehoods. Have there been any causalities on your side of this battle?"

Alden hung his head. "We have lost three of our number and several are wounded."

"Since this uprising has been based on lies, neither my father nor I will hold you responsible. If you agree to working things out without more bloodshed, I personally will make sure certain medical assistance is available to you."

"Why would you do this?" Alden asked. "Don't you want total control of Nalo?"

"Of course, we don't. We want nothing but peace. I had my fill of fighting when I served in the military. Your province is very important to the wellbeing of the entire planet. I have been told of the fertility of your farms and the bounty of the fish you harvest every year. My father heard of unrest and sent me here to meet with your governor."

Matos stood and held out his left hand to Palen. "I am the governor you have been sent to meet. When Major Domus asked for the leaders of the militants, I contacted them and insisted I needed to be allowed to sit in on the negotiations. I had expected one of your father's diplomats and was surprised when he sent his son. It reminds me of a story told of the One God who sent his only son and, according to the prophecies, he was killed. You are a brave man to come on such a mission and to meet with those who would have waged war upon our king."

Across the table, the expressions on the faces of the young militants went from jubilation at the fact they might be able to overthrow the king and kill the heir apparent, to one of disbelief over being deceived about the history of their planet.

Palen breathed a sigh of relief as his telecommunicator crackled. He got up from his seat and walked to the far corner of the room to talk with his father.

"What is going on there?" Hedro demanded.

"There was an uprising. There have been causalities as well as injuries. I am in conference with the leaders of the militants as well as the governor. We are dealing with someone spreading falsehoods about not only your reign but also the reason our people arrived on Nalo so many years ago."

"Are things under control?"

"I hope so, but I could use some back up, as well as someone to learn the identity of the traitor within our midst. I have offered medical aid to the wounded in the camp of the militants and I do have armed guards outside the door of this meeting room. These people came without weapons and I pray I have righted the falsehoods with words of the truth."

"I have already dispatched aid to your location. Are you certain you are unharmed?"

"Yes, Father. I think these young men and I have come to an understanding. I must get back to the bargaining table."

"Leave your telecommunicator on. I want to speak with Matos."

Palen swallowed hard and returned to the table. "My father wants to speak with you, Matos."

45

The older man nodded his approval. "I am pleased to be speaking with you, Your Highness. I am ashamed of these young men. Alden, their leader, is my grandson. I know what he has done is wrong and I would plead with you to have mercy in your punishment. I understand there are consequences for their actions."

"I consider you a friend, Matos. I have dispatched more troops to your location and the leaders of the rebellion will be taken into custody. What their punishment will be is up to a judge and jury here in Capitol City."

Without warning, the door to the meeting room opened and the guards who accompanied Palen to the meeting barged in.

"Stop," Palen shouted. "I am the one doing this, Father. I have promised these men they will be treated fairly. I will not stand for military intervention. I will handle this in the way I see fit. If we put them under arrest, we will be giving into the falsehood that predicated this uprising."

With that said, he switched off his telecommunicator and ordered the military to stand down.

"Now, are we going to come to a peaceful conclusion to this discussion? I don't want to see any of you severely punished. You are pawns in a cruel game of deceit. Between all of you, Governor Matos, and myself, we are going to have to find whoever is behind this. He is the one to blame. It is easy to spread falsehoods and whip young men into a frenzy of hate and mistrust. You have been led astray but I do not hold you accountable. Will you agree to help me right this wrong?"

One by one, Alden and his friends got to their feet and held out their hands toward Palen. "You are indeed a man to be respected, Prince Palen. If you will accept us, we are willing to talk to the men who have been fighting and explain what has prompted this. We know there must be punishment, but we will take it willingly, to spare the men who mistakenly followed us."

Palen clasped the hands of the men who now were pledging their loyalty to him. In the years to come, these men would be his peers when he assumed the throne.

~ * ~

Felda was pleased at how quickly her pilot was able to get her to the hospital. As soon as they arrived, she was whisked into the emergency room where her mother waited for her.

"How long have you been in labor?" Wasla asked.

"I went to the space port with Palen. He was sent to the other side of the planet on a diplomatic meeting. He no more than lifted off than I felt the first pains. I'm so frightened, Mother. Palen should be here, he should be with me when this baby is born."

"I know he should, but he thought you had more time before the birth. Unfortunately, babies don't always abide by schedules and this little one is more than anxious to be born. You and I will get through this together and have a pleasant surprise for Palen when he arrives back home."

Felda knew her mother was right. Palen would one day be king and as such he wouldn't always be able to be at her side for important events.

Three hours after arriving at the hospital, Prince Kratan entered the world, screaming his protests for all the world to hear.

It took almost two weeks for those responsible for the uprising to be rounded up and taken into custody. As they promised, the young men Palen met when he first arrived pledged their loyalty to him and were instrumental in the arrest of the men who were spreading the lies about, not only his father, but also all of the people who had come to Nalo to enrich the lives of the citizens of the planet.

Within hours of his meeting with Governor Matos, along with Alden and his friends, he learned his first son arrived two weeks ahead of time. It saddened him to think he had not been there when Felda needed him. While he quelled the uprising and made political allies, he let his wife down. When he returned home, he vowed things would be different.

Chapter Six

Palen couldn't believe it had been three weeks since he originally left home. Once the uprising was quelled, he was finally able to video-communicate with Felda and see his newborn son, Kratan. His arms ached to hold both his wife and his son. Instead, his duty to the planet had taken top priority.

The local news heralded him as a hero in not only the negotiations with the rebels, but with the capture of those responsible for sowing the seeds of doubt among the young men he now called friends.

He'd been surprised when he learned Alden was only in his late teens and rebelled against his parents. Even though Palen pleaded with his father for leniency, Alden and his friends were called to task. They were each to be held in custody until Palen returned to Capitol City. With a military escort, the young men would be transported to a military prison where they would await their trial. Palen was pleased it wouldn't take place until he could be there to testify. He wanted to make certain the court knew of their assistance in apprehending those behind the uprising.

He waited to board his sky skimmer until everyone else boarded their vehicles. "I will land shortly after you do," he said, clasping the forearms of Alden and each of his friends. "In my conversations with my father, I have made sure you will all be treated with the respect you deserve, regardless of your past actions."

Once he was buckled into the seat of his sky skimmer, he closed his eyes and allowed sleep to claim him.

~ * ~

The space port at Capitol City was on complete lock down, not only because of the arrival of the military squad with the prisoners but also that of Palen's sky skimmer.

As much as Palen longed to see his wife and newborn son, he knew he would have to face his father for a debriefing before he could be reunited with his family.

The flight was uneventful and as soon as he left his craft, he was met by a military escort to take him to a hovercraft waiting to transport him to the palace. Before entering the craft, he saw Alden and his friends. It saddened him to see them shackled. Before he could say anything, each of the young men raised their hands in salute, smiles gracing their faces.

The royal hovercraft waited for him outside the main building. Without having to go through customs or claim his luggage, Palen was seated in the vehicle and being transported to the palace in record time.

Upon his arrival, he was greeted by the palace guards as well as many of the servants. He enjoyed their jubilant greetings. At the same time, he dreaded meeting with his father. He knew he'd overstepped his authority by making an alliance with the former rebels.

Without hesitation, he made his way to the throne room where he knew his father would be waiting for him.

"Palen, it's good to have you back in Capitol City," his father greeted him.

The smile on his father's face immediately put him at ease. "It's good to be home, Father. The rebels have been brought here for trial, but I wish to appeal to you for mercy for them."

"I anticipated as much. When we first talked, I was angry and upset with you because of your decision to override my authority. I have since changed my mind. You have made me proud in the way you handled the situation. I've read all of the reports and from them I have realized you are more than ready to take over the throne once I am no longer able to rule. I have also reviewed your recommendations for the prisoners who came back with you. From those, I see no need for a trial."

Palen held his breath. Would his father be harsh in his judgement?

He prayed not. "Why will there be no trial? These young men deserve to explain their actions and the reason for them."

"As you know, those who were responsible for the unrest have been transported back here. Judgment was swift and they have been sent to the penal colony that is a satellite of our planet. They will no longer be able to do such harm to our planet."

"What of the others who came with me?" Palen was annoyed with his father for not answering his original question.

"Ah, my son, you are young. Patience comes with age. I have been in consultation with the advisors ever since our original conversation. I have been very impressed with the way you have turned the opposition you first encountered into trusted allies. All of these young men have the same thing in common. They gave up their education in order to follow a group of charismatic traitors. They thought what they were doing was for the best, but instead they all almost lost their lives. After you are rested and have been reunited with your wife and son, the two of us will interview each of them individually. At that time, they will be given the choice of spending four years on the penal colony or finishing their secondary education as well as getting their degree from the university here in Capitol City. During that time, they will not be allowed to leave the city nor will they be able to be in contact with their families."

Palen didn't realize he was holding his breath until his father finished speaking. He certainly hadn't expected his father to be so forgiving of the young men he now considered as his friends.

"I worried about your decision. I am pleased with your leniency. These are not hardened fighters, but troubled teens who were easily incited to violence."

"I have closely monitored your discussions with these young men. Knowing most of their parents and grandparents, I realized they could easily become close advisors to you. You have made me proud and I am certain these young men will do the same for their families in the future, with the proper education."

~ * ~

Felda's anger over her husband being away from her when she delivered her first child burned out during his absence from their home. Anger turned to fear when she learned of the war he'd inadvertently stepped into. Even though she thought the mission should have been carried out by the diplomats, she soon realized Palen was the only one qualified to make peace with the rebels and apprehend the troublemakers who had incited the riots.

She glanced at the clock and realized the time for Palen to land at the space port had long since passed. She'd received a message from the palace saying Palen had been summoned to the throne room of King Hedro and he would not come to their home until after the official debriefing meeting.

"It's not fair, Mother," Felda lamented. "Palen has missed the first month of our son's life and now he is forbidden from coming to us straight from the space port."

"This is the way with men. You have spoken with Palen several times over the past month and you know he is anxious to be back in your home. Unfortunately, this is a prelude to what his life will be like when he becomes king. Your children will be blessed with you for their mother. As you must remember, Palen's mother died when he and his sister were very young. He knows little of a normal family life. His father has been king for all of his life. He is doing what he has been trained to do. It doesn't mean he loves you any less, but you will always come second to this kingdom in his mind."

Felda nodded her head in agreement with her mother. She knew it was the stress of being a new mother that was ruling her heart rather than allowing her to make decisions with her mind.

Kratan's cries of hunger took her mind away from how long it was taking for Palen to return to them. She hurried to the nursery, where the nursemaid, Solidar, was trying to soothe the screaming child.

"I have come to feed the baby. Why don't you go down to the kitchen and have the cook fix you something to eat? It's well past the time when you should be having your midday meal."

"Thank you, Your Highness."

"I don't think I'll ever get used to people calling me that. I thought we agreed you would call me Felda in private."

"That is hard for me to do. I have been trained as a nursemaid for the royal family. My mother was nursemaid for Prince Palen and often for you as well. I was taught not to forget royal titles. Now if you will excuse me, I will go down for the midday meal while you see to Prince Kratan's needs."

Felda shook her head. She remembered Solidar's mother fondly. She took good care of not only the royal children but also any of the other children of the families who served the king. Le-le, as the children all called her, was strict in her discipline but loving as well. It was one of the reasons she and Palen had employed Solidar when they learned of her pregnancy.

As soon as the nursemaid left the room, Felda opened her gown so her son could nurse at her breast. She enjoyed these private moments when she had Kratan all to herself. She'd questioned the need for help with the child, but as the future queen, she would have no time for childcare. Even as Princess Felda, she knew soon her royal duties would begin. She had been excused from those duties because of the birth of her son but in another month, she would be done with her maternity leave and ready to do the things expected of her.

~ * ~

Palen left the throne room. After the long flight and the debriefing with his father, he was mentally and physically drained. Even so, he was anxious to return to his home. The telecom communication connections he'd had with Felda helped, but he longed to hold her in his arms and become acquainted with the newest prince in the royal family.

A hovercraft awaited him outside the palace, but he waved them away. His home within the compound was only a short walk away from the palace and he needed some time alone to digest his father's directive concerning the prisoners.

Once at the front door, he punched in the access code and waited for it to open for him. To his surprise the entry hall was empty. Instead of seeing his wife, Solidar came from the kitchen to greet him.

"Where is Princess Felda?" he inquired.

"It was time for her to feed your son and she told me to come down to the kitchen to get something to eat."

Palen nodded. He'd grown up with Solidar and for that reason he'd insisted on hiring her to care for their child. It seemed strange when he heard her refer to him with his official title. Times like these were ones when he wished he could be called Palen the way he had when he was a child.

Without stopping to even take off his traveling cape, he took the stairs to the upper level of the house, two at a time. At the top of the stairs he noticed the door to the nursery room standing partially open. Before entering, he took a moment to watch Felda as she breastfed his son. From what he could see the boy had a full head of downy soft hair. Unfortunately, the remainder of his body was hidden from his sight by the blanket that swaddled him tightly.

Wanting to see more of not only his son but also his wife, he pushed the door completely open and entered the room.

"Palen, you're home!" Felda exclaimed.

"Finally. I had to speak with my father before I could come home to be with you and our son."

"He is almost finished eating and you will be able to hold him and get acquainted. He has developed quite a personality during your absence."

Palen could hear the icy tone of his wife's voice. "I am so sorry I wasn't here for you. I thought the mission would be over before the birth of our child. Unfortunately, that wasn't the way things went."

"I've been told of how successful the mission was."

"I guess you could call it that. I ache for those young men who came back with me to face their punishment for their deeds. It was evident the quality of education we enjoy here in Capitol City is not being implemented in the outer regions of the planet."

"What do you mean?"

He marveled at the change in her voice. It had suddenly gone from anger to concern.

"There are very few members of the younger generation who are able to obtain a decent education. Most of them work with their parents in order to supplement their family's income with no time for higher education. Because of this, they were led astray by rabblerousers who insisted our ancestors came from Plantas in order to take over Nalo. Of course, we both know this isn't the truth."

"I'm shocked. I thought standardized education was available all over the planet."

"So, did I. I've learned this is the poorest province on the planet and feeding their families comes before education for their children. My father and I have been debating what to do about this and he is making some decisions that could help the situation, but I'm afraid it might be up to you and me to help with the process."

"How can we help?"

Palen hoped she would be pleased with what he was about to propose to her. It would mean more time away from their new baby than she might be willing to accept.

"The first part of the plan is for you to oversee the education of the young men who willingly came with me for their punishment. Father is offering them education rather than incarceration. It would mean you would have to spend at least two to three hours a day working with them, one on one."

"That sounds plausible. Why is it I think there is more to this than you are saying? With Solidar working for us I know the time away from the house will not be a problem."

"While you will be seeing to the education of these young men, I will be working on building up the economy and making provisions for the education of the children as well as the young men and women. In time, the two of us will be responsible for upgrading the educational needs. Their schools and universities are lacking and the ignorance of this leads us to what promoted the uprising."

He watched Felda's face as the impact of what he told her sunk in. Before his eyes, he saw her bewilderment and even anger turn to excitement over the possibility of making a difference in the area of education.

"When will this start? Will I have time to wean our child?"

"My part will begin immediately. Yours, on the other hand, will begin slowly. First you will be introduced to the young men you will be mentoring. To begin with they will have the best teachers available here in Capitol City. You will be expected to meet with them perhaps once or twice a week. Those meetings can be arranged to be held here, at the house, until Kratan is weaned. In the beginning, it will be just for you to get acquainted with them."

"Are you certain it is safe for them to be here?"

"I have gotten to know each of them over the days and weeks we were together. They openly admit it was their lack of education rather than aggression that led to the uprising. They are all from good families, but they do need guidance. Considering your passion for teaching, I can think of no one better to mentor them. As for having them in our home, you know we are always guarded. Nothing will happen."

Kratan allowed Felda's nipple to slip from his mouth, indication he was finished with his midday meal, and ready to be burped.

"Allow me," Palen said, when his wife lifted their son to her shoulder.

The smile that graced her lips told him, he was finally able to hold his son and help take over some of the parenting tasks.

Having never handled a small baby before, he picked up his son. From the education he'd received from his mother-under-the-law, he carefully supported his son's head. Once he held him against his shoulder and gently patted his back, he was rewarded with a healthy burp. Only then did he cradle his son in his arms and open the blanket to see his perfectly formed body.

"He is magnificent. I can't believe you were able to grow a child within your belly."

For the first time since his arrival, Felda laughed. "It seems to me I had a little help in that department. I see he resembles you more every day. He is a good strong boy and will grow up to be as good a man as his father."

Chapter Seven

The telecom unit on Palen's wrist alerted him to someone at his door. Rather than going to see who it was on his own, he allowed one of the servants to greet whoever might be there. It was not a good idea to go in person, since one never knew when there would be an assassination attempt on a member of the royal family.

A few minutes later, a messenger wearing the uniform of the royal family was ushered into the room Palen used as his home office.

"The king requests your presence at the palace, Your Highness," the man greeted him.

Why would my father send a messenger when he could have contacted me telepathically?

"What could be of such importance as to send a messenger?"

The man held out a computer tablet in his gloved hand, but Palen was reluctant to touch the computer. Within his mind he contacted his father. *Have you sent a messenger to my home, Father?*

I know nothing of a messenger. Delay him while I send the palace guard to apprehend this so-called messenger.

Fear clutched at Palen's heart. Only two rooms away, his infant son slept and in the adjoining room his wife was tutoring Alden and his friends. Unsure of when anyone would be coming from the palace, he telepathically voiced his concerns to Felda.

~ * ~

There is a stranger in the house. Take Kratan to the safe room.

Felda was in the middle of a history session with Alden and his friends. The message from Palen frightened her.

"Is there a problem, Your Highness?" Alden asked.

"There is an intruder in the house. The Prince has instructed me to take the baby and go to the safe room."

"Where is Prince Palen?" another of her students asked.

"He's in his office."

Alden was quick to take control. Within moments, he assigned two of his friends to stay and guard Felda, sent two more to the nursery and took the last three with him as he went to the office.

"We will go and protect Prince Palen. Both you and the child will be well protected. Do not leave this room until someone comes to tell you it is safe," he informed her.

Felda agreed and tried her best not to give into hysterics.

~ * ~

Palen eyed the man suspiciously. "What is this important message?" he asked, stalling for time.

"It is all in the tablet," the man replied.

Palen noticed beads of sweat forming on the man's forehead.

"Why would my father send you when contacting me telepathically would be instantaneous?"

From behind the man, Palen saw Alden and three of his companions silently enter the room. Before they could tackle the man, Palen felt he needed to give them warning about the tablet.

"Don't touch the tablet this man is carrying," he shouted, as Alden's men surrounded the messenger.

What happened next came so quickly, in the future, it would be difficult to put into chronological order.

The messenger was taken completely by surprise and he dropped the tablet to the floor. As soon as it left his hands it exploded, sending sparks throughout the room, igniting several small fires. While one of the men restrained the messenger, two others worked at extinguishing the fires and Alden shielded Palen.

Almost immediately, royal guards stormed into the room. In the pandemonium, they held their weapons on the men who came to save Palen's life.

"These are friends and the heroes of the day. Had it not been for them, I don't know how much longer I could have stalled this assassin."

"What weapon did he carry, Your Highness?" the captain of the guard asked.

"It was the tablet. Check the man's gloves. As long as he held it in his gloved hands, it looked harmless. As soon as it left his hands, it exploded and started the many fires you see have been put out around the room."

"Who are you?" the captain of the guard shouted at the prisoner.

When the man remained silent, Alden took a good look at him. "He is a member of the underground fraction who incited us to open hostilities before we met with Prince Palen. They call themselves The Pure of Nalo. They preach death to the outsiders who have come to our planet. I mistakenly thought when the leaders of this group were arrested and sent to the penal colony, the group would disband."

"Is what this man says true?"

"Are you one of them?" the man asked, answering the question with a question of his own. "Are you one of these so-called refugees who have come to take over our planet and destroy those of us who have lived here since the beginning of time?"

"Your question deserves no answer. That said, I am loyal to Nalo. I recognize those who came to our planet as the descendants of the 'sky gods' who came in the distant past to teach our people the art of the written language, mathematics and the science of medicine. They brought understanding when we were little more than animals, and when they came back to us it was as friends rather than enemies."

Palen finally found his voice. "Be certain to check his gloves," he said. "While he held the tablet, it looked harmless. As soon as it left his hands it exploded. I am not certain about how it was constructed, but somehow it became a weapon to be used against the crown. Do not touch it, even though it has been detonated, it could still be dangerous to be handled."

Before anything else could be said, King Hedro rushed into the room. "Have these men who I was lenient with turned against us once again?"

"Things are not as they appear, Father. We are blessed these young men were here for their tutoring session with Felda when this assassin came within our midst. They have saved my life, unlike the servant who allowed this man to enter my home. Find him, for I fear he is in association with the group who wants every one of the refugees who came from Plantas to be eliminated. Were it not for Alden and his friends, I only fear what would have happened, for I don't know how long it would have been before he would have tried to carry out his orders for my murder?"

Hedro turned to the young men who came to Palen's rescue. "Our planet owes you a debt of gratitude. Be prepared to be summoned to the palace for recognition of what you have done today. I am surprised to see there are only four of you, were there not eight?"

Alden, raised his head, locking his gaze with that of his king. "We were here studying with Princess Felda when Prince Palen warned her. Two of my companions are guarding the princess while the other two are guarding the nursery. Unlike others who formed the hate group, we have pledged our loyalty to the royal family. Unfortunately, this man is but the tip of the iceberg. There are others and until they are routed out, they will continue to be a threat."

Hedro moved closer to Alden and clasped his arm. "You are a brave man to speak the truth to your king. Most people would be less forthcoming. If our questioning of this prisoner brings about the names of those involved in this conspiracy, would you be willing to assist in their capture?"

Palen watched Alden and his companions as they allowed the question posed by their king to sink in. As though they rehearsed their response, they each dropped to one knee, bowed their heads and held they left hands over their hearts.

"We are at your service, Your Majesty," Alden replied.

With his response, the tension seemed to drain from the room. Palen realized just how close he'd come to death and his body responded by becoming overwhelmed with weakness. Alden was immediately on his feet and at Palen's side to guide him to the desk chair he had occupied before the assassination attempt began.

"Send for the healer," Hedro ordered.

"There is no need for a healer," Palen protested.

It was Alden who, after putting his hand on Palen's shoulder, ended the debate. "I can see where sparks from the tablet have hit your body. If, indeed, the tablet was poisoned, touching it would not only have burned you but have caused a poisoning as well. King Hedro is correct, the healer should be brought to make certain none of the poison has been inflicted on your body."

Reluctantly, Palen agreed with both his father and his friend.

It took only a matter of moments for Wasla to arrive and begin the examination of her son-under-the-law. After waving her medical wand over his body, she declared she wanted him to be taken to the hospital, immediately.

"Did anyone else have contact with either the tablet or the sparks from it?"

Two of Alden's companions nodded. Without hesitation, Wasla ran her wand over each of their bodies. With the results, she declared they also needed hospitalization for the treatment of poisoning that had been inflicted upon their bodies.

Before they were taken to the hospital, Hedro addressed the young men. "You have acted valiantly this day. From today, forward, all of you will not only be finishing your educations here in Capitol City, but you will be training for the royal guard."

The expressions on the young men's faces denoted their acceptance of their king's offer.

"Once everyone who has come in contact with the poison is released from the hospital, we will have a special ceremony to make everything official. At that time, your families will be flown to Capitol

City to be there to witness the appreciation of not only the royal family, but also the people of Nalo."

It was Wasla who interrupted Hedro. "It is time for my patients to be taken to the hospital. I have requested a hover-ambulance and I have been advised it has arrived. I have also arranged for the other young men, as well as my daughter, to be brought here to bid them farewell before they are transported to the hospital."

Although the four men who guarded Felda and the nursery were allowed to stand in the doorway, no one was allowed into the office.

Everyone in the room, including King Hedro and Wasla were transported to the hospital for a more complete evaluation. Even though they had not come in direct contact with any of the sparks or particles from the tablet, there could still be spores of the poison in the air.

Palen ached to hold Felda in his arms but knew he could easily contaminate her in the process. "Everything will be well, my darling. Care for our son and we will soon be reunited."

~ * ~

The hospital, that was usually very quiet, bustled with activity when the people possibly infected during the assassination attempt on Prince Palen were brought into the emergency area. The entire area where they were to be kept was quarantined and anyone who came to care for them dressed in protective gear.

Security was tight and no visitors were allowed. Even though the king was among those hospitalized, his close advisors were more than able to keep the planet running smoothly, without anyone knowing of how close they came to losing not only the crown prince but also their king.

After a week in isolation, Wasla and the other attending healers declared them out of danger. With that pronouncement, they were able to return to their homes as well as their regular activities.

Palen and Wasla returned to the home he shared with Felda. It was evident she'd been under a great strain without either her husband or her mother.

"Are you certain you are no longer carrying any of the poison in your systems?" she asked when she met them in the foyer.

"We are completely free of any trace of it," Wasla replied. "We were lucky not to have come into direct contact with it. We all had superficial contact and it was easily counteracted once we were at the hospital."

Palen immediately noticed the closed door to his office. "Has the room been decontaminated?"

"It has, but all of the furnishings have had to be taken out. The workers also stripped all the walls as well as the floor to the studs and subfloor. They say it will take at least two more weeks to complete. Have they told you what kind of poison was used? No one wants to tell me anything regarding the incident."

"We were informed the tablet was filled with a poison they are still trying to isolate. The reason the man carrying it was able to do so without worry, was it was set not to detonate until it left the protective gloves he wore. He was isolated with us, but kept under heavy guard. It soon became evident he'd contracted the poison, because once he confirmed the names of those who sent him, the effects of the poison finally took his life."

Tears formed in Felda's eyes. Even though the man had been assigned to eliminate her husband, Palen knew the thought of any living being losing his or her life would affect her deeply.

"What of the people he named before his death?"

"We've been told they were all arrested and they named others. They have already been transported to the penal colony. Their foolish actions have changed their lives completely."

Within hours of Palen's return, the news of the disaster that had been averted hit the airwaves. Immediately, the populace of Nalo turned from outrage over the attempt on the royal family, to cheers over the capture and deportation of those who were responsible for these atrocities against their king and prince.

Chapter Eight

Princess Felda thoroughly enjoyed her life as a royal princess. After the assassination attempt when Kratan was but a tiny baby, their lives had become routine and peaceful. Now, three years later, she was joyfully expecting the birth of their second child. While Palen anxiously awaited the birth of a daughter, she told him the child could easily be another boy.

"This child will be our next princess," Palen said, as they prepared to begin their day. "I just know it will."

"I don't know why you are so certain. As many times as I have asked Mother to tell me the sex of the child, she refuses. It is the same as it was when I carried Kratan. We will not know if I carry the next prince or princess until the moment I give birth."

As usual, Palen finished dressing to begin his duties for the morning and kissed her tenderly before he left their bedroom to break his fast. After leaving the breakfast room, he would be going to his office to begin his royal duties for the day.

~ * ~

Only hours earlier, Palen had been summoned to the royal chambers where his father, King Hedro, lay on his death bed.

Slowly, the people of the original flight from Plantas to Nalo were dying. Many of them were very young, like Felda's father and King Hedro, and had suffered from Time Warp Fever during the journey from Plantas. Grato had died of complications of the fever combined with a

64

disease of the people of Nalo less than a year earlier. Felda was pleased her father was still alive when her son, Prince Kratan, was born. He lived until Kratan was two years old before he succumbed to his illness.

As much as Felda wanted to be at her father-under-the-law's bedside as he lay dying, it was impossible. She was heavily pregnant and her mother warned her against exposing herself to any illnesses that gripped King Hedro's body.

She heard Kratan playing in the nursery. Even though she knew his nursemaid was there to care for him, she got up to go in and watch his imagination at work.

"Your Highness, there was no need for you to disturb what you were doing. Kratan is just playing," his nursemaid said.

"I know, but sitting with my sewing and waiting for news of King Hedro is too confining. It's such a nice day. Do you think we could take Kratan out to the park?"

"That is a lovely idea, Your Highness."

"I do wish you would call me Felda. We have been friends since Kratan was born, when Solidar was his nursemaid. I was blessed when you were available to take over her duties. As sisters, you are both more than qualified to care for my children."

"As I've told you many times before, it wouldn't be proper."

"It would be if I said it was."

Raina began to laugh. "You are right, Felda, but I will only call you by your proper name when we are in private. In public I will continue to call you Your Highness or Princess Felda."

"That would please me greatly. Has Kratan had his midday meal?"

"Yes, he just finished it. The question is, have you had your midday meal?"

"It was brought to me, but I am so concerned about King Hedro, as well as my mother, who is treating him, I have very little appetite. I much prefer to spend some time with you and my son."

"I understand, but you must keep up your strength for the little one you are carrying." Protectively, she placed her hand over the bump of Felda's belly that housed the precious new life she was carrying.

"I ate a little, so I am certain neither of us will die of starvation. Hopefully, by the time Palen and I share the evening meal, he will have good news about his father's condition."

It didn't take long for Raina to ready Kratan for the excursion to the park. Felda enjoyed the bright fall sunshine and loved watching her son play on the equipment meant to entertain the children in the park.

You are growing up so fast my little one. Soon you will have a baby brother or sister and I know you will be a good big brother.

From the corner of her eye, she saw Palen coming toward her. Her mother was with him. She knew the two of them coming to the park together was not a good sign.

Leaving Kratan in Raina's care, she got up to approach them. Mentally, she tried to prepare herself for the news her life mate and mother were about to impart to her.

"My father is dead," Palen said, before enfolding her in his arms.

She remembered when her father died and how Palen comforted her. As much as she wanted to do the same for him, Felda was so overcome with grief, her tears could not be contained.

"You are so lucky to be able to shed your tears in grief. Unfortunately, as soon as the funeral is over, the coronation will take place. I must stay strong for our people."

"Honestly, Palen, tears of grief are not considered the weakness you men make them out to be," Wasla told him. "When we left Plantas, every man on our ship shed tears for what we were losing, even your father and Grato. In private, Hedro grieved with me when Grato died. Show your people their new king is a compassionate man who is capable of shedding tears when he grieves."

"Mother is right. As I recall, you grieved with me when my father died. Allow me to do the same for you now. For the next two weeks, you will be the grieving son. The time for strength is when you have been crowned king. We will now retire to our cottage and prepare the royal proclamation to the people. You will continue your father's guidance to the people and make Nalo a much stronger planet."

Palen held her tighter. She could feel his tears washing against her cheek. She thanked the One God for allowing her mate to be able to grieve the passing of his father.

~ * ~

King Hedro laid in state for the entire two weeks, so people from all over the planet of Nalo could come to pay their respects to their beloved ruler.

Felda endured the endless hours of standing at the bier and accepting the condolences of the many mourners. It was only when her mother insisted that she rest did she allow one of the pages to bring her a chair.

At long last, the period of mourning was past and the funeral completed with the cremation of their beloved ruler's remains. Palen went alone to scatter the ashes over the ocean that represented the vast expanse of the space Hedro traveled to come to Nalo and become the ruler to reunite all the kingdoms of the planet.

The following morning, they were awakened early and readied for the coronation ceremony that would crown them King Palen and Queen Felda.

Even though Kratan had been sheltered from the sadness of the two weeks of mourning, this morning he was dressed in royal robes as he would also be crowned as Crown Prince Kratan. Felda looked at her son and wondered how he would behave as the heir apparent.

After the morning meal, they were escorted to the throne room. There, the top advisors to the king waited to pledge their allegiance to their new ruler and his family.

Felda was proud to see Alden and his friends wearing the uniforms of the Royal Guard. In the three years they had been in Capitol City, it was evident they had not only matured but also over and over again pledged their loyalty to the royal family. Each of the young men who came to her for tutoring so many years ago had become citizens their parents, as well as everyone on Nalo, respected.

Among the loyal subjects, Felda saw her mother kneel as soon as the royal family entered the chamber. For the first time, she realized their relationship might be compromised by her new title as Queen.

Squeezing Palen's hand she whispered, "Must my mother be made to kneel to us? She is the only parent either of us has left. Can we not give her a royal title on this special day?"

Palen's eyes which mirrored sadness ever since his father's passing, now twinkled with the merriment Felda knew so well.

"You are so right, my queen. Once the coronation is finished, I will issue a royal proclamation making your mother the Royal Mother Healer. It is only fitting as she was the healer for both my father and yours. She never left either of their sides from the moment they became ill until their deaths. For that matter, she has cared for our family and even put her life on the line when the assassin came with poison to take my life. No one could have been a more loyal subject."

The fact he referred to her mother as a loyal subject raised her hackles, but she said nothing. It was the way the royal family referred to anyone even if it was his own mother-under-the-law.

The ceremony was long and detailed. Even before it was over, Kratan was yawning, in need of his nap. When at last, they were pronounced king, queen and crowned prince, Raina immediately scooped Kratan into her arms in order to take him to the nursery for his afternoon nap.

Felda wondered how much of the ceremony her son would remember. He was but three years old and, for him, playing with his toys was much more important than being declared the crown prince.

"My first royal proclamation is that Wasla, as my queen's mother, will, from this day forward be called Royal Mother Healer, a member of the royal family. As a member of the Ministry of Medicine, she will become the leader of this group."

There was a gasp that turned to a cheer from everyone who was witnessing the coronation ceremonies. Even though Wasla was the most senior member of the Ministry of Medicine, she had never been granted the position of the leader of the group. Being a male-dominated profession, women were often passed over for advancement.

As soon as the audience quieted down, the head of the Ministry of Medicine stepped forward to kneel in front of Wasla. "My Lady Royal Mother Healer, the title of head of the Ministry of Medicine should have been bestowed upon you long before this. I will be more than willing to pledge my loyalty to you and offer my assistance in any capacity you see fit."

From her vantage point, Felda could see tears form in her mother's eyes.

"I have always admired your ability to lead the Ministry of Medicine. I accept your offer and if it meets with King Palen's approval, I will appoint you my second in command. Should anyone have difficulty dealing with me, as a woman, I will pray they will voice their concerns to you. With your expertise, I am certain we will make a perfect team."

The former head of the Ministry of Medicine touched his forehead to Wasla's extended hand. "I am your servant and grateful for the trust you have in me."

Getting to his feet, he faded back into the crowd and the other members of the Ministry of Medicine cheered. It was evident, they too, approved of Palen's first official appointment.

By the end of the festivities, Felda could feel the beginning of early labor. "I am sorry, my love, but I must retire to our apartments. This child is eager to be born."

The worried expression on her mate's face told her he was not only the duly crowned king but also a man concerned for her welfare, as well as that of their unborn child.

"Mother," he said in a hushed tone. "I think Felda needs your attention. This will be your first official duty to the new royal family."

Between Palen and Wasla, Felda was escorted not to their home, but to the apartment assigned to the king and queen. A page ran ahead and told the servants to prepare a place for the royal birth. While Kratan had been born in the hospital, this new child would begin his or her life in the palace where it would spend its life.

Felda knew this birth would be very special, as it would be the first official royal birth since the residents of Plantas came to Nalo, so many years ago. When King Hedro took the throne, his children Palen and Salina were children and the laws of Nalo said there were to be no more than two children per family. With Salina married to a military man, and Palen now king, Kratan's place as the crowned prince was secure. The birth of their second child was a royal event. Boy or girl, it didn't matter, because this child would be second in line for the royal throne.

~ * ~

Sweat beaded on Felda's forehead. With Palen holding her right hand and her best friend, Salina, holding her left, she endured the endless hours of labor. At last the urge to push became too great. With all her might she bore down until the squalling infant left the warm security of her womb to enter the world.

"She's small," Wasla declared, "but she is healthy."

Felda breathed a sigh of relief. "Can I hold her?"

"As soon as she is cleaned up, weighed and measured, she will be in your arms. From the way she is crying, she is anxious to be held by her mother and suckle at your breast."

Felda looked from the crying infant to her husband, her king.

"She is perfect, just like her mother. I declare this royal princess will be named Mira, in memory of my mother."

The fact her husband decided to honor his mother brought tears of joy to Felda's eyes. As a child, when Felda and Palen played together it was Mira who insisted on tea parties for Salina and Felda. With Wasla working as a healer, it was Mira who taught her to be a cultured young woman.

"Royal Princess Mira is the perfect name for the granddaughter of our first queen," Salina said before Felda could answer.

It pleased her to know her husband and best friend approved of her newborn daughter. Before the day was ended, Mira would be presented to the people and become the official Royal Princess of the planet of Nalo.

Chapter Nine

As king and queen of Nalo, Palen and Felda were often called upon to take royal trips to the outlying areas of the planet. Whenever it was possible, they traveled with their children, but often their trips clashed with the time when the children were being schooled. With Kratan now thirteen and Mira ten, they were both enrolled in a prestigious boarding school and each making top grades.

Shortly after Mira's birth, Wasla predicted her granddaughter would be the mirror image of her paternal grandmother and namesake. Now, at the age of ten, the prediction had come true.

"I am so excited to see the children," Felda said as they neared the landing area for their private air transport.

"I am too…"

"I hear a but in your voice. Something has been on your mind ever since we left the last stop on our trip."

"I have a lot on my mind right now. Before we left Capitol City a month ago, I received word that Earth has joined the Confederation and Seros is considering joining with them as well. We have allies on both of the planets. I'm not sure if we should stay neutral or not."

"I wish you would have confided in me earlier. This must be weighing heavily on your mind. Once we are back at the palace, I think we should have a teleconference with our friends on Earth as well as on Seros and see if these rumors are true. You have first-hand experience with the generals from the Confederation from your time on Bankos. Do you think this is a good move for our people, to say nothing of our allies?"

"I'm not sure. I honestly like the generals of the Confederation, at least the ones I had contact with. I don't think they wish us ill, but there are other planets in the Galaxy whose inhabitants aren't as friendly toward us."

"Are we in danger? Is an attack from our enemies coming soon?"

Palen took Felda's hand in his and brought it to his lips. "I shouldn't have voiced my concerns. I don't know if the Confederation is a threat. I do know they keep those who are evil at bay. When I confer with our counterparts on Earth and Seros, I will get their take on joining the Confederation."

~ * ~

Kratan paced in front of the school, waiting for his sister, Mira, to get her things together for the summer break. He certainly couldn't understand why it took her so long to get ready to leave for the palace. He could tell by the expression on the face of their pilot, waiting in the hovercraft, that Mira's tardiness upset him as well.

"It's about time," he admonished, when she finally came from her dorm, dragging a large suitcase behind her.

"I don't know what the hurry is. Mama and Papa aren't due to land until late this afternoon. I also have more things to pack than you do. You'll still be in the same dorm room next semester, even though you will be going to secondary school, so you can leave most of your stuff here. I'll be moving into a different dorm, so I had to clean out the entire room. I thought the house mother would help me. I mean, I am a princess, but she said be I a princess or a commoner, I had to take care of my own things. I've never had anyone talk to me like that before."

Kratan could tell his sister was on the verge of tears. He could handle her temper tantrums but not her tears. He had to remind himself she was only ten and still a child while he was thirteen going on fourteen. In the eyes of most of the people in the galaxy, he was a man. As much as he wanted to sit with his father and learn how to rule the planet, he knew his father valued the education he was getting not only at the boarding school but also at University when he finished secondary school.

His anger cooled and he helped Mira load her suitcase in the luggage area of the hovercraft. Once they were securely buckled in, their pilot announced it would take less than an hour for them to reach Capitol City since the weather was clear and the skyways were relatively quiet.

Kratan recalled other trips when it would take over two hours to reach their home because of either weather or traffic. He'd read stories about what life was like on planets like Earth before the use of hovercrafts became commonplace. If they had to travel on roads, like the ones in the city where the skies were too congested to allow hovercraft, the trip would take much longer.

After landing at the air transport, personnel from the palace came to help with the luggage and transfer everything to the waiting ground vehicles. In the distance, he saw the Royal Vehicle, waiting for the landing of his parents.

"Do you know when the king and queen are due to land?" he asked Joltan, a member of the Royal Guard.

"We were told they weren't landing until this evening, but they were able to leave earlier than anticipated. They've had good flying weather. They should be arriving within the hour. Would you prefer to wait here for them, Your Highness?"

"No, it is best that Mira and I return to the palace and bathe so we're ready to greet our parents without the grime of travel clinging to our bodies."

"That is a wise choice, Your Highness. I will advise them you are awaiting them at the palace." Joltan snapped to attention and saluted Kratan.

The gesture surprised Kratan. Never before had Joltan saluted him. Of course, never before had he reached the age of reason, as his father called it. It was common knowledge that Joltan was only two years older than Kratan when he entered the military and went to Bankos as a member of Palen's battalion, and his loyalty extended to pledging his life to his king.

Kratan wondered if things would be the same for him when he entered the military. It wasn't something he wanted to do, but it was his father's command, and Kratan was mature enough to understand what a royal command meant.

~ * ~

Mira saw her brother as a little boy pretending to be a man. When Joltan gave him a salute in the same manner she'd seen the older man salute her father, she realized something had definitely changed. She wondered if Kratan would still maintain his bedroom in the nursery wing of the palace or would he be assigned his own royal apartment?

Pondering the future was something she had no patience for doing. Instead, she concentrated on all the things she and Raina would do together, once she was free for the entire summer. When she'd been home during the winter break, Raina promised they would enjoy many outings during the coming summer.

"I will be going to the secondary school when we return in the fall," Kratan said, breaking into her mental musings.

"They say the courses at the secondary school are harder than the ones we have been participating in this year. You will have to study much harder to maintain the high grades our father demands. Do you think you are smart enough?"

"I am so much smarter than you. I will be taking courses I get to choose. I've already signed a document of intent to study military history, mathematics, Nalo history and Nalo law. Mother also wants me to study interplanetary history. I will be talking to her about it over the summer. It is possible she could teach me everything I need to know."

"You're crazy. Mother has many duties as our queen. As far as teaching you goes, she hasn't taught in a classroom since I was born. The story goes that on the day of my birth, she had just been crowned Queen of all of Nalo. In addition to two children, she had many things to do to help Father with ruling the planet."

"What you seem to forget, my dear sister, Mother is but a woman and women have no place when it comes to ruling a planet. It's best they do what they are best at, have children and run a household."

Kratan's statement angered Mira. Rather than questioning his thinking, she remained silent. By doing so, she wondered how her parents would react to this new concept her brother was putting forth.

The palace came into view and Mira strained to see if Raina waited for her. Finally, she found her nursemaid waiting for her at the top of the steps leading to the balcony of palace.

"See," she exclaimed, "Raina is waiting for us."

"She is waiting for you, not me," Kratan replied. "I am no longer in the need of a nursemaid. I am now old enough to be considered a man. You are still a child. My summer will be spent preparing for the military training I will be receiving when I go to secondary school in the fall."

Mira shook her head in dismay. She knew she would miss Kratan's company over the summer, but on the other hand, she would have Raina all to herself.

~ * ~

The hovercraft landed and it pleased Palen to see Joltan waiting for them. As soon as the hatch opened, he was the first to step from the craft, so he could hold out his hand to assist Felda in disembarking. What he never let on was this was something his father always did. He'd been crowned king in the wake of the assassination of the former president. The worry of assassination was always there. His father would always disembark first so if someone was ready to carry out the unthinkable, it would be him and not his life mate who would take the brunt of the attack.

As soon as he was on solid ground Joltan gave him a smart salute. At times like these, he would have appreciated Joltan clasping his arm in greeting, but the military training and protocol superseded the friendship they cultivated over the years.

"Was your trip productive, Your Majesty?" Joltan asked.

"Yes, it was. After all these years, I wish you would call me Palen when we are not in public."

"You ask this of me whenever you return from a trip. My answer is the same as always. When we were in the military, you were my commanding officer and I gave you the proper respect. It is the same now that you are my king. I refuse to disrespect you even in private."

"As you wish. What is the news in the capitol?"

"Prince Kratan and Princess Mira arrived. As per your instructions, Prince Kratan has been moved from the nursery to his own apartment in another wing of the palace. I have also taken the liberty of enrolling him in the summer military training for young men of his age."

"I didn't know you were planning on moving Kratan from the nursery, to say nothing of beginning his military training," Felda lamented.

"You must remember I took the same training when I was his age."

"You know I do, but you were not my child, you were my playmate, on your way to becoming king. I don't like the idea of our children growing into adulthood."

Without hesitation or embarrassment, Palen took her in his arms. "It is the cycle of life. Just as you and I grew up, it is the same with our children. I'm certain our parents felt the same way when we became adults."

"As usual, you are right. I just fear growing old. Each day we are growing older and our lives are closer to coming to an end. Once the children are grown, we will no longer need Raina. Do you have any plans for her future?"

"I have been giving that quite a bit of thought. Since she is excellent with children, I am thinking she should be in charge of a daycare for the children of working mothers. I would like to have her start designing the facility when the children go back to school in the fall."

"I have a feeling you have been reading my mind. I have been thinking about the same thing for several months now."

Knowing their belongings would be taken to the palace and everything put in its proper place, they made their way to the hovercraft. With Joltan piloting, they relaxed in the backseat.

Palen enjoyed Felda sitting next to him, but he couldn't stop his mind from focusing on the teleconference he had scheduled with

President Anthony Jacobson from Earth and Prime Minister Audra from Seros. As descendants of the exiles from Plantas, they had all taken their places in the government of their adopted planets.

~ * ~

Felda knew her husband's mind was occupied with the teleconference, but she was anxious to see her children. She knew she would find Mira in the nursery getting reacquainted with Raina. As for Kratan, she understood his new position in the household. She didn't want to intrude on him in his apartment, nor did she want to embarrass him in front of his friends. She made the decision she would let him come to her.

Even though she'd seen Mira just before leaving for this last trip, she could swear her daughter had grown several inches and matured.

"Mama, I'm so glad you're finally home. Raina was telling me about all the things she has planned for us this summer. Do you think you will be able to join us?"

"I think that could be arranged. I'll have to check my schedule against the one Raina has set up for your outings. For now, I want to hear all about what you did at school before you began your summer break."

For the next hour, she listened as Mira described the lessons that she enjoyed the most and the friends she'd made but would not see until school resumed in the fall.

~ * ~

Palen checked his schedule before walking through the familiar hallways to the apartment that would now belong to his son. He knew how Felda felt concerning the children becoming adults.

He remembered how he felt when his father first moved his residence from the nursery to the apartment for the crown prince. When he walked in for the first time, he felt as though he was a grown man, ready to take on the world, only to learn he was still little more than a boy with much to learn before proclaiming his manhood.

Over the past few weeks, he'd ordered his son's belongings to be moved here so he could take up his proper residence in the palace. Would Kratan be wise enough to understand this was just his first step in preparation for manhood and someday taking his place on the throne? He hoped so.

In reality, he knew the new status would go to his son's head as it had gone to his so many years earlier. It took him several months to realize, although his age denoted manhood, his maturity needed more experiences and education to catch up.

After acknowledging the bodyguard at the door, he put his hand on the door handle to the apartment which had at one time belonged to him. Without bothering to knock, he entered the apartment. From one of the inner rooms, he heard Kratan hurrying to see who had entered his sanctuary.

"What is wrong with the guard at the door? How dare he allow someone to enter without knocking or waiting to be…" he stopped his rant short when he saw Palen standing in the living area of his apartment. "Father, I didn't know it was you. I assumed…"

Palen held up his hand for silence. "I am certain you think now that you are situated in the apartment for the crown prince, you have the same authority as I do. I will tell you, my son, you do not. You are taking just the first step into manhood. When you return to school it will be secondary school, where you will prepare for university as well as your service in the military. Don't overstep your bounds and alienate those who, one day, will be your staunchest advisors."

"I thought when I moved out of the nursery, I would be considered a man."

"That is the problem: you thought. When I was your age, I did the same thing. I made many bad decisions and almost lost the love of your mother. We'd grown up together and I always knew I would make her my life mate. Unfortunately, I acted like a fool around several young ladies in the kingdom and she let me know if I wanted to dally with others, she would be doing the same thing. When I went to Bankos, we weren't even speaking to one another. As soon as I returned home, I went to the school where she was teaching and watched her with her students. In that moment, I realized how much I loved her and that I didn't want to ever lose her. Don't make the same mistakes as I did."

"I am different from you, Father, I have not met the woman I want to take as my life mate. How will I find a suitable mate, if I do not meet many women?"

"You have to go secondary school, university and serve in the military. During that time, you will find a woman who will satisfy you for the remainder of your life. It is not something you can rush into blindly. Pray to the One God and he will guide you in your quest. Just remember, it is important for you as well as your life mate to be virgins on the day you are mated to one another. I have never regretted waiting for my mating day to make love to a woman. Since that day I have seen many beautiful women, but none that can compare to your mother."

Palen watched as the words he just spoke to his son had a chance to sink in. In his mind, he was a thirteen-year-old boy who just moved into the apartment for the crown prince. He could sense his son's disappointment at not being able to become a womanizer. He wished his father had been as frank with him as he was now being with Kratan.

"I am sorry, Father. I understand what you are telling me. In anticipation of moving into my own apartments, I was not very polite to my sister. I told her women had no place in government."

"You are right, it was a terrible thing to tell her. I thought you were taught better than that. There is no way I could rule this planet if it weren't for your mother. If you don't change your attitude, I fear you will never become king in my stead. Perhaps I should seriously consider training your sister for leadership."

The expression on Kratan's face told Palen he had gotten the response he wanted. With the cold truth put forward to his son, he knew Kratan would work harder to change his attitude, not only about women but also about his importance.

"I am sorry, Father. I will seek out my sister and apologize to her. After that I will study hard and not make assumptions about the importance of anyone on the planet."

Palen wanted to take his son in his arms, but instead clasped his forearm in a manlier gesture.

Chapter Ten

Palen, along with Felda, made his way to the telecommunication center for the scheduled teleconference with Prime Minister Audra from Seros and President Antony Jacobson from Earth.

It took several minutes before both connections were made. Knowing both of the leaders he would be talking to had parents who originally came from Plantas and mated with those from their new adopted planet gave him pause to think about Kratan's chances of marrying within the parameters of those with ties to Plantas. With so few of their people actually arriving on Nalo, it was possible both his son and daughter would find love outside of their own race. It had been so with his sister. Her mating was not only a loving one, but also a productive union. They easily settled into the role of governors on the far side of the planet.

"Greetings."

Palen returned his attention to the screen. The face of President Jacobson came into view.

"The same to you," he replied.

Before he could say more, he saw Prime Minister Audra's image appear on the other side of the split screen.

"Am I late?" Audra asked.

"We both just got connected," Anthony replied. "I'm glad this conference could be established."

"I have a question for both of you," Palen began. "I've been told Earth has joined the Confederation and Seros is considering it. How close to the truth is this?"

"Earth still doesn't have one central government, so getting all of the leaders to decide on something like this has been difficult. It has been proposed, but we need to know more about what this affiliation will mean for us."

"That is where Seros is more advanced than you are, Anthony. I am the Prime Minister and representative of our ruling monarch. We have had many meetings with their representatives, but no decision has been made. What is Nalo planning to do, Palen?"

"That is why I called for this meeting. I didn't want to rely on the information I've received from the Confederation. I know many of their leaders from my time on Bankos. They can be very convincing but I don't trust them completely. Have you been approached about a meeting with the Confederation leaders?"

From the expressions on the faces of his counterparts, he knew they hadn't heard of any such thing.

"I have a feeling the Confederation leaders are trying to play one of us against the other," Anthony declared. "I don't think the time is right for such a meeting. I do think it is in our best interests if we become each other's strongest allies. The space program on each of our planets has accelerated since the refugees first arrived. At this point, traveling between our planets is not only feasible but something we each should be looking into. I know there are many descendants of those who came from Plantas who would like to reconnect with our counterparts on Seros and Nalo."

The suggestion from Anthony intrigued Palen. He knew the history of the people from Plantas, mostly from Felda, but also from his parents. He had a hard time comprehending what it would be like to know your home planet would be destroyed after the refugees left, making returning to the familiar impossible.

Even with the budding space program the scientists were working on, Palen knew interplanetary travel to such faraway places like Earth and Seros would not be possible during his lifetime. While he'd been in the military, he'd been deployed to a nearby planet. It had been a harrowing journey, so he couldn't comprehend traversing the galaxy to such distant destinations.

~ * ~

Kratan was intrigued with the idea of interplanetary space travel. While his father talked of more assistance to the space program, he wondered what the upside to such exploration would be.

Over the summer, he read all the history books his mother provided to him. He was disappointed by the fact she told him he should study with one of the teachers at the secondary school, rather than rely on her, as she hadn't been in a classroom in over ten years.

"I realize ancient history cannot be rewritten, but with all the advancements in the education community, I would do you a disservice to teach you in an antiquated way. Your instructors at secondary school will do a much better job than I can."

As Kratan thought back on the advice he'd received from his mother, he knew she made sense. Once he returned to school, he'd inquired about adding ancient history to his schedule. Although he wouldn't be eligible to study it for another year, he knew he'd made the right decision. From what he'd heard, the teacher was considered one of the best on the planet.

"Hey, Kratan, what are you doing tonight after classes?"

Kratan turned at the sound of his roommate's voice. He knew what many other students had planned for the evening. They were going to go to one of the drinking palaces and sample the local fermented beverages. Since they were all underage, it was possible they could be either thrown out on their ears or expelled from school.

"I have studying to do. Tomorrow is the big test. Besides, I doubt you would appreciate having my bodyguard accompanying you on your foray to the drinking palace."

"How did you know where we were going?"

"This is a small dorm and nothing remains a secret for long. You know I would enjoy going with you, but my father holds me to a higher standard. I won't betray you, but I also won't accompany you. Go with the rest of our friends and enjoy your evening. Your secret is safe with me."

Whether it was the refusal to join his friends or the thought of getting caught, he would never know, but that evening saw many of his friends, including his roommate, joining Kratan in the library, studying for the test that would be administered the next day.

~ * ~

For Mira, returning to school was different from any previous years. Before, even with the difference in their ages, she and Kratan were going to school on the same campus. Even though he was still technically on the same campus, his classes were being held at the secondary school and their paths would no longer intersect.

This year she had no older brother to run interference for her when the school bullies tried to intimidate her. Everyone knew she was a princess, but there were many who teased her for being the daughter of the king.

She was on her way back to the dorm after class when two of the boys who were her tormentors the year before approached her.

"Princess Mira, we would like to take your brother's place as your protectors," Baja said.

He was one of the original inhabitants of Nalo, without a drop of Plantas blood running through his veins. She observed that over the summer he'd grown and was now turning into a very handsome young man.

"Why are you being so nice to me?"

Baja's friend, Sorodo, broke into a wide smile. "It seems that the headmaster here at the school is a good friend of both of our fathers. When we went home for the summer break, we were admonished for the way we treated you last year. It was worse than the beating we took from your brother and his friends. We had no freedom for the entire summer and had to promise to become your protectors for this school year."

"That is if you will allow us to be your protectors," Baja

interjected.

"I will accept your offer. To be truthful, I worried about being here at school without Kratan to look out for me."

Both of the boys beamed at her acceptance. What she didn't know, at the time, was that the three of them would form a friendship that would follow them throughout their lives.

Chapter Eleven

With Mira approaching her nineteenth birthday and the end of her freshman year at the university, she marveled at how her life had changed over the past eight years.

Five years earlier, she'd said goodbye to Raina and delighted in how the nursery was transformed from an apartment for babies to one fit for a royal princess.

She, Baja and Sorodo had become like the Three Musketeers she read about in the history of Earth. All through their years at elementary and secondary school, her friends stood in solidarity against all the bullies who thought it acceptable to harass the young royal.

While she loved both Baja and Sorodo, she also knew one day she would be forced to make a choice between the two of them. She was of an age where she should be thinking of mating, even though her mother insisted she needed to finish her education before she considered becoming a wife and mother.

"Are you ready for the new school year to begin?" Baja asked when they reunited at the beginning of the term, outside her dorm.

"I am, but where is Sorodo? I thought he would be with you."

Baja's expression darkened. "Over the summer, he went to the far side of the planet with his parents. It was meant to be an educational vacation, but instead, they were in a terrible accident. It was a malfunction of their hovercraft and both he and his mother were killed instantly."

Mira gasped. "How could something like that happen?"

"I met with Sorodo's father, once he was brought back to Capitol City. He feels it was sabotage because of his standing with his company.

I don't know if I accept his accusations, but when I spoke to my father about it, he seemed to agree. He said back when King Hedro was in power there were assassination attempts on your father's life. At that time those responsible for them were called The Pure of Nalo. Recently, some fractions of that group have contacted my father and asked him to join their group. He declined their offer and reported these men to one of your father's advisors, Alden. He also reported them after he heard about the accident involving Sorodo's family."

"Is your family in danger?"

"Father says no. Those responsible have been apprehended and sent to the penal colony. It was all kept quiet, as everyone thought that movement was, indeed, long dead."

Tears rolled down Mira's cheeks. "When will the evildoers of this planet realize my ancestors came, not to destroy, but to enlighten and help everyone on Nalo? My grandmother, Wasla, has treated everyone with the respect they deserve and has saved many lives. My father, like my grandfather before him, has ruled without prejudice. Still, one of my best friends has given his life to those who want to destroy us."

"Please don't cry, Mira," Baja said, taking her in his arms. "Sorodo may be gone, but he will never be forgotten by anyone who knew him. Rest assured, I will never desert you. Together, Sorodo and I pledged our loyalty to you eight years ago. Nothing has changed."

Even though Mira believed Baja's words, she soon learned he was going to be inducted into the military. For the first time in her life, she would be entirely alone.

~ * ~

Kratan was home on leave when he first heard of the accident that took the lives of Sorodo and his mother. He'd been surprised when his father insisted he join him in the throne room.

"I am certain you have heard about the deaths of Sorodo and his mother," Palen began. "Back when you were but a baby, there was a group by the name of The Pure of Nalo and they made an attempt on my life as well as that of your grandfather. At the time, we thought we had eliminated everyone involved in their treachery, but we were mistaken. We have uncovered a cell of these militants and learned they were involved with the accident, since Sorodo's father wouldn't align his loyalties with them."

"How did you learn this?"

"You must know that Sorodo and his friend Baja proclaimed themselves your sister's protectors. It was Baja's father who came to Alden and explained how he had been approached by the same people. He didn't give them an answer to their proposition. Instead he alerted us. Alden also visited Sorodo's father in the hospital. Between the two of them, they have given us enough names to rout out the militants. I am ready to give you and your battalion the information as to where to find these militants. You are to arrest them and bring them to justice."

Kratan swallowed hard. What his father was suggesting was a full-out military operation, not on foreign soil but right here on Nalo.

"I know this is a dangerous assignment, and I wouldn't put this on your shoulders if I didn't think it was necessary. You, along with your battalion, are the best of the best and will carry out this assignment with precision and secrecy."

Pride filled Kartan's heart. "I will do my best for you and for Nalo."

For the first time, his father saluted him, as though he was any other military commanding officer. Had his father reacted in any other way, Kratan would have been disappointed.

~ * ~

Kratan's unit approached the headquarters of The Pure of Nalo. His heart pounded in anticipation of confronting the militants who thought nothing of killing innocent women and children. He revised his thinking. Sorodo was not a child. He would have soon been nineteen and eligible for military service. He was a man whose life was cut short in retaliation for his father's refusal to join forces with those who were against the rulers of their planet. In other words, these were the descendants of the men who tried to take his father's life over twenty-two years earlier.

He looked back at his men and gave the silent command for them to close in on the headquarters. They had the element of surprise in their corner.

In a tactical movement, they broke down the door, surprising the occupants of the house. Across the back wall of the room, Kratan noticed a handmade banner proclaiming THE PURE OF NALO WILL OVERCOME, written in blood.

Before any of the militants could reach for their weapons, the men of Kratan's battalion had them surrounded and were pointing their laser weapons at them. It turned Kratan's stomach to realize, although there were many men his father's age, the majority of the men in the house were closer to his own age. It was evident these people relied on recruiting uneducated youth. With this realization, he remembered one of his father's trusted advisors, Alden. He too had been seduced by these people, not because he held a grudge, but because he knew nothing of the history of their home planet.

"Bind them securely and prepare to transport them to Capitol City."

"What are we charged with?" one of the young men protested.

Kratan did the best he could to hold his temper. "First, you are charged with conspiracy to overthrow the government. Secondly, you are charged with the murder of a young man by the name of Sorodo and his mother, as well as the attempted murder of his father. You will find, in your case, justice will be swift and your lives will be changed forever. May the One God have mercy on your sorry souls."

To his surprise, his men came from a back room of the house with several young hostages. It turned his stomach to realize they were no more than twelve or thirteen years of age. Mere babies. It was possible they had been lured away from their families with the intent of brainwashing them with their political propaganda.

"These boys are no more than children. Keep them separate from the others and contact their parents. I am certain they have been searching for their children. I pray they have not been in the clutches of these fiends long enough to be indoctrinated into their warped ideology."

Hearing these words, the boys began to tremble and cry. "Our parents don't want us. The leaders told us they had been asked to take us."

Kratan knelt in front of the frightened boys. "Your parents do want you. These men have lied to you, just as they have lied to each other over the past twenty-five years. They are evil men with hatred in their souls. They would have led you into lives that mirrored their own."

"Who are you?" one of the boys questioned. "Do you know our parents?"

"I am Major Kratan. Unfortunately, I do not know your parents, but I know mine. They love me just as your parents love you. You have been deceived, but you have committed no crimes, yet. I want your promise you will stay in school and do your best in your studies. When you are grown, if you come to me, I will see to your future."

"I have heard of the name Kratan. My father told me someday he will be king. Do you know of him?"

"I'm the one your father has told you about. As for being king, that will not happen for a long time. My father, King Palen, is still a young man and he enjoys good health. I look forward to the time when my military service is over and I will be allowed to work more closely with him. For that reason and that reason alone, I will be monitoring your progress until you are old enough to make decisions about your futures."

Kratan followed the men who took charge of the children. He wondered if this was how his father felt when he first met Alden and his companions. They too had been inducted into the service of these evil men, but turned their lives around. From that day forward they remained loyal to not only his father, but all the royal family. He prayed it would be the same with these youngsters.

Rather than accompany his battalion back to Capitol City with the prisoners, he elected to join a few of his men to bring the kidnapped boys back to their parents.

Keeping them in a room at a local inn, he made certain every family was contacted. When they arrived at the inn, he met with all of them individually. Each set of parents told the same story, their children went out to play and never came home. All of the families contacted the authorities. It didn't take long before the disappearances became a rash of more and more incidents.

After speaking with each family, he addressed them all together. "My men and I were on a military mission for King Palen. Your children were kidnapped by a cell of militants who were planning to brainwash them to rise up against the government of our planet. Because of their age, I feel there is hope for them and for their future. As the crown prince of Nalo, I am returning them to your care. In doing so, I will be following them until they are old enough to become men. When they are, I will be more than happy to assist them in whatever endeavors they choose to pursue. Many years ago, my father mentored eight young men taken in by militants like the ones who took your children. Today they are among his trusted advisors. I plan to do the same for your sons as what he did for the eight young men he saved on that day."

"We are in your debt, Your Highness," the father of one of the boys declared. "We were afraid we would never see our sons again. Now, you have returned them to us not only for their safekeeping, but you have guaranteed their futures. We will never be able to repay you."

"Perhaps you will be able to repay what you feel is a debt before you think. As the eyes and ears of your king in this area, I would pray to the One God that you will feel free to contact either my father or myself should you hear of any other rumblings of The Pure of Nalo in the future. These are evil men who fear anyone who is different from them. My father, like his father before him, has been loyal to everyone on Nalo. Among his advisors are people from all over the planet. He cares not if they were with his father on the ship that arrived from Plantas. He did not come here to overthrow your government, but when it did happen, it was the will of the people that he should step into the position he'd been trained for on Plantas."

The grandfather of one of the boys stood up. "My wife and I have been raising our grandson ever since his parents were killed in a freak accident. I was a young man when the refugees first landed on Nalo. At the time, I feared them, but I soon learned of the good they brought to our people. I agree, we must all work together in order to eliminate those who claim to be The Pure of Nalo. My eyes and ears will be open to report any suspicious activity to the king."

The older man clasped Kratan's arm, as did all the other men and women in the room. He'd gotten his point across and made allies in the process.

Once the boys were reunited with their parents, Kratan knew his work was done. These children had been saved from the fate that awaited the militants who were now, most likely, on their way to spend the remainder of their lives on the penal colony.

Pleased with the outcome of this confrontation, he prepared to go back to Capitol City and debrief his father.

~ * ~

News of the confrontation with The Pure of Nalo and the prisoners who would be bound for the penal colony reached Capitol City quickly.

Ever since deploying his son on this mission, Palen worried about the outcome. These militants would like nothing better than to be able to brag about taking the life of the crown prince of Nalo.

Kratan's second in command arrived at the palace and was announced. Although Palen was shocked to hear it wasn't his son, he agreed to meet with the man who knew his son so well.

"Your Majesty," the man said, bowing low. "My commander, Major Kratan, has assigned me to come to you with a report of the capture of those we encountered at the headquarters for The Pure of Nalo."

"Come into my study, so we can speak in private."

Palen got up from his throne chair and led the way into the study. Once they were comfortable, he began.

"I have been told you have brought in prisoners with no casualties. I commend you for a job well done. What I don't understand is why you are sitting before me rather than my son?"

"The mission went off flawlessly. We had the element of surprise on our side. The militants were unable to even reach their weapons when we broke into their headquarters. As we were getting ready to take the prisoners and return to Capitol City, two others of our party returned from their search of the house and with them were six young boys. None of them could have been older than twelve or thirteen years old. It was Major Kratan's decision to remain behind with the children until they were reunited with their parents. I volunteered to stay in his place, but he said it was his duty."

Palen smiled at the man's story. It brought back the memory of when he stayed with the eight young men, Alden and the others, who became his trusted friends. It was inevitable his son would be doing the same with these youngsters.

"You have executed your duties well, Captain. You and your men deserve a month to rest before you return to duty. Use your time well so you can return well rested."

The captain bowed low and turned to leave the study.

Palen watched him, a smile gracing his lips. The son who had once degraded women had grown into a man of whom he could take pride. He would be the perfect choice to take his place when the time came.

Chapter Twelve

Mira read the last transmission she'd received from Baja. In it, he explained how his military service would be up in the spring, when he would be returning to Capitol City to ask her father for permission to mate with her.

She'd always delighted in the stories her mother told of how her father came back from his military duty and asked for permission for the two of them to be mated. It was such a romantic story, she prayed Baja would be as romantic as her father had been.

In the spring she would be graduating from the university and be ready to become a teacher, as her mother had been. Would Baja honor her wishes or would he insist she should be content to be a life mate and a mother?

She stored the text message away in her telecommunicator and hurried down to the main living area of the palace. She was home during the winter break and was anxious to meet her mother for luncheon.

"You look like you've received good news," Felda greeted her.

"I have. Baja will be finished with his military service in the spring. He is planning to ask Father for his permission for the two of us to be mated."

Felda smiled. "I remember your father doing the same thing. At the time I was disheartened when he had to return to his unit and we had to wait. Your father was like your brother and served as an officer. Thankfully, Baja has no such aspirations and will be free to mate with you. In the meantime, remember you still need to continue your studies. His asking doesn't mean the mating ceremony will take place immediately. Such a royal ceremony takes much planning and none of that can begin until your father gives his blessing."

Mira nodded her agreement. Much could happen between now and the time for Baja to return to Capitol City. The memory of Sorodo's untimely death reminded her just how fragile life was. With Baja being in the military, even though Nalo was not at war with anyone, other dangers could lurk around every corner.

~ * ~

Baja mounted the steps to the palace. During his military service he'd risen to the rank of sergeant. Even though he wasn't an officer, he was proud of the years he'd spent in the military. With his new status as a civilian and his position within his father's company, he prayed he would be worthy of becoming the life mate to Princess Mira.

In many of their conversations, Mira told him how her aunt married, and she and her life mate worked in the diplomatic corps. Would it be the same with them? He enjoyed working in the hovercraft industry. It wasn't like he was a common line worker. He'd done his share of the line work. Now he worked in the main office as the assistant to his father, the president and owner of the company.

As he made his way into the foyer of the palace, he was stopped by the palace guard. He immediately recognized the man as one of the Eight Elite. He remembered hearing the stories of how King Palen took pity on the young men when they had been enticed by the stories of a group called The Pure of Nalo. Taking pity on them, because of their age, he offered them education, rather than imprisonment. Within months of them accepting his offer, they were the ones to save his life from an assassination attempt.

"State your business," the guard ordered.

"My name is Baja and I have an appointment with King Palen."

He wondered if it was his imagination or if he noticed a smile cross the man's lips.

"You will wait here, while you are announced."

The man nodded toward a ranking officer, who came to Baja's side.

"I am Alden, I will take you to meet with King Palen, but only if he is agreeable to your meeting as well as your intentions."

Baja wanted to shout that he was planning to ask for Princess Mira's hand in mating, but he knew it would be an inappropriate response. He'd been around Mira for more years than he could remember. At first, it was as her tormentor because of her royal status. He smiled as he remembered taking a severe beating at the hands of her brother, Kratan, and later, punishment by his father for doing something so despicable. It had been the same with his best friend Sorodo. From the first day of the next school year on, they became her protectors and now he was ready to profess his love for the exotic beauty of the princess.

He watched as Alden left him standing in a reception room. Even though he had no doubts about gaining her father's approval, his heart pounded in nervous apprehension.

"The king will see you."

It hardly seemed possible that Alden had been gone long enough to even say anything to the King. Baja thanked him and hesitantly took the steps that would take him to the throne room.

"Baja, welcome," Palen greeted him.

"I am honored to be in your presence, Your Majesty."

"I have been expecting you. My daughter has told me of your intentions. Come and sit down, so we can talk of your plans."

Baja watched as the king led him to a more comfortable seating area at the far side of the room. This certainly wasn't how he expected to meet with his king. He thought the man would wear royal robes, along with a crown, and would look down on him from the raised throne. Instead, they each settled into comfortable side chairs. On the small table separating them was a tray with beverages and platters of pastries and fruit. Out of respect, he waited until King Palen filled his plate before indulging himself.

"I have known of your special relationship with my daughter and I thank you for being first her protector, before becoming her friend. Are you ready for the next step in your relationship?"

"Yes, Your Majesty, I am."

"If that is the case, you should probably address me as Palen in private. Do you understand what it will mean when you mate with Mira?"

"I do. She is a royal princess and as such is used to a lifestyle of luxury. I feel I can provide for her, as I have worked for my father in his hovercraft factory, doing every menial job assigned to me, during my years in secondary school. Now, with my military service finished, I have taken my rightful place at my father's side. I work in the main office and am learning everything I need to know to take over the business when my father is ready to retire."

Palen nodded. "I have been told you have an older brother. What of him? Will he not covet your position within your father's company?"

Baja let out a sigh of relief. "My brother has been studying at the University. Once his residency is finished, next year, he will become a healer. He is hoping for a position in one of the outlying provinces. My father is very proud of his accomplishments. Even so, my father is also proud of my military service. I enjoy working within my father's business and hope one day to be as respected by the employees as well as the community."

"Well said, young man. I know of my daughter's feelings for you. It was the same between her mother and myself. She is looking forward to teaching at the secondary level. Would you be content with a working mate?"

"I would. Even though we know it would not be necessary, I understand her desire to teach, at least until we have children and perhaps even after. I have no problems with a working life mate, as my mother has worked side by side with my father as he built his business."

"Would you have a problem living in a home on the palace grounds?"

Baja thought about what Mira's father just asked him. Before coming here, he'd been looking into a small house close to the factory. He never considered living in such close proximity to Mira's family.

"If that is what is necessary for her happiness, I would have no problem with it."

"That is a good answer. I have a feeling Mira might feel differently, but I am prepared to have a home built for the two of you once you are joined. Of course, that will not be for at least a year. Her mother will need that much time to plan for a royal mating ceremony. Do you have a gift of commitment to give to my daughter?"

"I have been looking at rings and trying to decide which one would be perfect to grace her finger."

Palen began to smile. "I am pleased to think you have not yet purchased a ring. Since we have been anticipating this event, it was her Grandmother Wasla's dying wish that Mira have her rings of commitment. Would you be willing to accept them?"

"I would. Even so, I would also like to purchase the ring I have been looking at. If nothing else, she can wear it on her left hand rather than her right, as is the custom of those who came from Plantas. I would do nothing to dishonor her heritage."

"You show great reverence and love for my daughter. I will be pleased to pledge her as your life mate and to call you my son-under-the-law."

Baja wanted to shout for joy, but remembering he was in the presence of royalty, he contained his enthusiasm. After thanking Palen, he got to his feet, and prepared to leave.

"Before you leave, take this."

Palen held out a box housing the ring with the beautiful violet stone that matched Mira's eyes. With it was an engraved mating band. The beauty of the two rings took Baja's breath away and, immediately, he could see it gracing her right hand. He remembered meeting her grandmother once, but at the time she was an old woman, looking at the end of her life. Even so, the rings that would soon belong to Mira caught his attention.

~ * ~

Mira waited in her apartment, her mother at her side. "What if

Father doesn't give his permission to Baja to mate with me?"

"You worry for nothing. Your father has approved of Baja being in your company ever since he took over as your protector, along with Sorodo, after your brother went to secondary school. It will be no different today."

A knock at the door interrupted their conversation.

"The young man, Baja, has come to see Princess Mira. Are you acceptable to his request?"

"Show him in," Felda replied. "I am leaving as I have other duties that require my attention."

Winking broadly at her daughter, she left by the private entrance so as not to encounter Baja on her way out of the apartment.

Mira watched as the outer door opened and Baja was escorted in. He looked dashing in the suit she'd helped him pick out especially for the occasion.

"I have just left your father. He has given his permission. Would you do me the honor of becoming my mate for the rest of our lives?"

He held out the box, but it wasn't one from a local jewelry store. As he opened the cover, she recognized the promise and mating rings she remembered seeing on her grandmother's right hand.

"H-how did you get these rings?"

"Your father gave them to me. He told me it was your Grandmother Wasla's last wish that these rings be given to you in preparation for your mating. I was pleased to accept them."

"Oh, yes, Baja, yes. I have waited for this day for so long. My only regret is that Sorodo will not be there to rejoice with us."

Baja smiled at her acceptance. "Even though I wanted to be mated immediately, I have agreed to wait for one year. In that time your parents will be able to plan a majestic royal mating ceremony and I will become more secure in my position with my father's company. I promise we will be happy. For now, I want to take you to the jewelry store and purchase the ring I planned to give you."

"I don't understand. Why is there a need for another ring?"

"This ring is an heirloom, passed down from your grandmother.

The one I plan to purchase will be special because it represents my love for you. It will grace your left hand, just as this one graces your right. Both will be special and have great meaning."

~ * ~

Kratan prepared to leave the military. He'd spent the last fifteen years of his life serving his planet. In that time, so much had changed in his life. Over those years, the young boys he'd released to their parents grew into young men. Only one of them joined the military, while others had pursued other paths in their lives.

One young man in particular, Jarom, stayed in close contact, as he went through secondary school, university and was now a practicing litigator. Through Jarom, he'd met Liona, Jarom's sister. As a child she was beautiful, but as she grew into adulthood, she was spectacular. Even with the difference in their ages, he'd fallen in love with her. Today, he would ask her father for permission to make her his own.

With the last of his packing finished, he recalled the meeting he'd had with his father to discuss his love for Liona. He'd expected opposition, considering she was not descended from the refugees who came to Nalo so long ago. He was pleasantly surprised when his father enthusiastically supported Kratan's choice for a mate.

"As soon as you obtain her father's permission to mate with her, bring her along with her family, to Capitol City, so we can meet them. I'm certain your mother, as well as the girl's mother, will be anxious to begin planning another royal mating ceremony."

Kratan was more nervous about broaching the subject of bringing Liona and her entire family to Capitol City than asking for the permission to be able to mate with her.

He picked up the last of his bags, and without a backward glance made his way to his personal hovercraft.

Within a matter of hours, he stood on the doorstep to Liona's home. As though he'd been expected, the door opened almost as soon as he knocked. The housekeeper who answered told him the family was in the sitting room and he was more than welcome to join them.

Over the past few years, he'd been a frequent guest in their home and felt comfortable finding his way to the sitting room.

"Have you come to speak with Father?" Liona inquired.

"You know I have. It's only proper for your father to give his blessing. Of course, there are other things we need to discuss."

"Other things?"

"In due time, my love, in due time."

It surprised Kratan to see not only Liona's parents, but also Jarom waiting for him in the sitting room.

"Liona said you would be leaving the military today and coming to our home," her mother said. "We are honored, as we always are, for your presence."

"Thank you. I have come for a special purpose. I would like to speak with Liona's father in private."

"There is no need for a private conversation. I have sensed your intent toward my daughter, and I am honored to give my blessing to your union."

Kratan didn't realize he was holding his breath until Liona's father, Jax, got to his feet, to clasp his arm, before drawing him into a loving embrace. This was the kind of family he'd always wanted, but his father's position as reigning monarch of the planet meant he had been raised by nursemaids, as the duties of the throne always came first.

"I-I don't know what to say. I had everything planned, but with your acceptance and blessing I'm at a loss for words. I met with my parents on my last leave and they want your family to come to Capitol City. That is where the preparations for our royal mating ceremony will be made."

To his surprise, the expression on the faces of Liona's parents was one of shock, rather than excitement at the prospect of going from the fringes of the planet to Capitol City.

"We are not worthy," her father said.

"Why would you say such a thing?"

Jax took a deep breath before he began to speak. "Although we are considered to be comfortably wealthy, we are little more than workers in one of the local factories. We know nothing of the ways of the king and the palace."

"And my father would have no comprehension of the life you live. In the past he has met Jarom and even helped him with his studies of the law. When we last spoke, my father was securing a position for him with a prestigious law firm in Capitol City."

"Did you know of this?" Jax asked his son.

"King Palen sent me a communication about a month ago. He told me of the position and I have told my employers of my intensions to move to Capitol City."

"Oh, Father, with Jarom, as well as myself, moving away, what reason do you have to remain here?" Liona pleaded.

"What of our jobs?"

"There would be no reason for you to work once you relocated, but if you insist on doing so, I am certain there would be a position available to you at the hovercraft factory my sister's life mate and his father manage. I am aware his father is looking to retire and Baja will be taking over his responsibilities. He told me there will be a position in management that must be filled, but he has been unable to find anyone to take over what he has been doing. If you would be willing to be the second in command at such a facility, the position would be yours."

"I have a feeling Liona's young prince has countered each of your excuses not to relocate to Capitol City," Liona's mother Nada said. "We would be pleased to accept your offer, Prince Kratan. How soon would we be expected to make the move?"

"My father wanted me to bring you back with me, but I told him it would not be so easy to close up your life here. Whenever you are ready to make the move, just contact me and I will make all the arrangements. I am prepared to take Liona with me when I return to Capitol City. I am aware Jarom will need some time to tell his current employers of his move."

For the remainder of his visit, the talk was of the relocation to Capitol City. By the time Kratan was ready to leave, Jarom had spoken with his employers and was also ready to leave immediately with Kratan and Liona.

Even Jax and Nada were getting excited and were certain they would be ready to make the move within the next month.

"Where will you, as well as our children, be living, once you return to the palace?" Nada inquired.

"I have a large apartment in the palace where Jarom can stay until he is able to arrange for his own accommodations. As for Liona, she will be taking over my sister's apartments in the palace. Since my sister mated, she and her life mate have moved into a house close to the manufacturing plant. Although my father wanted to build her a home on the palace grounds, my mother overrode his decision, saying Mira and Baja needed to be on their own, and not under the watchful eyes of her parents. Once we are settled, we will begin to look for accommodations for you and Jax. I'm certain Liona will be able to find something that will meet your expectations."

"I can't believe how quickly things move around you," Jax commented. "With this one visit, you have changed our lives for the better. I never envisioned living in Capitol City, to say nothing of being in administration at such a well-known manufacturing facility. If we are able to sell our home, we should be ready to move within the month. I know my wife will not be satisfied until she is once again living in close proximity to our children."

Chapter Thirteen

Felda anxiously awaited the arrival of Kratan, along with Liona and Jarom. Even though she'd met Jarom when he visited Capitol City, she'd never met Liona. However, she felt as though she knew her soon-to-be daughter-under-the-law intimately, from the many conversations she'd participated in with Kratan.

As soon as she received word of when Kratan would be bringing Liona and her brother to the palace, she'd ordered the apartment once occupied by her daughter Mira be aired out and cleaned before Liona's arrival. At the same time, she ordered that Kratan's apartments also be refreshed in anticipation of his arrival with Jarom.

Knowing her instructions would be carried out to the letter, she went down to the main reception hall to wait for Kratan and his fiancée, along with her brother, to arrive.

"You are pacing like a caged animal, my love," Palen said, coming to her side before engulfing her in his strong arms.

"It has been so long since I've seen our son. I am anxious for his return."

"I think you are more anxious to meet the woman who has stolen his heart. When I am gone, you will become the Queen Mother. At that time, Kratan and his bride will rule in our place. Do you think she will measure up to your high standards?"

"My standards matter not. She is the choice of our son, and as such, the only standards she needs to measure up to are those of Kratan. He has made it quite clear she is the woman of his choice, even though there is a great difference in their ages."

"I have been giving the matter much thought and, with Liona having no Plantas blood, their union should put an end to those upstart followers of those who call themselves The Pure of Nalo. It is bad enough Kratan and I have had to deal with them. This union should be good for the entire planet."

"Are you certain that Liona's parents will have a position with Baja's company?"

"The arrangements have been made, and Baja has been in contact with Jax's current employers. They were thrilled with the position he was being offered and will be helping with the sale of their home. I am certain they will be an added asset to Capitol City."

Felda shamelessly hugged her husband within the sight of the palace guards. "You have been more than generous in accommodating Liona's family."

A commotion from the outer courtyard ended their conversation. The exuberant shouts of the guards as well as many of the townspeople, heralded the arrival of Kratan.

Felda resisted the urge to give into the excitement of the moment and run out to the courtyard as though she was a young woman rather than the queen of this planet.

"Mother, Father," Kratan declared, as soon as he entered the main reception hall. "It is good to be home. This is Liona and her brother, Jarom."

Jarom bowed deeply and Liona curtsied.

"There is no need for such formality, as you are soon-to-be members of our family," Palen said, as he stepped forward to embrace Liona and clasp Jarom's forearm.

"We are pleased to be here, Your Majesty," Jarom said, taking the obligation of conversation from his sister. "Prince Kratan has had a great influence on my life. Without his intervention, I am certain I would be serving a life sentence on the penal colony, had he not stepped in and turned my life around."

"I am aware of what transpired between the two of you while you were under the spell of The Pure of Nalo. I had the same experience when

I was in the military, and the young men I mentored have become my closest friends. They serve as not only some of my top advisors but my most trusted personal guards. I have heard good things about the work you have been doing with your former employers. I expect the same from you when you serve with the royal litigators."

"These children are tired," Felda interrupted. "Their return to Capitol City has been a long journey. They need to rest and wash the space dust from their bodies. I will escort Liona to her apartment while you and these young men continue your conversation in Kratan's apartment."

Turning away from the men, she embraced Liona and led her away from the reception hall. "I have been looking forward to your arrival and you are just as lovely as my son has told me. I've missed having my daughter living at the palace. Even though we wanted to build a cottage for her and Baja on the palace grounds, they wanted to live closer to the hovercraft plant. I cannot fault them for not wanting to be under our watchful eye, especially since she is not in the line of royal succession."

"Kratan has told me much about his sister. I am anxious to meet her. I hope we will become fast friends."

It was the first time Felda heard the girl speak and, to her, Liona's voice sounded like the sweet sound of the morning birds that heralded the dawning in the palace gardens.

~ * ~

"I fear I am overwhelmed by the grandeur of the palace, Your Majesty."

"Did you not hear my husband? We are to be family. If you do not want to call me Mother, you have my permission to address me as Felda. Within the palace we are very informal."

"Thank you, Felda. I have been afraid my brother's affiliation with The Pure of Nalo, would be a stumbling block between my family and yours."

"On the contrary. My husband approved of the way our son handled the situation all those years ago. With your joining, this business of the royal family being not of this planet will be dispelled. It is true that my parents, as well as those of my beloved life mate, were of the refugees who came from Plantas so many years ago. I am certain you have heard the story of their arrival. It was a terrible time for our people. Our planet was dying and the majority of our contingency was destroyed in a meteor storm. Only the ship carrying our families and a few others were able to land safely on Nalo. We thought all the rest were lost. It was many years after our arrival when we learned the last ship in our group was able to survive and make it to Earth."

"I cannot imagine surviving such a harrowing journey. I have studied the history and look forward to going to the libraries here in Capitol City to increase my knowledge. My mother and father insisted on it when my brother got into trouble when he was so young."

Felda nodded. "I am certain you and Mira will become friends."

~ * ~

Kratan walked through the familiar rooms and halls of the palace, reliving many of his childhood memories. For the time being, he would be sharing his apartment with Jarom. It wasn't as though he was a stranger to sharing his accommodations with someone. Until he reached the rank of officer, he'd lived in the barracks with other soldiers. Still, he was concerned about sharing his apartment. This had been his sanctuary ever since he left Mira behind in the nursery.

Memories of Mira and the nursery that became her apartment brought to mind the fact Liona would be occupying Mira's apartment. With it being on the far wing of the palace, he knew the distance between their two apartments would be but a minor hindrance to the two of them getting better acquainted.

His musings were interrupted when his father opened the door to the apartment that he would be sharing with Jarom. For him, he was home. For Jarom, the grandeur caused him to gasp when he stepped into the sitting room.

"I am unworthy of this," Jarom protested. "Perhaps I should look for accommodations in the city, closer to the offices where I will be practicing law. I am certain Prince Kratan would appreciate the solitude in preparation for his joining with my sister."

Kratan applauded when Jarom made, what he felt, were the obligatory suggestions. As much as he relished the aloneness the apartment always meant for him, he wanted Jarom to become comfortable in Capitol City before he ventured out looking for accommodations within the city.

"Nonsense, my boy," Palen replied, before Kratan could make a comment. "Unlike your sister, these accommodations are only temporary. I have spoken with the partners of your firm and once they get to know you, they will be able to help you find the perfect apartment to fit your needs. They, like you, are of the younger generation and you will find their assistance invaluable. For now, allow us to enjoy your presence in the palace."

Jarom simply nodded his head in acceptance of Palen's suggestion. "I am anxious to meet the members of the firm where I will be working."

"All in due time," Palen said. "You will stay at the palace until your office space has been refurbished for you. The senior partner in the firm assures me everything will be ready for you within the week. Once you become familiar with the workings of the firm, you will learn they are the main litigators for the palace. From what they tell me, you will be assigned to the account for my son. In time, you will be the chief litigator for the king. It will give you the most prestigious position on the planet. From everything I have learned from your instructors, as well as the firm for which you worked before; you are most certainly up to the challenge."

Kratan was pleased to see the pride in Jarom's eyes at the encouraging words from his king. He, too, checked out the younger man's credentials before suggesting his father use his pull to get him affiliated with a good law firm. In the years to come, he knew the two of them would work well together, not only as king and king's attorney, but also as brothers-under-the-law. Theirs would be a good partnership that would stand the test of time.

~ * ~

Liona took in the opulence of the apartment that had been assigned to her. In all her life, she'd never seen anything like this.

Once the queen left the apartment, she took time to examine every inch of the accommodations that was now hers. Each piece of furniture looked too delicate to be serviceable. In order to test it out, she seated herself in one of the chairs. To her surprise, the piece was completely comfortable and seemed to be sturdier than she originally thought it to be.

A knock at the apartment door came as a surprise. Before she could get up to answer it, the maid she'd been introduced to earlier greeted whoever it was on the other side.

"Oh, Mistress Mira, it is good to see you. Mistress Liona is in the salon. I'm certain you know the way."

"I most certainly do. It is good to see you again, and I am so pleased to see you have been engaged to take care of my soon-to-be sister-under-the-law."

Suddenly, Liona felt her mouth go dry. Meeting the queen had been informal. She was not so certain about confronting the one person who knew Kratan the best. Before she could contemplate the situation further, Mira entered the salon.

"You must be Liona. Kratan's description of you did not do you justice. I am Mira and I know we are going to be great friends. I just couldn't wait until the official dinner tonight to meet you. Baja and I have left the children with their nursemaid. He is as anxious to meet your brother as I am to meet you."

Mira's kind words soothed Liona's misgivings. Before she could drop to a curtsy, Mira pulled her into a loving embrace.

"Please, I don't need such reverence. I am no longer a royal princess. I gave up that title when I followed my heart."

"I was hoping we could be friends. I know no one in Capitol City and I am anxious to go to the Royal Library to read more of the history of our planet. I want to know everything so I can be a helpmate to Kratan."

Mira led Liona to one of the couches in the room where they both seated themselves. "I cannot believe you have an interest in history. Before I was mated, I too loved history. I will enjoy taking you to the Royal Library. If I know my mother, she will want to keep you busy with plans for your mating ceremony, but we will find the time to do that which you desire. Mother can be overbearing, but between the two of us we will be able to talk her into joining us, as she was one of the best teachers of history on the planet before she and my father were mated."

For the first time, Liona relaxed. She liked Mira and could feel an instant friendship blossoming.

~ * ~

Jarom was surprised to see his belongings had been unpacked and put into the second bedroom of Kratan's apartment. At the insistence of the king, Kratan's personal valet was now assigned to him.

After Jarom had taken a refreshing bath, Picor, the valet, was there to assist him in choosing the proper clothing for tonight's royal dinner.

From the sitting room of the apartment, he heard Kratan speaking to another person. He was almost afraid to interrupt their conversation.

"Perhaps I should wait in here and not intrude on Kratan and his visitor," Jarom commented.

"What nonsense are you speaking, Master Jarom? Prince Kratan's visitor is his brother-under-the-law, Baja. When he arrived, he said he was anxious to meet you. Not only is he the owner of the largest manufacturing plant on Nalo, he is also good friends with Prince Kratan, as well as several of the partners of the firm you will soon be joining. They were all in the military together and have been close friends ever since."

Jarom took a deep breath and nodded his agreement to Picor before going into the salon, where he knew he would be meeting with Kratan and Baja.

"We thought perhaps Picor drowned you while you were in the bath," Kratan teased. "This is my brother-under-the-law, Baja. He is anxious to meet another soon-to-be member of our family."

"I'm sorry I took so long. When I heard you speaking with Baja, I did not want to interrupt. It was Picor who told me who your visitor was. I am pleased to make your acquaintance, Baja. The opportunity you have made available to my father is more than anyone could ask for."

Baja crossed the room and clasped Jarom's forearm in greeting. "It is I who am excited to meet you. When I read the credentials for your father, I was more than impressed. I am certain we will make a good team in running our operation. I've been told several of our friends, who work for the firm where you will be working, will be at tonight's dinner. They are as anxious to make your acquaintance as I am."

"I feel overwhelmed." Jarom said. "I am not used to such adulation. I know I proved myself as a litigator in my former position. I hope I can do the same now that I am here in Capitol City."

Kratan put his hand on Jarom's shoulder. "You will find things are no different here than they were in your former position and home. Even though my father has ruled fairly, I'm hoping I will be a more personable leader. Now, let us enjoy a drink together before we go down to the dinner my mother has orchestrated for your first night in Capitol City."

Jarom worried about what Kratan planned to give him. Other than wine, he'd never indulged in strong spirits. In the past, his friends did things unfitting of proper gentlemen while out drinking. He never wanted to disgrace either himself or his family by such actions.

"This wine is made especially for the royal family," Kratan said, as he handed Jarom and Baja each a wine glass. "It is said one of the people who came from Plantas brought the precious seeds with them. Their family had an award-winning winery on their former planet, and they hoped to find fertile ground once they arrived on Nalo. As we all know, things were much different here, as the land wasn't receptive to growing plants and food. Thankfully, the greenhouses were in place, and the refugees were able to obtain land and build greenhouses for the vineyard."

"That is ancient history, my friend," Baja commented. "It's one of the blessings that the refugees brought with them the ability to rehabilitate the soil and now farming flourishes without the use of the greenhouses. We have much to be grateful to the refugees for."

Jarom took a sip of the wine. It was, indeed, the best he'd ever tasted. As he savored the sweet flavor, he thought about what Kratan and Baja said.

When he'd affiliated himself with The Pure of Nalo, he'd been convinced the refugees brought nothing good with them. He'd never heard of the advances they brought with them. It was terrible to think of the ground being so polluted it was unfit for growing food. Had it not been for Kratan, he would have continued to do so much damage to those who had done so much good for the people of Nalo.

"How do you like the wine?" Kratan asked, breaking into Jarom's thoughts.

"It is excellent. I could become used to drinking it."

"You shall," Baja chimed in. "As Kratan's brother-under-the-law, it is always served when there is a special occasion to celebrate. In other words, my father-under-the-law is very generous with his friends and family."

Jarom wondered how much of what Baja just said would come to pass. He certainly wasn't marrying the king's daughter. He was merely Liona's brother. Once he was settled into his accommodations in the city, he doubted he would be a frequent visitor to the palace.

"Is everything in place for Jax and Nada's arrival?" Kratan inquired.

Jarom was pleased to have the conversation no longer centering on him and his opinions.

"I have been in contact with both Jax's employers as well as Jax. Things are moving quicker than we ever expected. His former employers have bought their home and I am making arrangements for them to move into the home of my parents."

Jarom came to immediate attention. "How can that be? Will your parents be content to share their home with my parents?"

"Hardly. My parents are much older than yours. They are ready for retirement and Mother has been adamant about getting rid of their large home, even though she had servants, and moving into a smaller home. There is a new retirement community on the far side of the city. At her insistence, Father commissioned a new home to be built for them as well as all new furniture. Your parents will be able to move into a fully furnished home complete with a full staff of servants."

For a moment, Jarom was at a loss for words. "W-will they be able to afford such a luxury?"

"The house, as well as the servants, are financed by the company. It's the same with the home Mira and I share with our children. Things are much different here in Capitol City, especially since the refugees arrived. They brought so many advances it has been a benefit for the entire planet."

"I know you're thinking of the days when you were enticed by The Pure of Nalo," Kratan said, coming to Jarom's side. "It's taken longer for all of the advances to reach the farthest provinces, but my father and I are hoping to change those things, now that we are able to work together. I saw a lot of resentment when I was in the military, but soon it will all come to an end. With Liona at my side, I know we will do great things."

"Have you spoken to my sister about your plans?"

"Not yet. We have a full year to wait for our mating. In that time, we will be making a plan for our future. I have no doubts about the viability of our union. I understand she is young and is going to be overwhelmed for the first few weeks. Once she is comfortable, we will begin making our plans."

Jarom hoped his sister was up for the task of becoming queen one day. For now, it was a fairy tale, but in time it would be a reality.

"Where will you live once you are mated?" Baja questioned.

"Certainly not in the palace. You must remember, when you and Mira were mated, my parents commissioned a cottage to be built for you on the palace grounds. Since you preferred to live in the city, it was never built. There is also the cottage my parents inhabited when they were first mated. It has sat empty for so long; it will be completely refurbished. That means we will be able to design the interior to suit our needs."

Jarom knew his sister would be thrilled to design her new home. She'd always enjoyed decorating her room differently with each changing of the season.

~ * ~

The banquet hall was ablaze with lights. Felda was in her element. She enjoyed entertaining and tonight was extra special. Her beloved son was home with the woman he would be mating within a year. She was also excited to get to know her future daughter-under-the-law along with her brother. Considering there would now be young people in the palace again, she'd invited Mira and Baja, along with many of their friends. It was her hope these young people would become close to Liona and Jarom as well.

As the guests began arriving, she made it a point to greet each and every one of them. These were the young men and women she'd known as children. Their parents had been her peers before she became queen and had still remained close, although they didn't get together as often as they once had, they still kept in touch.

When Kratan and Liona entered the hall, all Felda could do was gasp. It was evident Mira had helped her with her clothing as well as dressing her hair. She had no doubts why her son loved this woman with all his heart.

"Good evening, Mother," Kratan greeted her. "It is my honor to present Liona to you. She is excited to experience her first official state dinner."

"I am, indeed, honored to be in your presence," Liona said, as she dropped to a formal curtsy.

"I will have none of that. I told you earlier we do not observe such formalities in our home. Even though this is a state dinner, you, as well as the rest of our guests, are friends and family. For tonight we are not the king and the queen. We are your hosts and are excited to have each and every one of you at our table. I pray the meal with meet with your expectations. Now find your places at the table and we can begin the celebration."

~ * ~

"I didn't expect your mother to be so…" Liona whispered, until Kratan silenced her with a kiss.

"Believe me, Mother is as nervous as you are over this dinner. She has told me, many times over, how nervous she was the first time Grandfather invited her to the palace for dinner. My grandmother died long before my parents were mated. Therefore, she had no one but her mother to guide her in the ways of becoming royalty. Even being brought up with Father as her playmate, she was apprehensive about sliding into the role of rulership. She completely understands your qualms about the new role you will soon be undertaking."

Liona relaxed. These were the things she feared the most all through the times when Kratan was coming to see her. What if she was unable to become accustomed to this new path her life was about to take? With Kratan's reassurance, she knew she would be able to accomplish anything, as long as it helped her to be the perfect mate for the future king of the planet.

Chapter Fourteen

Time seemed to fly and soon, Liona was in the midst of plans for the royal mating as well as meeting with the contractors who were working on the cottage that she and Kratan would be living in once they were mated.

Although Kratan was busy working with his father and learning everything he would need to know in order to be able to rule the planet, they still found time to be together and learn each other's innermost secrets.

"In a week, we will be mated," Kratan announced when he came to her apartment. "Are you as excited as I am for this to happen?"

"You know I am. How could I not be excited? Everything has turned out so well for my entire family and it's all because of you. Mother and Father have been accepted into Capitol City society and Jarom is now a respected litigator with his firm."

"I understand your pride in your family, but how are you adjusting? Will you be content in our cottage? We will have household help, but will you miss the palace?"

Liona took a long moment before answering Kratan's question. This was something she had been thinking about for many days. "I am looking forward to beginning our lives in our cottage. I would love to be the one keeping your house and cooking your meals. I doubt they would be the gourmet fair you're used to eating."

"I can understand what you're saying. I've had long talks with my mother about this. She felt the same way as you do when she mated with my father. At the time she was teaching history and the servants were essential. It didn't take long for her to find her duties as a royal princess made even her teaching more than she could handle, to say nothing of running a household. I'm certain you've been told of the duties that will be expected of you. That said, I think we can come to an acceptable agreement. We will have a housekeeper/cook. Whenever you wish to work in our kitchen, she will be more than willing to take some time for herself. I will continue to retain my valet, Pecor. He has been with me, with the exception of when I was in the military, ever since I was able to have my own apartments. If you require a personal maid, we will find someone to fill that position."

Liona smiled uncontrollably. "I had no idea how to broach this topic with you. As much as I love to cook, I detest housekeeping. This way, when I have the time to cook for you, I will be able to do so, without depriving you of the meals you are accustomed to. I am so glad your mother insisted on putting an addition onto the house for servants' quarters. I think everything is going to be perfect as soon as we are mated."

She allowed Kratan to enfold her in his arms and dispel all of her fears. For almost a year she'd lived in the palace and been pampered beyond compare. She was ready, although hesitant, to leave the palace and begin her life as Princess Liona.

~ * ~

Kratan nervously awaited the beginning of the mating ceremony that would seal their futures together for a lifetime. Dressed in his formal uniform, adorned with medals, the reflection he saw in the gazing glass didn't bely his nervousness.

"You look much more confident about this day than I did," Baja said.

"Outward appearances can be conceiving. My insides are as jittery as they can be. What if I cannot complete the duties of a husband on our mating night?"

Baja laughed loudly, adding to Kratan's uncertainty. "I doubt you will have any problems in that department. From what I am told, the men from Plantas are more than adequate in the mating bed. Just because you have no personal experience doesn't mean when the time is right your body will perform as it is meant to."

"Just remember," Jarom interjected, "Liona is also a virgin. Go slowly with her, as I have been told there is pain that will soon turn to pleasure. I'm sure she is just as nervous as you are about going to the mating bed."

"Of course, you are right. As a male, I've been well schooled in the ways of men and women. I can only pray it is the same with females."

This time, both of his brothers-under-the-law were laughing at him. "I remember the first night I was with Mira in that way. She knew more than I ever thought she would. I assure you the females are as well schooled in that department as we males are."

Baja's teasing, along with Jarom's words of wisdom, seemed to calm his nerves. Within the hour he would be able to proclaim Liona as his life mate forever.

~ * ~

Liona took one last look into the gazing glass. She could hardly believe the reflection that stared back at her. She looked resplendent in the wedding robe her mother, with Felda's help, fashioned for her to wear on this special day. It was made of the whitest of silk, with purple embroidery adorning the hem and sleeves. Into her hair, Mira wove purple ribbons, and she carried a magnificent purple flower that had been brought with the refugees from Plantas. She was grateful for the number of plants the refugees were able to bring to Nalo. With the soil now restored to accept the plants, they added beauty as well as new foods for the people to eat.

"You look beautiful, Daughter," Jax said, when he entered the room where she dressed for the mating ceremony. "I can't believe everything that has happened in the last year. I would have never thought my daughter would become a princess, nor that my wife would become best friends with Queen Felda. Soon Prince Kratan will become my son-under-the-law and my little girl will become a woman. The One God has blessed us, indeed."

"He certainly has. I thought having to wait a year for this day would be terrible, but in that time, I learned so much about what will be expected of me as a member of the royal family. It also gave Mother and Felda the time needed to plan the mating ceremony. I am ready for this next chapter of my life to begin. Kratan and I have discussed the need for household help and have come to a compromise where I will be able to prepare some of our meals."

Her father chuckled softly. It was as though he knew something she didn't, but she wouldn't let it bother her. Instead, she allowed him to take her arm and escort her to the main chapel of the cathedral.

She watched while her childhood friend, Tata, walked down the aisle where Jarom waited to escort her toward the altar. Next to make the walk was Mira, who was greeted by Baja. Once they stood at the altar, it was Liona's turn to take the long walk toward her future.

~ * ~

Kratan stood at the altar and listened to the music from the string quartet. Although he'd never met Tata, he knew she was a special friend of Liona's. He'd heard her speak of how she wished Tata lived in Capitol City. If he wasn't mistaken, it wouldn't be long before Jarom made the announcement of asking her to be his mate. He could see the love that radiated from his soon-to-be brother-under-the-law's eyes as she walked down the aisle in order to take his arm. It was she same look he knew Baja reserved for Mira and Mira alone.

The only time he saw his sister looking this beautiful was on her mating day. On that day she was looking forward to the beginning of her life with Baja. Today she was rejoicing in his mating with Liona.

The music changed and as it did, he inhaled sharply. He'd never questioned the beauty of his soon-to-be mate, but today she looked more beautiful than she ever had before. Love radiated from her eyes and he knew the same emotion showed in his.

It seemed to take forever for her to reach his side, and when she did, he watched as Jax gave her a kiss on her cheek before giving her hand to Kratan.

"All I ask of you, son, is to love her with all your heart. I also ask that you never send her back to us hurt and in tears."

"You have my pledge," Kratan replied.

Even though he'd never heard any other man make such a pledge on his mating day, he realized even in this, his mating ceremony, changes were beginning to be made on Nalo.

~ * ~

With the vows exchanged and the ceremony ended, the wedding party made their way back to the palace, where the lavish reception was waiting for the guests as well as the newly mated couple to arrive.

Felda and Nada watched as the guests began to arrive, as excited as two children in anticipation of the celebration of their naming day. They'd worked so hard in the planning of this day and now all of their efforts were about to pay off. A cheer went us as Prince Kratan and Princess Liona entered the grand ballroom.

"They make a perfect couple," Nada observed. "In my wildest dreams I never thought my daughter would someday become a royal princess."

"I know what you mean," Felda replied. "I was beginning to think my son would remain unmated for his entire life. From what he tells me, he was waiting for the perfect woman to be his life mate."

Once the mating party arrived, they were escorted to the head table, where waiters served them before serving the remainder of the mating guests. Everything transpired under the watchful eyes of both Felda and Nada. It wasn't until Palen and Jax insisted they take their places at the table reserved for the parents of Kratan and Liona, leaving the servants to oversee the process of making certain each of the guests were completely satisfied, did they seat themselves.

~ * ~

"How long must we wait before we retire to our cottage to begin our mating night?" Kratan whispered in Liona's ear.

"We can't desert our guests. There are traditions that need to be observed. I'm as anxious as you are for us to be alone, but we must be polite. The orchestra will be here once we finish eating and we are obliged to start the dancing."

Kratan agreed with his life mate, but still felt a strong desire to be alone with Liona. The thought of the delights of the mating night made him harden. Knowing he had to observe the obligations of his station did little to quench the fire burning within him.

The delicacies placed before them were ones he knew the palace chef, as well as the cooks who helped him, considered to be the best they could provide. Kratan had to admit they outdid themselves. Everything was orchestrated around the favorite foods of both himself and Liona. With these choices, it was evident the guests would be totally satisfied with the meal.

As soon as the dishes were cleared away, the orchestra began to play the music that signaled the time for the dancing to begin.

"Ah, my love, it is time for us to dance. Once we finish, we can slip away to our cottage. I've been assured we will be totally alone there. This may be the only time in our lives we will not have either servants or children monitoring our time alone."

"You are wicked, Kratan, but I totally agree. I am looking forward to being alone without anyone else knowing our every movement."

"After our mating night, we will be going on a trip. My father says it is something that was practiced on Plantas. There is a resort in the southern hemisphere of the planet that is perfect for our mating trip. Our official duties will not begin until we return and I plan to enjoy every minute of our solitude."

Liona giggled as Kratan took her into his arms and swept her across the dance floor. He'd always enjoyed dancing and was pleased he insisted she be schooled in the dances his family brought to Nalo.

"You are a worthy partner not only on the dance floor, but also in life. On this day you have made me the most blessed man on Nalo."

He leaned back and enjoyed the way she blushed at his compliment.

"It is I who am blessed. With you as my mate, I see nothing but happiness in our future."

As soon as the dance ended, they took only a few minutes to bid their guests farewell. Since his friends brought him to the cathedral as well as the palace, he allowed the royal chauffeur to take them back to their cottage. In the morning, they would leave for the resort where they would enjoy their mating trip.

Chapter Fifteen

The incessant pounding on the cottage door roused Kratan and Liona long before the break of dawn.

"Who could be at our door at this hour?" Liona asked, her voice laced with fear.

"You stay here. I will go down and see what this is about."

He didn't take the time to put on the trousers he had worn the night before. Instead, he grabbed the robe Picor laid out for him when he brought Kratan's wardrobe, as well as that for Liona, from the palace to the cottage.

He waved his hand as he passed through the darkened rooms to bring the lights to life. When he opened the door, he was amazed to see the royal guard standing on his doorstep.

"What is the meaning of this? Has something happened at the palace?"

"Yes, it has," the captain of the guard answered. "A note was found when the servants were cleaning up after the banquet. It was a threat to you and Princess Liona as well as to the remainder of the royal family. King Palen was alerted and he has sent us to bring both of you to the palace for your safety. Once you and the princess are dressed, we will be taking you to the palace."

"That won't be necessary. My hovercraft is packed for us to leave on our mating trip. We will take that to the palace."

"Very well, Your Majesty."

Kratan hurried up the stairs to the bedchamber where he'd enjoyed the delights of the mating night. Once he entered the bedroom, he alerted

Liona to the danger. Hurriedly, they both dressed and rushed down the stairs. To Kratan's surprise, the captain of the guard stood in the salon, waiting for them.

"What is the meaning of this? I told you to go back to the palace without us."

"I know you did, Your Majesty, but we were instructed to check out your home. As part of our check, your hovercraft was inspected. They found a bomb that was set to detonate within moments of lift off. You are much safer with us. We know our vehicle hasn't been tampered with."

Kratan felt the blood drain from his face. How could this be happening? "Was the note signed?"

"I'm afraid it was. It was signed The Pure of Nalo."

"I thought our mating would put an end to that group," Liona lamented.

"I did, too, but we were mistaken. It is possible I have angered them by following my heart and taking you as my life mate. We must waste no time in getting to the palace. Your safety is my most important duty."

~ * ~

The palace was in an uproar. Palen and Felda were the first to be alerted to the note threatening all of their lives. One by one, the guests who spent the night of the mating ceremony began to gather in the main salon.

"I can't believe this is happening. I thought the mating of our children would bring an end to this abomination," Jax said. "Tell me again where the note was found."

The servant who brought the note to everyone's attention explained where the note had been found. Before anyone could comment on this, Kratan and Liona arrived.

The composure Liona exhibited on the trip from their cottage to the palace began to crumble. Tears flowed readily down her cheeks. It was Jax who pulled her into his arms to comfort her as he had when she'd been a child. In those early years, he could chase away all of her childish fears. Now he could only hold her while she cried.

"What does the note say?" Kratan asked. "Has the military been alerted?"

"Nothing has been done, until we are all safely within the palace walls," Palen replied.

"Are we safe here? When the royal guard did a sweep of our home, they found not only an explosive device in our main salon but also one in our hovercraft that would have ignited as soon as we lifted off. Had it not been for the royal guard, we would have both died in our haste to get to the palace."

The color drained from the faces of both Felda and Nada. "Has the palace been checked for explosives?" Felda questioned.

"We have members of the guard doing that now. Unfortunately, the palace is much larger than the cottage and the inspection is taking considerably longer. I pray to the One God nothing will be found."

"Even if something is found, I am certain there will be no problem in disabling it," Kratan said. "They were easily able to disable the devices they found in our home as well as our vehicle. For now, I would like to know what the note said."

Palen picked up the note from the table as though it was a poisonous viper.

This is a warning to the invaders who have taken over our government. Up until now, we have been tolerant of your reign. What is unacceptable is that the young prince has stolen one of our own to turn her into a princess. This will not be tolerated. Death to Prince Kratan and Princess Liona, along with the rest of the royal family. It was signed, The Pure of Nalo.

"I am sorry to have put you in such danger, my love."

Liona turned from her father to find comfort in the arms of her life mate. "If I am to die, I want it to be within your loving embrace. This is no one's fault but those horrible people who have plagued our planet for far too long. I thank the One God for you saving my brother from their clutches and coming to love me as much as our parents love each other."

From behind them, they heard a woman cry out. Everyone turned to see Tata making her way toward Liona. "This is terrible. We were just told about the threat."

Liona disentangled herself from Kratan's embrace in order to allow Tata to throw herself into her best friend's arms. "We are safe, for now," she said. "Kratan and his father will get to the bottom of this. They have encountered these monsters before and I pray they will eradicate this threat once and for all."

~ * ~

Jax watched his daughter and the young woman who was like a second daughter to them. Through all the time they were discussing the problem, he'd been focusing on where they found the note that brought about this concern. When he was told where the note had been found, he envisioned the seating assignment for the mating banquet. He was horrified when he realized who occupied the seats at the table where the note was found.

"What is all this nonsense?" Zardo, Tata's father demanded as he entered the salon. "I resent being awakened at this ungodly hour of the morning."

While King Palen explained what was going on, Jax watched the expression on Zardo's face. They'd grown up together and entered the military at the same time. While Jax worked in the intelligence area, Zardo was assigned to the bomb squad. As much as he didn't want to admit it, his one-time friend, the father of his daughter's best friend, was the only one who sat at the table where the note had been found with the ability to plant the explosive devices the royal guard found.

"Does anyone have any idea as to who is behind this organization?" Palen asked.

Jarom shook his head. "When I was recruited, it was by one of the older boys. None of us knew who was behind all the hatred."

"I'm certain this is all a hoax," Zardo commented. "You are all making too much out of this. I, for one, am going back to my quarters to pack for my journey back to my home. I suggest you do the same, Tata."

"I think not," Jax said.

"What are you saying?" King Palen asked.

"Knowing where the note was found brought to mind the only person who could possibly be responsible for not only the note, but also the explosives that were found at Kratan and Liona's home. As I recall, before the dancing began, Zardo excused himself. He was gone longer than it takes to relieve oneself. Even if he didn't place the devices, he played an integral part in this. The note was found under the cloth at the place where he sat. He is one who knows the most about these devices. When we were in the military, he was trained with these."

"You know nothing," Zardo shouted. "All you can think of is the prestige you and your children have gained because this alien prince has taken in your family. I always thought Liona was destined for great things, but in her choice of a life mate, she has become an abomination."

"No!" Tata declared. "You can't be responsible for this. You are my father and I love you with all my heart. How can you even think of destroying Liona? Tell me you have no connection to The Pure of Nalo."

"I cannot tell you what you want to hear, Daughter. I am The Pure of Nalo. It is my creation and I am proud of it. It is time we rid ourselves of these refugees. We have waited too long for this to happen and they have been breeding like rats. Their numbers are increasing and they are a threat to those of us who inhabited this planet from the beginning of the time. They are like a plague upon the land."

Jax ached to watch his friend sink deeper and deeper into madness. Two members of the royal guard seized him and dragged him away from the salon. As they did, Jax took Tata into his arms.

"There is no reason for you to return to your home. I'm certain no one holds you responsible for the doings of your father. We have plenty of room for you in our home and I am certain arrangements can be made for your belongings to be brought there."

From beyond the main salon, Zardo's screams of protest could be heard as the royal guard continued to take him to a secured area.

~ * ~

"Who will be questioning Zardo?" Jarom inquired.

"I hadn't given the matter proper thought," Palen replied.

"If I may be so bold, I would like to suggest Joltan and I be the ones who question him. In our youth, both of us fell under his spell. I also have known him since childhood. I spent many hours at his home, never knowing his connection with The Pure of Nalo. I am certain even though he may think this was his idea, he is actually too young to have been the instigator over forty years ago."

"You summoned me, Your Majesty?" Joltan said as he entered the salon with more of the Royal Guard.

"Yes, I did. I'm certain you've met Jarom. He is to Kratan as you are to me, as they met under the same conditions."

Jarom extended his hand in greeting and was pleased when Joltan clasped his forearm. "Yes, I have met this young man. It seems he, like myself, fell under the spell of The Pure of Nalo. Speaking of that despicable group, have you any leads as to which of their followers are behind this?"

"Not only have we captured the so-called leader of this group, but Jarom has suggested the two of you be the ones to question him."

"I can understand why you have made the request, Jarom. Do you know the name of this leader?"

"It is Zardo."

Joltan's eyes widened at the mention of Zardo's name. "Zardo? I never thought I would hear his name again. He was indoctrinated into the group at the same time as my friends and myself. He did not accompany us on the mission where we encountered King Palen. As I recall, he was infiltrating the military. I haven't thought of him in years. It is no wonder he has risen in rank."

Jarom took the opportunity to voice the thoughts crowding his mind. "I'm afraid he has allowed this situation to drive him into madness. He is convinced The Pure of Nalo is his conception. Perhaps it is because he has risen in the ranks of the organization and no longer has anyone above him. I am now more certain than before that you and I are the perfect people to question him. You knew him as a youth and I knew him as the father of not only one of my childhood friends, but also of the woman who is my sister's best friend. We should be able to rely on our relationship with him in order to bring out the truth behind this organization."

Everyone agreed with Jarom's plan for the questioning of Zardo He prayed between himself and Joltan they would be able to find some semblance of the truth.

Once the explosive devices that had been found within the palace walls had been disposed of, the other guests were allowed to leave the palace. Although Kratan and Liona planned to take their personal hovercraft to their destination, they agreed it should be checked over completely before they were allowed to use it. Baja and Mira were more than happy to take them to their destination and to go back to pick them up at the end of their scheduled visit.

With the salon devoid of people, Jarom and Joltan went down to the cellar of the castle where Zardo was being held.

"It's about time you came to see me, Jarom. You're a litigator, get me out of this mess."

"I haven't come here to save your sorry soul. I am here to question you about The Pure of Nalo."

"As am I," Joltan said.

"Who are you? You wear the uniform of the Royal Guard. Are you here to torture me?

"It is no wonder you don't recognize me, Zardo. Had I not been told of your identity, I would never have recognized you either. I am Joltan. You and I were recruited into The Pure of Nalo at the same time. I was blessed when I met King Palen and along with my friends was granted mercy. You, on the other hand, were not as lucky as us. Your mind was turned to evil thoughts. Now, it is our job to find out how many operatives you have in the city."

"If that is the case, the two of you are fools. There is no one in the organization I would trust with this operation. Only my second-in-command, who has trained under me, was able to handle the small job of placing the explosives in the house of the alien prince and his hovercraft. I am sorry he didn't try to take off in it and the royal line would be ended. It was I and I alone, who placed the devices in the palace."

Joltan nodded toward Jarom. Now, he was certain, was the time to find out more about the hierarchy of the organization.

"From what Joltan has told us, you are far too young to have been the original organizer of the group. What happened to those who were your superiors?"

"They, like you, were fools. Once I was dismissed from the military, my skills far exceeded theirs. It took very little effort for the ones who were in charge to disappear with no one ever knowing what happened to them. It was only a short time before I was in charge and running The Pure of Nalo in the way it should have been for years."

"Who is the second in command you spoke of?"

"It makes no difference, because he no longer exists. When he reported to me after the banquet, I made certain he would in no way be able to incriminate me. I eliminated him in the same way as I eliminated those who once thought they were superior to me."

Joltan and Jarom looked at each other skeptically. They weren't at all convinced Zardo acted on his own. There had to be others involved. The man was delusional. Deciding they would get no more information from the man, they returned to the throne room to meet with King Palen.

When they entered the throne room, they were shocked to see King Palen consulting with the Captain of the guard.

"What have you learned?" King Palen asked.

"Nothing of value, Your Majesty." Joltan replied. "He insists he had an accomplice but once the explosives were installed at Prince Kratan's home, Zardo says he was eliminated and his body would never be found."

Palen nodded. "We found a laser gun when we searched the room that he was assigned for the mating ceremony. We also found more materials for making explosives when we conducted the search. That being the case, I have instructed the royal guard to check out the home of

Kratan and Liona more thoroughly as well as that of Jax and Nada. We have had Mira and Baja's children brought to the palace, while they take Kratan and Liona to their destination for their mating trip."

Jarom inhaled deeply. "Have you had my apartment searched as well? His anger is at not only the royal family but also at the members of my family. He has never been happy about the feelings I harbor for Tata. I was planning to ask his permission for the two of us to be mated once Liona's mating ceremony was completed."

"We thought of this and you will be staying in Kratan's former apartment, while Tata will be in the apartment Liona occupied until the day of their mating ceremony. Until we know everyone involved will be safe, you will remain here, under protective custody. We have also contacted your firm and they completely understand the circumstances. It is the same for your father and his position with the hovercraft factory."

"What about the other members of The Pure of Nalo?" Joltan asked.

"The military has been alerted and are searching throughout the planet for their outposts. They are also searching his residence as well as his office at his place of employment for any files they are able to find."

~ * ~

Justice was swift. Once the search of Zardo's home and office was completed, it took little time for the authorities to make the necessary arrests. The Pure of Nalo finally came to an end when Zardo was hanged and his followers sent to the penal colony for the rest of their lives.

Chapter Sixteen

Princess Liona rubbed her ever-expanding belly. Although she didn't know the gender of her babies, she had been told they were going to be identical twins. In this, the last month of her pregnancy, she'd been confined to the bedchamber on the first floor of their home. She missed sleeping next to Kratan each night, but knew he would get no rest with her constant movement in search of a comfortable position.

This morning the babies were engaged in a tussle. She knew it represented a struggle to be the first to enter the world to be given the title and its position in life.

Kratan entered the room, carrying her breakfast tray.

"I can't believe you are bringing me my morning meal."

"Why shouldn't I? I despise eating alone, and thought this would be a good time for us to partake of a meal together."

"What of your duties at the palace?"

"Whatever they are, they can wait. Unlike my father I intend to be with you when these babies are born. As my mother tells it, Grandfather sent Father to quell an uprising of The Pure of Nalo. While he was away, my mother gave birth to me. I was several weeks old before my father even held me. It is the one thing in his life he regrets. Missing the birth of his first-born son has always distressed him."

"Don't you mean his only born son? What if these two children are girls? By law we cannot produce more than two children."

"In that case, one of them will be Nalo's first natural born queen."

Liona put the first piece of toasted bread to her lips, when an unfamiliar pain slashed its way through her body.

"Is something wrong, my love?" Kratan inquired.

"Not really wrong, but perhaps you should be in contact with your father to let him know you will not be coming to the palace today. I have a feeling these babies are so anxious to come into the world, that today will be the day. Once you do, you should contact the midwife. I am certain we will be in need of her services before this day is over."

"Are you certain?"

Liona nodded. "I know my body, and the pain I experienced is different from any other I have encountered before. It is like when you first felt the babies move and you asked me if I felt it. Whatever these children do is known to me and at this time I am certain they are ready to be out of their confined space."

While Kratan went to summon both sets of parents as well as the midwife, Liona's maid came to help her into her birthing gown and place the birthing sheet on the bed. By the time Kratan returned to her side, the pains were coming on a regular schedule.

After a brief examination by the midwife, they were assured the babies were, indeed, ready to be born. Kratan pulled a chair to the side of the bed and allowed Liona to clasp his hand with each pain. It was shortly after midday when Miro was born. For a moment, the pain subsided, only to be replaced by the pain of the second baby making his way into the world. Younger by two minutes, Nicos would always be referred to as the spare heir and would be forced to be subservient to his older brother.

"You have two healthy sons," the midwife declared. "Since they are a mirror image of each other, I will tie a purple string around the wrist of the older of the two boys. In that way you will be able to tell them apart until they are old enough to bring forth their unique personalities."

Kratan picked up both of his sons, examining them from head to toe. "I have seen twins born in the wild and have heard of such births among our people. I never expected the One God to doubly bless us in such a manner."

Tears were running down Liona's cheeks. "They are beautiful, but I pity the life Nicos has been born into. He will always be the younger of the two. I pray their struggles in the womb will not carry over into their adult lives. It would have been different if one of them had been born female. In that case she would have been protected as a beloved younger sister. I fear these two will be at odds for all of their lives."

~ * ~

It didn't take long for Liona's prediction to come true. As the boys became old enough to be mobile, it was always Miro who was in the lead, forcing his younger brother to trail behind as though he was his brother's personal servant.

The animosity Miro showed toward Nicos tore at her heart. She had little time to be concerned with the behavior of her toddlers, as word came from the palace saying King Palen had become gravely ill.

The request to come to the palace came early one morning. Thankfully, the nursemaid was able to keep the twins entertained in the nursery without unduly upsetting them.

"What is happening?" Kratan demanded as soon as they arrived at the palace.

"Your father hasn't been feeling well," Felda replied. "He has done a good job of hiding it, but the physicians here are baffled. They put out the call for information on his illness and found a clinic on Seros who has been doing research on his condition. We have made arrangements for a hyper-wormhole transport to take us there."

"Seros? Wasn't that the name of one of the planets where the refugees from Plantas were sent?"

"One and the same. The contingency that went there was composed of the some of the most brilliant physicians Plantas had to offer. When they combined their skills with those of the physicians of Seros, they became one of the foremost centers for disease control in the universe. With the rise of the hyper-wormhole transport system, we will be able to travel there in a matter of days. For this reason, we will be making a proclamation, making you king over all Nalo."

Kratan was in complete shock. "Father is a young man. How can this be?"

"We have conferred with the physicians as well as the religious scholars. This is the will of the One God. It is not a certainty that the physicians on Seros will be able to save his life, but through him, they will gain more information on this illness. From what we have learned it affects many of the descendants of Plantas who have pure bloodlines."

Liona could not stop the stream of tears cascading down her cheeks. "How will we survive without Palen's guidance? He has been a just king and you a caring queen. How will we ever be able to take your place?"

"Please don't cry, Daughter. As you know, I have studied the ancient histories of both Nalo and Plantas. Each of these histories are founded in the fact life is followed by death and rulership is passed from one generation to the next. With our journey to Seros, it is possible more information will be ascertained to help others of our ilk, for I, too, am experiencing the early effects of this disease. We have both willingly agreed to be transported to Seros for experimental treatment."

Unable to shed unmanly tears, Kratan could only comfort his wife. Finally, he was able to question his mother. "When will all of this be taking place?"

"The announcement will be made later today. Your coronation is set for tomorrow, just before the transport departs for Seros."

"Is Father able to receive company?"

For the first time, he saw his mother's composure begin to crack. "He is further into the illness than I am, therefore, he tires easily. He wanted me to explain everything to you before you go into see him."

Kratan left the salon and went into his father's bedchamber. Although Palen sat in one of the overstuffed chairs, he looked thinner and frailer than he had just days earlier.

"Why didn't you tell me of this before?" Kratan asked.

"Everything came on so fast. I thought it was nothing major until I consulted my personal physician. He consulted the physicians of the universe and learned many of those with pure Plantas blood have been contracting this disease. It is more prevalent on Earth and Seros than it is here, because they had larger contingencies that made it to those destinations. They have been researching this on Seros for years and we are going there to participate in their research program. Since my recovery is not certain, it is important that you be crowned as king before we leave."

"Are you certain this is what is happening to you?"

Palen nodded sagely. "We are positive. When it was first diagnosed, the physicians on Seros were contacted. They sent their top physician here. He arrived yesterday and confirmed the diagnosis. Since you are well aware of the histories of our people, you know the name of Ragnar. He was on one of the ships sent to Seros and became one of the best physicians and professors of medicine on that planet. It is his grandson who came here."

Allowing the statement to sink in, Palen motioned to Joltan. On the far side of the room, a door opened and a young physician entered the room.

Kratan was surprised to see a young man who definitely carried the bloodline of Plantas in his background.

"I am Tarol, the grandson of Ragnar. I have been sent here to examine your father as well as to accompany both him and your mother to Seros. It is imperative that I take them back with me. We have the facilities necessary to care for both of them. I don't want to give you false hope, since your father's case is in the advanced stages. As for your mother, I am certain the disease is only just beginning."

"What about those of us on Nalo who carry the pure bloodline?"

"I am glad you asked. I brought with me the vaccine we have perfected. Your physicians have been given instructions to vaccinate all of your citizens with the pure bloodline. I will be giving you the vaccine as well as your sister."

"What of my children as well as those of my sister?"

"They will be vaccinated by your physicians. They are the ones who know of the children who carry the bloodline of Plantas."

"Can't you do the same for my parents? Why take them all the way to Seros?"

"Because the disease has just now manifested itself within them.

When that happens, it is too late for the vaccine to be of any good. Trust me, the decision to accompany me back to Seros is one that was not taken lightly. We are doing great research and they are more than willing to become subjects in that study. This disease does not discriminate between rich or poor. It is devastating, as you can see by looking at your father. His condition deteriorates by the hour. As soon as you are crowned king of Nalo, we will be departing."

~ * ~

Before the suns of Nalo began to set, the announcement had been made to the people and Kratan had been given the lifesaving vaccine.

Early the next morning, the arrangements for Kratan's coronation were in place. Rather than the pomp and circumstance surrounding previous coronations, the people were saddened to be saying goodbye to their beloved King Palen and Queen Felda.

Everyone was understanding about the reason for their departure and worried about their friends and neighbors who carried the Plantas bloodline. It was newly crowned King Kratan who put their minds at ease. Everyone on Nalo who carried Plantas blood would be vaccinated in the next few days. It was his first royal command.

After the abbreviated ceremony, Kratan, Liona, Mira, Baja and their children accompanied Palen and Felda to the spaceport to board the craft for their trip to Seros.

"I don't want you to go," Mira lamented.

"It is for the good of all the refugees from Plantas and their descendants. As soon as we arrive on Seros, we will be in contact with you," Felda promised.

"We mustn't tarry," Palen commented. "We have a schedule to keep. Just remember I love you all and know we are leaving the future of Nalo in capable hands. If I do not return, it will be because of the will of the One God. I pray your mother will be returning to act as Queen Mother to all of you."

~ * ~

By the time Kratan and Liona returned, all of their belongings had been moved from their cottage to the palace. The apartment that had been home for Liona when she first came to Capitol City had been converted to a nursery for the twins.

For the first time in years, the palace rang with young voices as Miro and Nicos ran from spacious room to spacious room.

"Are we ready for this?" Liona asked.

"We have to be. I have been trained for this all of my life. I remember being the age of our children and starting my education."

"You forget, there is only one of them who will one day be king. Miro knows one day he will be king and Nicos will be his underling. I fear the two of them have been fighting about this since before they were born. I ache for our younger son."

"I have seen their rivalry and have come up with a solution. While Miro will follow my footsteps by going into the military, Nicos will become the one who will pursue an education. Father was the one who suggested this. He feels Nicos will become a great diplomat. With the inter-planetary flights becoming commonplace, the diplomatic corps will be a more important position than any king in the universe. Nicos is destined for great things."

"I pray you are right. I love both of the boys equally, but I have to admit, Miro tends to be overbearing where Nicos is concerned. I hope the two of them don't kill each other before they grow to adulthood."

Kratan laughed at Liona's statement, although he'd seen it for himself and worried about the animosity between Miro and Nicos, he prayed that over the coming years, they would be able put their differences aside and work together for the good of Nalo.

Chapter Seventeen

Felda buckled herself into the seat provided for her, while Palen was taken to the infirmary the ship afforded them.

"How long does Palen have?"

Tarol finished buckling himself into his seat before he answered. "We have the best physicians and nurses tending to his needs during this trip. Although his diagnosis is dire, we will be safely on Seros before anything can happen."

Felda wanted to know more about this disease that took over Palen's body and threatened to do the same for her.

"What of your grandfather? I have read much about him in the history of Plantas. While most of the ships sent to Nalo were lost in the meteor storm, all of the ships destined for Seros and Earth arrived safely at their destinations. From what we have been taught, Ragnar made it to Seros and was able to revolutionize the educational system for all of their medical students. He was a great man and you are blessed to carry his bloodline."

"You honor me, Your Majesty."

"I am no longer known as your majesty. With the crowning of my son as king, I am Felda, the Queen Mother. The title of queen belongs to my daughter-under-the-law, Liona. The future of Nalo belongs to the young. Our time of leadership is past."

"As you wish, Felda. To answer your question, you asked of my grandfather. He and my grandmother made a great couple. She was a well-respected scientist and educator, while he had the medical background. He brought with him the ideas of teaching medical students about the necessity to know about the food that fueled their bodies in order to take the best care of their patients.

"My grandfather was the first to diagnose the mysterious illness of those who came from Plantas. It has to do with the differences between Plantas and our adoptive planets. It wasn't until the disease afflicted his brothers that he started working on the vaccine."

"If that is the case, why has it not affected anyone on Nalo before this?"

"It is possible it did affect them. Those who first contracted it on Earth called it Time Warp Fever. Back then, that was the only name they had for it."

Felda nodded her head. "I lost my father-under-the-law as well as my father to what my mother called Time Warp Fever. My mother was a great healer."

"May I ask how she died?"

"She sickened very quickly and passed, but it was long after the passing of my father and King Hedro."

"The disease has gone undiagnosed for years. It wasn't until my grandparents began their research that they realized it was more than Time Warp Fever. Through their research they were able to isolate the illness and perfect the vaccine. Unfortunately, it was too late for my grandfather. He was in the final stages of the disease and lost his life."

Felda wiped a tear from her eye. "Do you think it is too late for Palen?"

"It's hard to say. Once we are back at the hospital it will be up to the team of physicians who will be overseeing, not only his, care, but yours as well."

"We have been airborne for quite a while now. Can I go back and visit with Palen?"

"Unfortunately, we are about to enter the wormhole. Once we do, we must remain in our seats. Moving around the ship will be too dangerous."

Felda was a bit nervous as to the meaning of what Tarol told her. Had they left their home for an even more unsure fate? "How will this affect Palen's treatment?"

"You are wise to question his treatment. The team that goes with this ship is highly skilled in the transportation of patients with the disease. They are well trained and able to handle the wormhole."

Felda closed her eyes in frustration. She didn't like being separated from Palen for any reason, whatsoever.

~ * ~

The trip from Nalo to Seros, which would have normally taken several months or even a year, was completed in only a matter of days. As soon as they landed, medical personnel were waiting for them. With Palen's condition stabilized enough for him to be taken from the ship, a young female physician came on board to take Felda's vitals.

"Both you and Palen are cleared to be transported to the University where an entire wing has been devoted to the treatment of this ailment. We have been advised the two of you are of the first generation of those who came from Plantas to Nalo."

"That's correct. Our parents were on the lead ship of those who came as refugees. For many years, we thought we were the only survivors of our contingency, until we made contact with Ragnar, Nina and Tarena. I am afraid once our parents were gone, we no longer kept in such close contact with our counterparts on these planets."

"Here you will meet many of the descendants of the original refugees who went to Earth and Seros. Most of them are half-breeds but have also been affected by this disease, only not as badly as you have. They have all come here willingly to participate in the ongoing research."

Felda felt completely overwhelmed but made no protest when the physician who had been caring for her insisted on taking her from the ship in a wheelchair. As the young woman explained it, in her weakened condition, walking would be difficult after the flight through the wormhole.

~ * ~

Audra waited in her office for the notice that Palen and Felda had landed and been safely transported to the Ragnar Wing of the University Hospital. She wished she'd known of the disease that held Palen and Felda in its grip sooner. It was evident there would be little that could be done for Palen. Luckily, the information she'd received on Felda gave her hope that the former queen could not only be cured, but returned to her home planet.

As she reread the reports, she remembered when her parents first contacted Nina, Tarena and Grato. At that time, she was hoping to talk to the children, but was told they were, more than likely, already in their beds for the night.

In the past she had met Nina and Rand's children, Dyna and Betsy, when they came for the research program. A year later, they were ready to return to Earth, when Tarena and Paul's children Bridget, Ragnar, and Anthony came for the same study.

With the arrival of Felda and Palen, she would finally be reunited with the children of the survivors who were able to make it to Nalo. When she was informed of the outbreak of the disease on Nalo, Bridget was willing to stay and make Felda feel welcome, while her brothers returned to Earth.

The page for her to come to the isolation wing broke into her internal thoughts about the man and woman she was about to meet.

~ * ~

Felda felt as though she was settling into one of the luxury apartments in the palace instead of a suite in the hospital. Before being taken to her suite, she was allowed to go to the isolation unit of the hospital to see Palen.

She'd tried not to shed any tears in front of him, but she hadn't been successful. The journey from Nalo to Seros had taken its toll on him.

Please don't cry, my love, his words echoed in her mind. *We knew my condition was critical when we left Nalo. With luck, I will be able to help in the research they are conducting here.*

"Oh, Palen, how will I ever be able to go on without you," she lamented aloud.

To her surprise, she heard a knock at her door.

Quickly, she dried her eyes. "Come in."

The woman who entered the room reminded her of her mother, Wasla. It was evident she carried the blood of the Plantas refugees.

"You must be Felda," the woman said. "I am Audra, the daughter of Ragnar and Gina. I have been informed you are the daughter of Grato and Wasla. You are the last of the refugee families to come here."

"As a teacher, I am well versed in the history of our people. Up until now, the royal family of Nalo has been of a pure link to the original refugees. My son as well as my daughter have followed their hearts and mated with those not of our home planet."

Audra nodded her head. "That is where we are different. My parents mated outside of the refugees, as did the children of two of those who went to Earth. Unfortunately, the daughters of Rand and Nina returned to Earth, but Paul and Tarena's daughter, Bridget, decided to stay and get to know you."

"I don't know how I feel about that. Before the fated contingency going to Nalo ran into the meteor storm, my father and her mother were to have been mated."

"She is well aware of that. It is the reason she is so excited to meet you. Like your parents, her parents found a more mature love once they landed at their destinations. I assure you, she is someone you will enjoy meeting."

"When will this meeting take place?" Felda asked.

"In due time. Once you are settled, our techs and residents will run some tests. When you are finished with them, it will be time for the evening meal to be served. At that time, you and Bridget will be introduced."

Felda nodded. If she never met Bridget, it would be too soon. She wanted nothing to do with the daughter of the woman who thought she would be mated to Grato when they arrived on Nalo.

~ * ~

Bridget Carter paced the length of her suite. She'd stayed behind on Seros, not because she was infected with the disease, but because she wanted to meet the daughter of the man her mother once thought she would marry.

All her life she'd heard the stories of how her mother and grandparents were the last ship in the contingency traveling from Plantas to Nalo. At the time, they watched as the ships ahead of them were destroyed in a meteor shower.

They'd been lucky to be far enough back that they escaped the horror of being destroyed. Being closer to Earth than to Seros, they changed course and at last landed. They hadn't been heralded as gods, nor had they met with open hostilities. The people who came to their rescue helped them to assimilate into the society of their new planet.

It was at the wedding of her best friend, Nina, to Rand Jacobson, that Tarena met Paul Mathews. At the time, she was still mourning the loss of her beloved Grato, but she soon fell in love with Paul. Now all these years later, most people on Earth didn't know who carried Plantas blood and who didn't. The refugees had spread all over the planet and been accepted as valued members of society.

She was just cleaning up to go to the dining hall when there was a knock at her door. It came as no surprise to see Audra standing in the hall.

"Your counterpart from Nalo has arrived," Audra greeted her. "She is close to your age, but I fear she is a bit apprehensive about meeting you."

"I don't blame her. From what I am told, her father was the man my mother always thought she would marry. I've been thinking about this myself. Had things been different, we wouldn't be meeting each other today. Can you tell me what she is like?"

"Until she left Nalo, several days ago, she was the queen of that planet. While your people have made great strides in the educational and diplomatic fields on Earth and ours in the medical field here on Seros, their people became the leaders of their planet."

"That is interesting. As a child I always enjoyed playing dress up and pretending I was a great queen. Isn't it ironic that I should be meeting a real queen this evening?"

"The two of you aren't very different from each other. As soon as her son was crowned as king of Nalo, she became the Queen Mother, but in reality, she is a woman like so many other women in the universe. Royalty is nothing more than a title that has been bestowed on someone. You will like her. I pray the two of you will become great friends before your scheduled flight back to Earth."

~ * ~

By the time the technicians were finished with her, Felda felt more like a pincushion than a human being. She was surprised there was still blood flowing through her veins.

Instead of feeling sorry for herself, she made her way to the dining hall to partake of the evening meal. It came as a surprise when she noticed several others already gathered around the individual tables. Audra motioned her to come to a table on the other side of the room.

"You look overwhelmed, Felda."

"I fear I am. It is interesting to see how many tests have been performed on me in such a short amount of time."

"I know the feeling," the woman who was already seated at the table said. "I'm Bridget Carter, the daughter of Terina and Paul Mathews."

Felda nodded. "I have read the histories and know about your parents. My father, Grato, mourned the loss of your mother, until he finally allowed himself to love again."

"I hope we can become friends. I want to learn about the life you've lived on Nalo, just as I'm sure you are interested in my life on Earth. Audra tells me you are a queen."

Felda relaxed. "Before I became queen, I was a teacher of history. I'd been raised with the children of King Hedro, who became my father-under-the-law. My mate, Palen, is here also. Unfortunately, he is in a more advanced stage of the disease. Although I have been assured I can be cured, I will be returning to Nalo without him. It is his hope that his demise will help in the research about this disease."

"You are lucky to still have your husband. My husband, Dirk Carter, was working on the roof of our home and lost his footing. He fell and broke his neck. We had no time to even say goodbye to each other."

"Do you have children?"

"We do. Our son, Johnathan, is married to Dyna Jacobson's daughter, Claire. They live in Florida, which is many miles from our home in Wyoming. They are both physicians and were on a team who were looking into this disease. Dyna's mother, Nina, became ill and died before she could be sent to somewhere that she could get help. It was the same with my grandmother and my mother. It was one of the reasons I consented to come to Seros to be part of the research program."

Felda tried to take in all the information. How could she ever live without her children and grandchildren close to her? As soon as the question popped into her head, she realized she was now lightyears away from Nalo and had no idea when or if she would ever return.

"What about you? Do you have kids?"

She brought herself back into the conversation. "Our son, Kratan, was crowned king in his father's place, just before we left to come here. He and his wife Liona have twin sons, Miro and Nicos. They now live in the palace. Before that they had a cottage on the palace grounds. Our daughter, Mira, is mated to Baja, the son of the owner of the largest manufacturing plants in Capitol City. Their children are Sorodo and Anja. They are older than the twins and are already in school."

"I envy you. I wish Johnathan and Claire would take the time to have children. They are so busy with their careers. They keep telling me they have plenty of time to have a family. Since coming here, I've had a lot of time to think about my future. For this project, I left my teaching position in Wyoming, and have realized there is nothing there for me anymore. My brothers are both living in the southern United States as are my son and daughter-in-law. Therefore, I have no reason not to relocate.

When I return to Earth, I will be selling my home and moving to Florida. At least the winters will be much milder. Even though I will have to live with the threat of hurricanes, I will be closer to my family."

Tears formed in Felda's eyes. She couldn't imagine being separated from her family. She also understood the storms Bridget described that threatened all areas of Earth. It made her glad her family had landed on Nalo, with its temperate environment. There were four seasons, but not the horrific disasters that were visited on Earth and seemed to plague everyone on that frightening planet.

Chapter Eighteen

While Kratan adjusted well to life in the palace, Liona constantly worried about being able to fulfill the responsibilities expected of the queen.

A year after the coronation, they received word Palen had died from the illness, while Felda flourished under the care of the physicians.

"I have word from Mother," Kratan announced during the morning meal. "She will be arriving at the spaceport in two weeks' time. I wish my father was physically coming with her, but she is bringing his ashes back to Nalo."

"I grieve for the loss of your father, but rejoice to think your mother will be returning to us. My mother helps, but she has no idea how to handle the royal matters. I look forward to having your mother back at the palace."

"Are you certain? I remember Mother telling us how she often wished her mother would not have been living in the palace. Even though they loved each other unconditionally, as adults, even living somewhere as large as the palace put a strain on their relationship. If it were so with her mother, how will it be with your mother-under-the-law?"

"It will be different. I get along well with your mother and I have so many questions about being queen that I would like to confer with her about. I know the twins miss her as well. They see my parents often, but it's not the same."

~ * ~

Felda held tight to the urn which held Palen's ashes. This had been a long hard journey in both directions. The healing she anticipated receiving helped for herself but it wasn't the same for Palen. He'd passed away peacefully, even though he wasn't on his beloved Nalo. Now she was returning to her home and bringing his ashes with her.

She thought of returning to the palace. The memory of having her mother in such close proximity to her was foremost in her mind. They'd always been close, but having her live in the palace with them was more togetherness than either of them craved.

Her telecom talks with Kratan assured her there were apartments waiting for her within the palace, but she knew this wasn't what she wanted. She much preferred moving into the little cottage she and Palen, as well as Kratan and Liona, shared when they were newlyweds. As soon as they landed, she would make plans for the move. Even with the renovations made by her son and daughter-under-the-law, she knew the cottage would have to, again, be completely renovated to suit her needs, but she felt she was up to the challenge.

"We will be landing on Nalo within the hour, Your Highness," the pilot of space shuttle advised her. "I suggest you fasten yourself into your seat."

Felda nodded her agreement. "How many times must I tell you I am no longer the Queen of Nalo."

"Ah, Your Highness, you still deserve the title. I know your new title is Queen Mother, but you are still a member of the royal family and deserve the recognition of your position in life."

"I suppose you are right, but I much prefer to be simply Felda, a member of the older generation. I have many plans for the future and they don't include royal duties. I made many friends on Seros and some of them are from Earth. I may decide to do some traveling in the future."

"If that is what you decide to do, I pray you will remember me. I would be honored to pilot the space shuttle that would take you anywhere in the galaxy you would like to go. I have enjoyed our time together on this flight back to Nalo."

Felda knew she would be taking this young pilot up on his offer.

She knew his parents; they'd grown up together, and she considered them among her friends. "I appreciate your offer and will consider it, Natrum. You have shown your abilities to the utmost degree. Your parents have reason to be proud of you."

Natrum didn't reply to Felda's statement. The preparations for re-entry had begun and he needed to focus his attention to the readings on the instrument panel in front of him.

It didn't matter to Felda. She needed to take some time to reflect on everything she'd experienced over the time she'd been on Seros. She thought of the last words of her beloved life mate. Palen, in his last moments of life, held her hand and made what could only be called a prophesy.

My darling, Felda. My life is ending, but you have much to do. I fear for the future of Nalo. While our son, Kratan, is a fair and just man, I fear it will not be so for Miro. I have already seen how he lords his birthright over Nicos. In time, Nicos will leave Nalo and make a name for himself. I know not whether it will be on Seros or on Earth, but he will be sent away by his older brother.

I fear Miro will suffer for his part in Nicos' exile. In the end it will be the seed of Nicos who will be the salvation for Nalo. I have seen enough of Miro's behavior to know what kind of a man he will become. I am thankful to the One God for allowing me to leave this body.

What I ask of you is to watch over and guide Nicos. He needs your love, for being the younger of the two, he will never enjoy such love from his parents.

Tears sprung to Felda's eyes as the memory filled her mind. She knew everything Palen told her was the truth. Even as young as her grandchildren were, she could see Nicos being forced to be subservient to his older brother. It would take much wisdom for a king to rule Nalo and she feared such wisdom was not something Miro possessed.

~ * ~

"When do you expect the craft bringing the Queen Mother back to Nalo to return?" Kratan asked of the supervisor of the space port.

"I just had a transmission from the pilot, Natrum. They have entered into the gravity pull and will land within the hour, Sire."

Kratan nodded his approval. He was pleased to think that one of his childhood friends, Natrum, was the pilot of the shuttle carrying his mother back to Nalo. They'd played together as children and studied together at the University as students. When Kratan entered the military, Natrum opted for the training the space force offered. With that training, he'd become one of the best space shuttle pilots in all of Nalo, and perhaps all of the galaxy.

The announcement for the arrival of the space shuttle brought Kratan out of his thoughts of the past and he prepared to meet not only his friend but also his mother.

It always amazed him how flawlessly these massive crafts were able to descend from the heavens to arrive at a designated landing area.

Within moments of the arrival, he watched as his mother made her way through the tunnel to come into the greeting area.

"Mother, it is so good to see you. Did you have a good flight?"

"How do you describe good? It was very smooth and uneventful, but knowing I am returning to Nalo alone distresses me greatly."

She held out the urn she'd cradled so protectively throughout the entire flight from Seros.

"I know your father's spirit will be with me for always and ever. Even so, it is hard to have only his ashes to bring back to his beloved home."

"I understand, Mother, I honestly do. I have so many questions only he could answer, but I am trying my best to do as he would want me to. He trained me well."

"I am pleased you are doing that which would make your father proud. Where is Liona? Has she come to meet me as well?"

"She has remained at the palace. She is preparing your apartments for you."

"I wish she wouldn't do that. I would much prefer renovating the cottage where your father and I, as well as you and Liona, lived when we were newly married. I don't know how long I will be staying on Nalo. I made many friends among the descendants of those who went to Earth and I think I would enjoy going there to visit them and become better acquainted with those who share the same background as your father and myself."

"We have much time for such conversations. Your hovercraft is waiting for you. I know you won't mind, but I would like to spend some time with Natrum."

"I think that's a lovely idea. I remember the many times the two of you were together in your youth. Be certain to give him the praise he deserves. He made my trip through the galaxy an enjoyable experience despite the reason for my journey. For now, I am anxious to see Liona and my grandsons."

Kratan watched as his mother left the terminal. He knew the pilot of her hovercraft would be waiting for her. He also understood his wife as well as his sister would be waiting for her at the palace. This was the time she would be surrounded by the women in her life and he as king wouldn't be missed.

He turned to see Natrum striding toward him. It had been far too long since he'd seen his childhood friend and he marveled at how youthful he looked. Even with the responsibility of piloting a space shuttle throughout the galaxy, it seemed as though he hadn't aged since they both entered the military. On the other hand, he thought his position of King *had* aged him. For the first time in far too long, he put his position behind him and planned to spend a few enjoyable hours with his friend.

"Natrum, it is good to see you my friend," he exclaimed, holding out his hand to grasp Natrum's forearm.

"It is good to see you too, Your Highness."

"We will have none of that. We have been friends longer than I have been king. For a short time, I plan to renew our friendship."

"As you wish. I would have thought you would be as anxious to be with your family as I am to be with mine."

Kratan admonished himself for not thinking of the wife and children who were awaiting Natrum's return to Nalo.

"How inconsiderate of me. After such a long trip, I know you need to be with your family. I will not delay you any longer. I will be in touch with you before your next mission and your family will join mine at the palace for a long overdue reunion. I know the twins attend school with your children and I am told they all get along well."

~ * ~

Liona made one final check of the apartment her mother-under-the-law would be enjoying. In every room, fresh flowers were perfectly arranged in elegant vases.

"When will Grandmother be here?" Nicos asked.

"Soon, very soon. I had a communication from your father saying her shuttle arrived several minutes ago and her hovercraft pilot is waiting to bring her back to us."

The joy that radiated from Nicos' face was the complete opposite to the scowl on the mirror image face of Miro's. She knew Miro was jealous of his brother's attachment to their grandmother. While King Palen had doted on the oldest twin who would one day be king, Queen Felda lavished her attention on Nicos. It was the one flaw in Miro's character that bothered his mother the most. It didn't matter that the two boys were only minutes apart in age. Miro felt as though he should be given all the attention all the time. For his brother to get anything Miro didn't made him angry.

"I don't know why anyone would be interested in a mere woman," Miro said, his voice laced with disrespect. "I don't know why Grandfather was the one to die on Seros. He was the important one."

"Miro," Liona scolded. "What a thing to say! Your grandparents were beloved rulers of this planet. It is sad that King Palen had to die, but we are blessed to still have Queen Felda with us. I for one am looking forward to her arrival. I have missed not only her presence in the palace, but also the guidance she will give to me on a daily basis."

Miro's dark mood radiated from his eyes, while Nicos' joy spread sunshine throughout the room. She knew she would have to have a long talk with Kratan when they were alone in their bedchamber that night.

~ * ~

As the hovercraft neared the palace, Felda looked longingly at the cottage where she planned to spend the rest of her life. She knew her decision bothered her son. It was her life and she no longer needed the adulation of the royal lifestyle. While on Seros, she'd been Felda, just another patient at the hospital. No one bowed to her and the conversations she enjoyed with her newfound friends were enlightening. It was fun to be just a normal person and not a queen.

Still thinking about the cottage and her plans for the renovation project, the hovercraft landed. She waited until one of the guards came from the palace to assist her in alighting so he could escort her to the palace.

"Mother," Liona greeted her. "You look fabulous. I am so pleased you were able to be saved from that terrible disease."

Felda looked down at the urn she carried and thought about the last hours of Palen's life. "Yes, my dear, I was lucky to be spared the ravages of the disease. The trip there as well as all the medical procedures exhausted me. Therefore, the time I spent there after Palen's passing was necessary for me to rest and regain my strength."

She heard the sound of little footsteps and smiled to see Nicos running to greet her. The only way she could distinguish one twin from the other was Nicos had a small mole on his right cheek, while Miro's mole was on the left.

"Grandmother, I am so happy to have you home," Nicos said.

The only thing that stopped him from throwing himself into her arms was the urn she still carried. Aware the boy wanted to be cuddled, she set the urn on a small side table. She got down on her knees, at the boy's level, and pulled him into a loving embrace.

"I would pick you up," she said, just loud enough for him to hear, "but you have grown so much I don't think I could lift you. I can't believe how tall the two of you boys have become while I was away."

"Welcome home, Grandmother," Miro said, coming to her side.

"Ah, Miro, you boys have not only grown, but you're more handsome than I remember. I missed both of you terribly."

Miro beamed at the compliment, but stood to one side, while Nicos clung to her tightly.

"I'm certain your grandmother is tired from her long journey. Why don't you boys run off and play, while I take her to the apartment that we have made ready for her?"

Reluctantly, Nicos released his grip on Felda and slowly walked away to join his brother. It was evident the two of them would be going to the nursery where their nurse would keep them occupied until it was time for the family dinner Felda knew would be planned for this evening.

"The twins are growing up. I am sorry to have missed so much of their lives," she said to Liona.

"That is something I meant to talk to you about. I fear for Nicos. Miro demands all of everyone's attention. At times I feel like Nicos feels as though he isn't as important as his brother."

"Palen and I talked about this before his passing. We both agree with what you are saying. I love both of the boys dearly, but it is Nicos who needs my attention. Perhaps when I am settled in the cottage, he will be able to visit me often."

"The cottage? You mean the one where you and Palen first lived? I remember living there when Kratan and I were first married. It is a lovely place to live, but are you certain this is what you want?"

"Yes. I have been working on some sketches for renovating it to suit my needs. When I was queen, my place was in this palace, but it was never where I was the happiest. By moving into the cottage, I will be close enough to play mother and grandmother but far enough away that I will not be involved in the day to day running of the palace."

"I-I had no idea. I never considered you living anywhere but with us. I so need your guidance."

"It won't happen overnight. The renovations will take several weeks and by that time, I am certain you will welcome the time when you are alone with your family and seeing to the needs of being queen. Believe me, it will all work out for the best."

~ * ~

Felda's homecoming brought changes to the palace. While she relished the renovations to the cottage, both Kratan and Liona pleaded with her to change her mind.

"You know you're welcome to stay at the palace with us, Mother," Kratan pleaded. "What will you do in the cottage all by yourself?"

"What you don't understand, my son, is that I no longer belong in the palace. As I told Liona, I long to return to the cottage where your father and I were so happy before he took over the monarchy from his father. You'll see, everything will be for the best. I will have my privacy and so will you."

"What about the twins? They will miss you."

"Miro doesn't need or miss me as much as Nicos does. I will still be on the palace grounds and although both boys will be welcome to come and visit any time they wish, I know it will be Nicos who comes to my door most often."

Kratan shook his head in dismay. As much as he wanted his mother to stay in her apartment in the palace, he understood her need for the independence that living in the cottage would bring her.

Since the renovations to the cottage would not be completed for several weeks, they had lots of time to discuss what Felda thought about establishing diplomatic relations with both Seros and Earth.

"We have more reasons for allying ourselves with Seros and Earth than with any other planets in the galaxy," Felda rationalized. "You know the history of those of us who came to Nalo so many years ago. We were only one third of the population of our home planet. We have distant relatives on both planets. I've met with many of the descendants of the original refugees and they all have high ranking positions within the governments of both planets. With the threat of Time Warp Fever eliminated, there is no reason for us to remain in isolation. I think this is something you should look into in the near future."

Kratan agreed but she knew he would be reluctant to act on her suggestion. It would, undoubtedly, be Miro who would take the major step once he became king in his father's stead.

Chapter Nineteen

Nicos loved spending time with his grandmother. When he wasn't in school, it was his favorite place on the palace grounds to be.

He'd been in the last year of military service when he received the news of his grandmother's passing. He was able to return home immediately. Since he and Miro were deployed with different units, he made the trip back to Capitol City alone. Their separation had been at Nicos' request. With Miro the heir apparent, Nicos had become disgusted with his brother calling him the spare heir. Being separated meant Nicos' promotions came because of his accomplishments rather than his identity. To most of the men in his company, he was their commanding officer and not the spare heir for the planet of Nalo.

His shuttle arrived at the spaceport on time. No one was there to meet him. He hadn't expected anyone to come for his arrival. He knew when Miro arrived there would be bodyguards to escort him to the palace. It wouldn't be the same for him. He would have to hire a hover driver to take him back to the palace. It was just as well, since he preferred to be alone with his grief.

Upon his arrival at the palace, it was evident a subdued celebration was in progress. After taking his duffel bag to the apartment that had been made available to him when he was old enough to leave the nursery, he went back down to the main reception hall.

Even in their sorrow over the loss of Felda, his parents were greeting Miro. It was the arrival of the heir apparent and the entire palace staff was in a joyous mood.

"Nicos," his father greeted him. "Why didn't you tell us when you would be arriving? We could have had a hovercraft waiting for you."

"I much preferred the solitude of traveling alone. Besides, I was able to hire a driver to bring me here."

"I had your apartment aired out for you," his mother said.

"You shouldn't have gone to all the trouble. I am planning on moving to the cottage as soon as my enlistment is up."

The expression on his mother's face was one of shock. "Why would you consider moving out of the palace? This is your home."

Nicos didn't know how to answer his mother. The palace was Miro's home, not his. Over the years he'd spent more time with his grandmother at the cottage than he ever had at the palace. Had he been born a girl rather than a boy, things would have been different. As the mirror image of his older brother, he knew this wasn't his place.

"I have been giving this a lot of thought. I will soon be mustering out of the military and want to begin my career working with the diplomatic corps. It is best I have my own home, away from the palace."

While his mother voiced her disapproval over his decision, Miro joined them and agreed with Nicos, possibly for the first time in their lives.

"I completely agree with my brother. He has a life that is not within the palace walls. The last time we were together he mentioned joining the diplomatic corps. It was at that time when I told him that with Grandmother getting older, perhaps it would be for the best when he finished his enlistment for him to move into the cottage with her. In her advanced age, she could certainly use not only his help, but also his companionship. The way I see it, with her passing, she is now with Grandfather and it is a shame for the cottage to stand empty as it did for so many years while they lived in the palace."

By now Kratan joined the conversation. He tended to agree with Liona but each of his arguments were put down by his sons.

With the memorial set for the next day, all discussion of Nicos moving to the cottage was tabled.

~ * ~

The day after the memorial service for Felda dawned bright and clear. With his leave extended for two weeks, Nicos was anxious to go over to his grandmother's cottage to see what renovations he wanted to make.

Even though his grandmother had remodeled the cottage to her specifications several years earlier, he knew there were changes he wanted made before he made this his permanent home.

One of his best friends from the University, Oman, now owned the construction company his father had established. Together they explored every inch of the cottage, like excited teenagers.

"What are you thinking of doing?" Oman asked.

"To begin with, I want to increase the size of the kitchen. Grandmother had her meals prepared by her cook, but I wanted to learn how to cook for myself. Her cook was more than willing to teach me how to make Grandmother's favorite dishes as well as some she knew I would enjoy."

"I can't believe a Prince of Nalo would stoop to doing his own cooking."

"You forget, it is Miro who is the Crown Prince. As Miro loves to tell me, I am nothing more than a spare heir. I also want to put a sonic shower into the bathing room. I've been aware of the shortage of water on Nalo for years. That said, I want to be as ecofriendly as possible. I've gotten spoiled with my accommodations at my current post. Being an officer does have its privileges."

After going over the rest of the renovations Nicos wanted, they went back to the palace to enjoy the midday meal with Liona. When he'd told her about contracting Oman to do the work at the cottage, she'd immediately insisted they take their luncheon with her.

"It was nice of your mother to include me in the luncheon invitation," Oman said.

"You should withhold judgment until we are finished eating. She is going to try to get you to persuade me not to move to the cottage. My mind is made up and this is what I want to do. I'm a grown man and I need my own accommodations as well as my own life."

"Are you thinking of taking a wife?"

"Not right now. Working for the diplomatic corps, who knows how long I will be in Capitol City, especially since once Miro takes the throne, he won't want me in close proximity to him."

Oman shook his head. "I don't understand the relationship between you and your brother. Even though my brother is two years younger than me, I can't imagine my life without him by my side."

"I feel the same about Miro, but it is he who wants to forget he has a brother who was born within minutes after his birth. He has always known he would someday be king of Nalo and has seen me as his inferior. It matters not to me. I'm sick and tired of being referred to as 'the spare heir.' I want to make my way in this world not because of my attachment to the royal family, but because of who I am."

Before Oman could form a reply, they arrived at the palace and went to one of the private dining rooms.

Nicos noticed the table was set for three, meaning the only ones dining together would be his mother, Oman and himself. He was grateful Miro would not be joining them. He had enough togetherness with his twin brother at the memorial to last him an entire lifetime.

"I just don't understand why you think you need to move into the cottage. Don't you agree with me, Oman?"

"Far be it for me to disagree with you, Your Highness, but the decision is Nicos' to make. What we talked about when we were over there today sounds very logical to me. His life will not revolve around the palace and therefore he should have his own accommodations."

The expression on Liona's face was one of disbelief. Nicos was certain his mother thought she could sway Oman to her way of thinking. He silently thanked his friend for standing up for him.

~ * ~

Six months later, Nicos' enlistment was up. He was glad to be back in Capitol City and living in the cottage.

By the time he moved in, all of the renovations were completed. The first guests he hosted were his parents. They were shocked when they realized he hadn't employed a cook.

"How do you plan to live without a cook?" his father questioned.

"It's simple. During the many visits I made to Grandmother, her cook delighted in teaching me the skill. I enjoy cooking and I'm certain you will agree, once you've tasted the dinner that I've prepared for you."

"You are the one responsible for the delicious smells wafting from the kitchen?" his mother asked.

"I most certainly am. I've prepared squab in cream sauce with leeks, baked tubers, and new greens. For dessert, I've made a pudding I think both of you will enjoy, along with clotted cream."

"Are you certain you're my son?" Kratan asked. "I would be lost if I had to make food that was palatable, as I know my mother would have been."

"This is something I enjoy doing. It is one of the reasons I wanted to live in this cottage. I doubt if the cooks in the palace kitchen would allow me to come into their territory."

While his parents seated themselves at his dining room table, he served first a salad made of fresh greens and a dressing made from some of Nalo's finest wine and oil. He followed it with the entree, and finally the dessert.

"I must admit," Kratan said, as they enjoyed an after-dinner drink in the sitting room, "that was one of the most delicious meals I've had in a long time. I think our chef at the palace could take lessons from you."

Nicos beamed at the compliment. "I am pleased you enjoyed it. I fear I wouldn't get such praise from my brother. Speaking of Miro, when is he due to return to Capitol City?"

"Don't you know?" Liona inquired. "His shuttle will be arriving at the end of the week. He's planning a party at the palace. Didn't you get your invitation?"

Nicos choked back the tears he wished he could shed. "If there is to be a party, it will be without me, as I received no invitation. Miro has no more use for me than I do for him. Whatever his plans are, they do not include me. I will be leaving in the morning for training in the Southern Hemisphere and will be gone for at least a month. That is the reason I invited you to enjoy the evening meal with me tonight. I have obligations and I wanted to apprise you of them before it was time for me to leave."

He could see tears forming in his mother's eyes. No matter what animosity there was between Miro and himself, she didn't want to see or acknowledge their differences.

~ * ~

Miro took a month to relax after his enlistment was up by spending time in a resort on the far side of Nalo. It was there he met Bria. She was the most beautiful woman he'd ever seen and he wanted her to be his mate and the Queen of Nalo.

Her father was reluctant to grant Bria's new suitor's request, but as soon as he realized this young man was the Crown Prince, he relented. By the time the month was up, Miro contacted the palace and told them to prepare Nicos' old apartment to accommodate the woman he was bringing back with him to become his bride.

He knew the mating ceremony wouldn't take place for at least a year, since his mother would want to plan the extravagant ceremony he deserved.

In planning the celebration that he wanted to have for his return to Capitol City, and introduce the woman who would become his mate, Miro debated sending an invitation to Nicos, but decided against it. The last thing he needed was to have the Spare Heir putting a damper on his special night.

~ * ~

Miro and Bria arrived at the shuttle port and were welcomed by the royal guard. He loved seeing the shocked expression on Bria's face. He knew she had no idea what her life was about to become.

At the resort, she'd been one of the serving girls who supplied expensive bottles of the finest of Nalo wines. Although she was beautiful, she certainly wasn't a royal princess, yet. He knew his mother would mold her into a perfect companion to be his mate for life.

Having met her parents, he knew they would never fit into Capitol City society. Her father worked as a street sweeper while her mother cleaned houses for the upper echelon of the people in her city. He doubted if Bria had much education but that would be a point in her favor. Being uneducated, she could become whatever he wanted her to be.

By the time they arrived at the palace, he could tell she was becoming extremely nervous. On the flight to Capitol City, he'd instructed her the proper way to curtsy when she was presented to his parents, but he wasn't at all certain if she grasped the concept.

~ * ~

Liona could not imagine her son finding the love of his life at a resort on the other side of the planet. What had he told her? The girl was a common server at the resort. She knew she should withhold judgment until she was able to meet Bria. She had been but a commoner herself. Still, she and Kratan knew each other for several years before he made his intentions known to her. What could Miro know of this girl who had he only met days rather than weeks, months or even years ago?

There was a commotion in the entrance hall and she hurried to be the first to greet her son and the woman who had stolen his heart.

As soon as they entered, she was shocked at the appearance of this young woman. She was, indeed, young. Younger even than she had been when she first came to the palace as Kratan's future mate. Her hair, rather than carrying a natural color, had been bleached blonde and looked terribly dry. As for her facial features, it was hard to tell because of the amount of cosmetics she wore.

She'd heard of girls who painted their faces and dyed their hair. Even as a commoner, she had never encountered someone like this before. Other than the finest of facial soap, nothing else ever touched her face in all the years she lived in the palace.

If her appearance came as a surprise, her apparel was completely shocking. Rather than the robes or the more modern clothing preferred by the younger generation, the gown she wore was very low-cut and form-fitting. Her breasts literally were falling out of the bodice and it amazed Liona to see how anyone could even walk in such a tight garment.

"Mother, this is Bria."

Liona held out her hand as the young woman made a clumsy curtsy. "Such a gesture is not necessary as we will soon become family."

The girl took her hand and thanked her profusely.

"We have made ready the apartment of Miro's brother for you. Since he no longer lives within the palace walls, it seemed a shame to let it sit unoccupied. I am certain you will breathe new life into these old walls. Now, I'm certain you are tired from your journey. I have assigned a personal servant for you. Her name is Helda and she will show you to your accommodations."

Helda seemed to appear as though she was waiting for her name to be mentioned. "It is my pleasure to be serving you, Mistress," she said as she took Bria's hand.

Once they were alone, Miro embraced his mother. "It's good to be home. I thought perhaps Father would be here to meet me."

"Your father is in an important meeting with the diplomatic corps about the possibility of beginning a diplomatic relationship with Earth and Seros."

"Ah, I see. He's making a plan to get rid of the Spare Heir."

"He is doing no such thing. Your brother is far from being ready for such an assignment. He is now training at the facility of the Southern Hemisphere. I can't believe you would say such a thing."

"I wouldn't say it if it weren't true. Had he been born a female rather than a male, he would be married off and not included in palace life. Nicos has no place here. We talked about this when we were home for Grandmother's memorial service. I think the diplomatic corps is the best place for him. Once he has a placement, he won't be interfering with the royal duties. He knows his place, just as I know mine. We were never meant to be friends."

Liona was appalled to hear his affirmation of what Nicos had told her less than a week earlier. She'd prayed they would be friends and work together for the good of the planet. Now she knew it would never happen. She feared for what would become of Nalo once Miro took over as the reigning monarch.

Chapter Twenty

Nicos thought about the mating ceremony his parents planned for Miro and Bria. Everything had been perfect, with the exception of the woman Miro was mating with for life. She reminded him of the bar girls he met whenever he was on leave from the military.

Although his mother had tried, she still looked like a garish caricature on their mating day. Her face was plastered with more paint than he'd ever seen on anyone before. As for her mating dress, it left little for the imagination. It made him wonder if Miro had sampled the pleasures best left for after the mating earlier than he should have been entitled to.

Now, five years later, everything had changed. While Bria became pregnant on three different occasions, she lost all three of the babies before the third months of her pregnancies.

Even with that shadow over Miro, they were further bereaved when Kratan took a bad fall, hit his head, and passed away within hours of the accident.

Nicos had been at his father's bedside when he slipped away. As soon as the funeral was held, Miro was crowned king of Nalo, and Bria his queen.

Miro's first royal duty was to send Nicos to Earth to represent Nalo at their embassy. Secondly, he ordered that his mother should move to Nicos' cottage, rather than remain at the palace.

Nicos knew moving out of the palace broke his mother's heart. He was thrilled to think she would be occupying his cottage. The little house needed someone to love it as much as he did. Through the years, his mother visited often and even insisted on learning how to cook in his gourmet kitchen.

~ * ~

The pilot of the space shuttle announced they would be landing in Washington, DC in half an hour and the passengers should secure their belongings. Nicos thought of all the stories he'd heard about the long trip his ancestors took from Plantas to Nalo. Now it took only a matter of two weeks using the time warps and wormholes to get from Nalo to Earth.

He wondered what kind of reception he would get once they landed. Would there be a welcoming committee or would he have to find his own way to the embassy in the same way he did when he arrived at Capitol City for his grandmother's memorial service?

The landing was one of the smoothest he'd ever experienced. To his surprise, there was a delegation holding a sign with his name on it. He was glad his family kept up the practice of implanting the translator chip at birth. It would certainly come in handy now that he would be encountering many different dialects and languages. Even on Nalo, he'd been able to understand the many different languages of the members of the military from every corner of the planet.

Deliberately, he walked toward the people holding the sign. "I am Ambassador Nicos."

"I didn't think there would be many people on the shuttle from Nalo, but we couldn't take any chances. I'm Stephanie Jacobson. My great-grandmother came on the original flight from Plantas. I've been assigned as your attaché. I'm to take you to your apartment within the Embassy."

"Thank you, ah…Stephanie."

"Please, call me Steph. It's much easier to pronounce and we will be working very closely. Therefore, we will be seeing a lot of each other."

Nicos enjoyed the easy banter between the two of them. She was indeed a beautiful woman and her violet eyes belied her connection with the refugees from Plantas. For the first time in his life, he felt an immediate attraction to a woman.

After she introduced him to the remainder of his staff, they went out to where her hovercraft waited for them.

"This is a nice vehicle," he said, running his hand over the butter-soft upholstery.

Growing up, he'd toured his uncle's hovercraft factory many times. He'd been excited to learn how the vehicles were built and he knew the function of every part of them. Of course, Miro had never gone with him. Touring his uncle's plant was too mundane for the future king of Nalo.

"Oh, this isn't mine. I could never afford a craft with all the bells and whistles, as my father would say. This one belongs to the embassy. In other words, it's yours. I'm just pleased to get to pilot it until you're ready to solo."

"How long will that take?"

"Even though you have a pilot's license on Nalo, you will have to pass the test for one here on Earth. I'll be happy to help you study for the test."

Nicos smiled at her. She intrigued him. He would be content to have her pilot him for as long as she was willing. He knew he would have much more to do in his new position than he expected. He'd been trained for this and would be content to spend the rest of his life on this planet, lightyears away from Nalo and Miro.

The flight from the shuttle port to the Embassy took less than half an hour. Once they arrived, he was impressed with the opulence of, not only the building, but also his apartment. To his surprise, Steph told him she occupied an apartment on one of the lower floors of the building.

"Does that make us neighbors?"

"I guess it does, Your Highness."

Nicos was taken by surprise. "How did you know?"

"The former Ambassador told us about you. I can't believe a Prince would be content to come here as an Ambassador."

"I was born a prince, but I was never destined to be of the ruling class. My twin brother is but two minutes older than me and the one who was destined to become the king. Since my father died just before I came here, he is now the king and welcome to it. I wanted nothing to do with the royal duties kingship involved. To my brother, I have always been the 'Spare Heir.' Since he outlived our father, it is now a moot point."

"I'm sorry. I didn't know. From now on you are Ambassador Nicos."

"If I were an Earthling, would I have a nickname like you do?"

Steph laughed at his question. "If the two of us grew up together, I have a feeling I would have called you Nicky."

"Nicky, I like that. From here on, you're Steph and I'm Nicky. I think I'm going to like living and working on Earth."

~ * ~

Steph left Nicky to get settled while she went back to her apartment. Her orders had been to take him to one of the best restaurants in DC, but she had questions that needed to be answered.

As soon as she was back in her apartment, she connected her computer and placed a call to her best friend, Krissy Mathews. They'd met at a reunion for refugees from Plantas. Even though the original refugees had long ago died, there were many descendants who still enjoyed getting together and reliving the history passed down by their ancestors.

"Hey Steph, what's up?"

"The new Ambassador from Nalo arrived today. Oh my god, Krissy, he's the most handsome man I've ever met. If I can believe the former Ambassador, he's the great-grandson of the man who was engaged to your great grandmother."

"Oh, I've heard of him. His name was Grato and he was in the first ship that left Plantas for Nalo. My great-grandmother was in the last ship. The remainder of them were lost to the meteor storm. From the stories I've heard, my great-grandma was devastated at her loss, at least until she met my great-grandfather. They were surprised when they learned Grato had survived and married one of the women from Plantas who was on the ship with him. If I'm not mistaken, she was a doctor."

"What a coincidence, right?"

"I don't care about coincidences. I want to hear more about this new guy. He must be a real hunk if he's got your juices flowing."

"Who says my juices are flowing?"

"I do. I've never seen you this excited about a guy. I mean, I've tried to hook you up with any number of Jason's friends. Especially Robby Maxell, you know, the best man at Jason's wedding. He was so disappointed that you didn't want to hook up."

"There was really nothing wrong with good old Robby, but he just wasn't my type. Nicky on the other hand…"

"Nicky?"

"His real name is Nicos, but he wanted a nickname that sounded like he was born on Earth. Get this, the guy is a prince. I mean a member of the royal ruling family on Nalo."

"You're kidding, right? A prince? You're calling a prince Nicky?"

"I called him Your Highness and it was like I slapped him in the face. From what I can gather, he wants nothing to do with the royal family, especially his brother King Miro."

"Well, keep me posted. I want pictures, lots of pictures. So where are you taking him for dinner tonight? You're still taking him out to dinner, aren't you?"

"Yes, I am. I thought we'd go to Savvoy. They serve traditional foods from Nalo, Seros and Plantas as well as a darned good Texan steak. I'm looking forward to it. I hope he likes it."

*

Nicos, or Nicky as she had dubbed him, couldn't believe his good fortune. Steph was a beautiful woman. She was also a descendant from the refugees from Plantas. In other words, they had more in common than he ever expected.

She promised she'd return to take him out for the evening meal. He knew he would need to freshen up and change from his traveling robes to something more suitable for his life on Earth. After several transmissions between the embassy and the palace, he learned what he would need in order to fit in. He'd found a tailor in Capitol City who was more than willing to create a wardrobe of dress and casual clothing for his new life.

He chose a blue suit made of the finest wool from the sheep of Nalo, along with a white silk shirt and a tie with stripes to complement the outfit. It had taken him watching many videos to learn how to tie it, but once he mastered the art, it was relatively easy.

Once he showered and dressed for an evening out, he checked out the rest of the apartment. To his surprise, the kitchen, although smaller than the one he had installed at the cottage, was state of the art. He would have to try working with the appliances, but he was certain his cooking abilities would adjust to his new environment as well as new foods. With luck, it wouldn't be long before he would be able to ask Steph to come to his apartment for a home-cooked meal.

The ringing of a bell brought him back to the present and his anticipated evening with Steph. In his training, he'd watched hours of video transmissions about the life and traditions of the people of Earth as well as those of Seros. These were the two closest allies with Nalo, as people from Plantas has been sent to each of those planets several generations ago.

He passed a gazing glass and assessed his appearance before he answered the door. As soon as he saw Steph, he was pleased with his selection of apparel for the evening. She wore a stunning midnight-blue dress studded with something that made it look like the stars in the night sky. It left her right shoulder bare and covered her left shoulder. Seeing a woman's skin, other than hands, legs or faces, excited him more than the pictures of naked women he saw in his art and biology classes in college.

"Good evening," she purred. "Are you ready to go out and do a little exploration of the city? I made reservations for us at a restaurant called Savvoy. I thought you might enjoy it, as they serve dishes popular on Plantas, Nalo, Seros and Earth."

"It sounds interesting."

He took her hand and brought it to his lips. Having no idea of the proper way to address a young woman on Earth, Nicos decided it was best if he execute the greeting that was acceptable on Nalo. It surprised him to see her face color to a delicate pink.

"How gallant," she said. "I didn't think anyone used such an ancient form of greeting anymore."

"Ancient?" Nicos questioned.

"I am told this was an acceptable form of greeting between a man and a woman on the planet Plantas. Before the Exodus, all of our people practiced it, but once they arrived on Earth, the expression was changed. Here people shake hands. I always thought it was nowhere near as romantic as the way our people greeted each other in that bygone era."

Now it was Nicos' turn to feel the blush of embarrassment creeping into his face. "This is the way of greeting between a man and a woman when they meet on Nalo. I have read all of the history books and realize it was something those refugees who made it to Nalo initiated. My father and grandmother were well versed in the legends of those who were the first to arrive on Nalo. They brought many different practices to the people there."

Steph smiled and he relaxed a bit. "We can talk more about this when we get to the restaurant. Our reservations are for seven, and I never like to be late."

He followed her from his apartment to the elevator tube that transported them to the underground garage where the hovercraft was located. The technology of this planet amazed him. On Nalo, people took the stairs, rather than stepping into tubes that transported them from one level to the other.

"Are you all right?" Steph asked as they made their way to the hovercraft.

"It's just that things here are very different. We have no multi-storied buildings, like the ones here. Only the palace and some of the governmental buildings rise from the ground in the way they do here. I've never ridden in one of these things you call elevator tubes before."

"Wait until you see the escalator at the restaurant. It's a moving staircase. We even have moving sidewalks that connect us from one place to another."

"With all of these moving devices, how does anyone stay fit? I mean, it seems as though people here have no way to get natural exercise."

"Tomorrow I will introduce you to the gym that's in the building. We all use it. Do you have any exercise clothes with you?"

"Exercise clothes? I don't think I know what you mean."

"I thought as much. Once we finish our dinner, we'll go to one of the stores in the building where the restaurant is located. We'll be able to pick up what you need when we get there."

Steph pulled up in front of an impressive-looking building. At the top was a revolving sphere with lights coming from it as though it was a space ship like those used by the ancients when they first explored the universe.

A man in a jumpsuit with the logo of a transport company on his lapel came to valet their craft as they entered the building.

"Impressive, but can this man be trusted with…"

"Of course, he can. Although everyone pilots their crafts, they never park them. It's not safe to walk from such lots into a building, especially if you're a woman. These men are highly trained in martial arts and they carry weapons for their protection."

Nicos shook his head. He would have trouble getting used to what seemed like a violent society.

Inside the building, he was awed by the array of retail shops, each displaying fabulous items for sale. Rather than stop at any of them, Steph ushered him toward the moving staircase. Even though the prospect of riding on this metal monstrosity scared him, he knew he had to conquer his fears. He'd been in the military and knew this could never be as frightening as leading his men into hostile territories.

He watched as Steph effortlessly stepped onto the staircase and begin her ascent. Putting his fears behind him, he did likewise. To his amazement, it was exhilarating. It only took them to the second level of what she called the mall. From there, they went to an elevator tube to take them to the revolving sphere at the top of the building.

When they stepped from the tube into the restaurant, they were greeted with rich scents of foods that were both familiar and at the same time alien.

"Have you eaten here before?" he asked.

"Yes, many times. It is a particular favorite of my father when they visit the city. His grandfather was the first ambassador to work between the United States and those who came from Plantas. Of course, much has changed over the years. Earth has come under a central government and recently joined the coalition. Everyone in the diplomatic corps was thrilled when Nalo established an Embassy here and joined the coalition as well."

"That was my father's doing."

Before he could say more, the hostess greeted them and took them to a table.

"What do you suggest we order?"

Without looking at the menu, Steph replied, "I like everything here, but for tonight I think I would like to order from the Earthly menu. They make a mean steak and lobster that I'm particularly partial to. Of course, they do have foods from Plantas, Seros and Nalo. We have a lot of diplomats who visit Washington and the chefs here learned to make all of the traditional dishes from their planets, as well as the long-forgotten recipes that came with the refugees."

"I think I will try what you are having. If I want food from Nalo, I will make it for myself when I learn which foods from Earth mirror those of Nalo."

Before they could enjoy further conversation, the waiter came to take their order. Following Steph's lead, he ordered the lobster with steak done medium rare. He also ordered the same salad as she did, including the blue cheese salad dressing.

Steph looked at him with a shocked expression on her face. "I hope you know what you're getting into. I mean, blue cheese is an acquired taste. It was always my mom's favorite but it took a while for my dad to become accustomed to it. Getting back to what we were talking about, what do you mean you will make it for yourself? Are you telling me you know how to cook?"

Nicos smiled back at her questions. "At home, I insisted on taking over my grandmother's cottage. Once I did, I installed a gourmet kitchen. As a child, I spent many hours with my grandmother, learning from her cook how to prepare the meals she and I loved the most. I found I enjoyed cooking and have done so every chance I got. Of course, between the military and my studies, I haven't had much time for such things until I finished my education to be able to work with the diplomatic corps. Before you arrived tonight, I was exploring the kitchen of my apartment. I think, once I become acquainted with the foods on Earth, I will enjoy preparing a meal for you."

"Well, if that don't beat all. From working with the previous Ambassador, I never expected to find out you are an experienced chef. I remember my grandmother telling me about how when her mother first arrived on Earth, she was surprised to find that my ancestor, Rand Jacobson, knew how to cook."

"Do many men on Earth cook?"

Steph laughed at his question. "Many of the top chefs from around the world are men. Although they are touted as the best cooks, not many of the men here cook. They leave that job up to their wives or the hired help. I do admire a man who can cook. All of my uncles as well as my brothers know how to cook and are quite good at it. They even share those duties with their wives."

"Brothers? Is there not a ban on the number of children a family can have?"

"What a strange question. I know for a fact that families on Earth as well as Seros have multiple children. It was the same, or so I'm told, on Plantas. Is it not the same on Nalo?"

"I'll answer this one question but for the rest of the evening, I plan to get to know you better. On Nalo, sex before mating is prohibited. It is the same with the number of children couples can have. Each couple is allowed to birth two children. Since my brother and I are twins, we have

176

no other siblings."

He could tell Steph was formulating many more questions behind those violet eyes, but as he said, he wanted to get to know *her* better. That wouldn't happen unless he stopped describing the life that he left behind him.

Chapter Twenty-One

Nicos had been on Earth for over three years and to be truthful, he was disenchanted with his position of Ambassador. He wanted something more to challenge him. There was little actual work for him to do and, in all honesty, he was bored.

"What are your plans for the future?" Steph's brother Alex asked when they were attending the reunion for Plantas refugees.

"I honestly don't know. All my life I have been trained to be a diplomat, but to be honest, it's not the rewarding work I hoped it would be."

Alex nodded. "I gathered as much from what Steph has said. I've been looking into a business to invest in. With more and more interplanetary flights and people from various planets coming to Earth, I've been considering opening a chain of restaurants that will be like Savvoy, only more reasonably priced to accommodate the immigrants or tourists on a budget. I know you are a gourmet cook, so would you want to partner with me to oversee the operation?"

Nicos could feel the wheels in his brain beginning to spin. For weeks he'd been thinking about doing something different, but he didn't know what it would be. Alex proposed the perfect solution. "What kind of monetary investment would you be asking for?"

"I don't want or need your money, my friend. I have all the backers I need for this project. What we would need from you is your expertise. Steph has told me of your skills in the kitchen. You would be overseeing all of the chefs and doing the training. With this kind of restaurant there will be little room for error. The food we serve will have to be of the same quality, no matter which location people are visiting."

"How soon are you planning to begin this venture? I would need time to contact my brother and resign my commission. It's not something I can accomplish overnight."

"Are you telling me you'd be interested?"

"I most certainly am. I need something different in my life. Something that is steady and yet enough of a challenge for me before I can ask Steph to mate...I mean marry me."

Alex's expression was one of surprise, mingled with excitement. "We'll make a great team. You've got the brains and the expertise while my partners and I have the money. As for Steph, I'm sure she'll be over the moon. Welcome to the family, Nicki."

~ * ~

Nicos couldn't believe how quickly things moved. His video conversation with Miro went much better than he ever expected. When he said he was planning to resign as Ambassador, there was no talk of when or if he would be returning to Nalo. He knew Miro was happy to have his twin brother many lightyears away.

A week later, he received a video call from this mother. She told him she was content to be living in the cottage but it saddened her to think Miro and Bria lost yet another baby before it could even be born.

"Once I am settled," Nicos said, "I would like to have you immigrate to Earth. If I am not mistaken, you are very lonely."

He could see tears running down her cheeks and wished he could take her in his arms to give her comfort.

"It is hard living here, on my own. I have a good staff, but it's not the same as family. I rarely see Miro and Bria treats me as though I was one of her servants rather than the Queen Mother. I can understand why your grandmother was so thrilled to travel to Seros. Do you actually want me to come to Earth to be with you?"

"I do, Mother. Steph and I are planning to be married in three months. I would appreciate having you meet my soon-to-be wife and be able to attend my wedding."

"I don't quite understand what you are saying, but have you found a mate among the Earthlings?"

"I've told you about her in many transmissions. She is descended from the original refugees who came from Plantas at the same time we came to Nalo. I have even met descendants from Tarena. She was the woman Grato was to be mated with. I'm learning more about the history of our people. There is so much more than I read in all the books in Grandmother's library. I want you to come here. I can tell you are unhappy living outside of the palace. I can't understand the position my brother has taken."

"Don't blame Miro. He has many responsibilities and none of them include me. I would be pleased to join you on Earth. I will start making the arrangements to be on the next transport between Nalo and Earth."

Nicos broke the connection with his homeland. It saddened him to see his mother and know how unhappy she was. Over the years she had lost her brother and his wife, as well as her parents. The only family she had left on Nalo was Miro and knowing how self-centered he was, she was all alone.

Over the past three years, he'd questioned the reports of his father's death. It was highly unlikely his father had accidentally fallen down the stairs. As much as he didn't want to admit it, it was likely that somehow, his brother was behind the accident that took his father's life. Now his concern was for his mother. Miro's lack of concern for her bothered him. The sooner he could get her to Earth and settled, the better it would be for her.

~ * ~

Liona could hardly believe Nicos wanted her to come to Earth. Nalo had become unbearable for her. Miro no longer visited her at the cottage as he had in the beginning. With the remainder of her family no longer living, she had no one. As Queen of Nalo, she'd never cultivated any close friends. Kratan's sister and her life mate had retired and moved out of Capitol City. With them gone, the only family she had left here no longer wanted her.

She thought back to when she first came to Capitol City. Kratan's parents made her feel wanted and loved. Having her parents and brother at her side, she thought she lived in the best world possible.

Her thoughts turned to the day Kratan died. He and Miro had been participating in a heated argument. From what she was told, Miro left the room in a rage and Kratan followed him. It was then that he'd fallen down the stairs and hit his head.

Was that what actually happened? The thought that popped into her head was one she knew she would never know the answer to. Kratan had been maneuvering those stairs for his entire life. In no way did she believe such an accident could have happened.

She dismissed the thoughts she knew were accusatory of her oldest son. As difficult as he was to deal with, she couldn't bring herself to believe he would ever do such a dastardly thing.

As soon as she could, she would go to the palace to ask Miro to approve her transport to Earth.

~* ~

Miro was surprised when his mother asked for a private audience. She rarely visited the palace and he certainly didn't have the time to go to her cottage. Between his duties as reigning monarch and the demands Bria made, he barely had time to think of anything else. If only Bria would get pregnant and carry the child to term, things would be much better. If he didn't have to spend so much time in the bedroom, without any successes, he might be able to make more time for his mother.

"Mother, it's good to see you."

Liona took his hands in hers. He could tell she had something on her mind.

"I received a vision call from Nicos and he wants me to move to Earth to be with him. Can you arrange for my transport?"

Miro could hardly contain his excitement. With his mother lightyears away on Earth with his brother, he would be free to run the planet in the way he thought was best.

"Are you certain, Mother?" he finally managed to ask.

"Yes, I am. Nicos wants me there and I have learned I have nothing to keep me here. I am looking forward to starting a new life."

"If that is what you want, I will make arrangements for you to be on the next transport leaving for Earth. Unfortunately, I will not be able to allow you to take anything more than your personal belongings. All of the furnishings of the cottage do, in fact, belong to the monarchy. I will transfer enough credits to an account for you, at the same bank on Earth where we send the credits for the running of the Embassy as well as a salary for Nicos. From what he told me he is leaving the Embassy. Therefore, the new Ambassador will be going with you."

Liona dipped into a deep curtsy before she left the audience chamber. He waited until she was completely out of the palace before he gave into the gleeful laughter he'd been holding inside. With his mother gone, he would be free of the old ideas from the past and could move into the future.

Chapter Twenty-Two

Nicky and Steph waited at the shuttle port for his mother's flight to arrive from Nalo. So much had happened since he and Alex spoke in the early months of Earth's summer.

As he predicted, Miro was overjoyed with his resignation and his desire to remain on Earth. His brother insisted that as soon as the new Ambassador arrived, he should be ready to vacate the apartment.

It took little persuasion for him to agree to move to the Jacobson family compound just outside of Santa Fe. At the time, the architects were busy constructing the home where he and Steph would live after their wedding. As soon as he knew his mother would be coming to Earth to be with him, he commissioned a small cottage to be built on the grounds for her as well.

Although his new position would require a lot of traveling, it was best if he maintained a home close to the headquarters of Interplanetary Cuisine, as their new company was called.

While wrapping up the final work that needed to be done at the Embassy, he'd taken time to look over the variety of recipes that had been sent for his approval. Ones he wasn't familiar with he tried out in his kitchen, to decide if they were of the quality necessary for the chain of restaurants he would be overseeing. It took several weeks, but he finally put his stamp of approval on the menu for the restaurants that would be under his supervision. As soon as they arrived in Santa Fe, he would begin instructing the chefs that Alex and his fellow backers hired. He would be making certain each recipe was executed to his specifications.

The announcement came of the arrival of the transport from Nalo.

Although they had spoken through video chat three months earlier, he wasn't prepared to greet his mother. What the video screen hadn't shown were the worry lines around her eyes and the streaks of silver in her hair. Perhaps he had seen them, but hadn't wanted to acknowledge their existence.

"Nicos, I am so pleased to finally be here," Liona said as soon as he embraced her.

"Was it a difficult flight?"

"Not really. Of course, I have nothing to compare it with. I was treated with the upmost respect but at times there was turbulence. I don't think I was cut out for space travel. I pray I will never have to take such a harrowing journey again."

"You won't, I promise. Although, in the morning we will be taking a shuttle to Santa Fe, where our new homes are waiting for us. For now, I want you to meet the woman who has agreed to be my wife. Mother, this is Stephanie, although everyone calls her Steph."

"Santa Fe? Why is the name of your new home familiar to me?"

"It is in the history books as the place near where the last ship destined for Nalo landed when they came to Earth," Steph replied. "We have strong connections to the Mathews family. It was Paul Mathews who married Tarena. He and Rand Jacobson were best friends, so the family have been close ever since. For a while Rand and Nina lived at the family compound in Peru, but eventually they moved to Santa Fe. The grounds of the family compound are the landing site for the lost ship of the Nalo contingency. For many years, the land was deemed off limits to anyone. It was Rand and Paul who lobbied the government to allow them to build a family compound there."

Nicos knew that although his mother read all of the histories of those who left Plantas so many generations earlier, she didn't feel the close ties to these people that he'd experienced. Many of these people should have arrived on Nalo along with his family. Meeting them was like going to a family reunion many generations in the making.

Steph held out her hand and immediately Liona pulled her into a tight embrace. "My son told me you were beautiful and he didn't exaggerate. He also told me you are descended from the refugees from Plantas."

"I am, and my family as well as my friends are anxious to meet you. Especially my friend Krissy. Her great-grandmother, Tarena, was promised to Nicky's great-grandfather, Gratos, before they left Plantas. It was the meteor storm that separated them and sent her to Earth, in the same way it sent Gratos to Nalo. To be truthful, the refugees from Plantas are still a very close-knit group here on Earth."

"I hope I will fit in. My family can trace its roots back many generations to almost the beginning of time on Nalo. I have no Plantas blood in my veins."

"It matters not. As Nicky's mother, you will be welcomed with opened arms. My grandmother told me stories of meeting your mother-in-law when they were both on Seros at the Time Warp Fever treatment center."

Nicos silently thanked Steph for making his mother feel wanted in this alien world. Together they went out to where his rented hovercraft was waiting for them. Having shipped all of his belongings to Santa Fe at the beginning of the week, he and Steph had been staying at a hotel for one more night before taking the shuttle to Santa Fe in the morning. There, Alex would be meeting them. He would take them out to compound and the new homes they had waiting for them.

"For tonight, you and I will be sharing a bedroom in our suite," Steph said. "Neither Nicky nor I believe in living together before marriage."

"Speaking of marriage, when will the two of you be joined?"

"Since we will be arriving in Santa Fe on Tuesday, everyone will be assembled for the ceremony on Saturday. My parents are arranging everything."

"Before I left Nalo, I took the liberty of having something made for your ceremony. I pray it will be suitable."

Nicky thought of the wedding robe his mother wore when Miro mated with Bria. Would what she had made resemble the ceremonial robe she'd worn on that day?

~ * ~

Liona marveled about everything she found in this new, alien world. Although she'd spent the entire journey with the new Ambassador to Earth, Atos, he was met by a delegation from the Embassy and spirited away almost immediately upon their arrival.

Nicos, or Nicky as she knew she now must learn to address her son, made arrangements for her baggage to be sent immediately to Santa Fe, before they left for the hotel where they would be staying until the next morning.

As they made their way through the airways toward their hotel, she marveled at the congestion of the city. Nicky told her there were no limits on the size of families. She thought how much more civilized it was on Nalo where only two children were permitted to each family.

The hovercraft her son so skillfully piloted from the shuttle port to the hotel was of the same quality as the ones produced at the plant which her nephew now ran. With her sister-under-the-law both dead as well as her brother and parents, she was proud of the way her nephew stepped up and continued the tradition of his family.

The hotel surpassed her expectations. The bathroom provided not only a water shower, but a sonic one like she had used while living in the cottage. While Nicky advocated for conserving natural resources, Miro didn't share his commitment to the environment. The size of the suite also came as a surprise. It exceeded the size of one of the smaller apartments at the palace. The sitting room was enormous, as well as the bedrooms. The kitchen, although small, afforded top-line appliances, in case the guests wanted to cook for themselves.

"Will you be preparing the evening meal for us, Nicky?" she inquired.

"Not tonight. You will have enough time to get sick of my cooking once we arrive at our new homes. For tonight we are going to enjoy the restaurant at the hotel. They have excellent food and it's always a treat for Steph and myself to go there."

"Speaking of restaurants, when will your first restaurant be opening?"

"Not until after the first of the year. With my duties at the embassy, I was only able to approve the menus. Steph's brother, Alex, has a test kitchen set up at the compound where the recipes will be perfected and the chefs trained. Our first restaurant will be opening here in Washington, since that is the most diverse city in the area. Once that one is opened there are several others planned."

"If you are not open and you are not working for the Embassy, how will you be able to support yourself, to say nothing of your mate?"

Nicky laughed at her question. "Living at the Embassy, I was able to save a good deal of money. Even so, I am being compensated generously for the work I've been doing prior to leaving the Embassy."

Liona wondered if she should be worried about the fact her son was drawing a salary from the government of Nalo.

"I can sense you are concerned. There is no need. The work I did for my new employers was done on my own time. I worked evenings and weekends, trying out recipes and making them in my kitchen. Nothing I did took away from my duties."

She nodded. Nicky was her sensible child. He was the one who should have been king. She knew the kingdom would have been better off with him on the throne instead of Miro.

Thoughts of her oldest child brought to mind the questions surrounding the death of her life mate, Kratan. Was it possible his fall wasn't as accidental as Miro proclaimed it to be? Were the rumors of Miro's bid for power that lead to Kratan's untimely death true?

Putting thoughts of Miro and Kratan from her mind, she turned her attention to Nicky and Steph. "As long as I will be living on Earth, perhaps I, too, should have a name that does not sound so foreign."

"Are you certain you want to do that?" Steph inquired. "Liona is such a beautiful name, why would you want to shorten it?"

"Liona was a little girl on Nalo who fell in love with the Crown Prince. She is also the woman who became first a princess and finally a queen. Once my life mate died, everything changed. Liona belongs to the history of Nalo. What do you think of the name Lia?"

From the smiles on both Nicky and Steph's faces, she knew of their approval.

"Then Lia is who I will be for as long as I live on Earth. I'm afraid I will have to find a job once we are settled. I was given a stipend from your brother, but that won't be enough to support me for the rest of my life."

"Do not think that way, Mother," Nicky assured her. "You will never have to worry about how you will be able to live. With our homes in the compound, your expenses will be minimal and they are nothing that Steph and I won't be able to cover."

Nicky's assurance eased Lia's mind. She was ready to start a new life on a new planet, far away from everything she'd ever known in her life.

Chapter Twenty-Three

Their arrival at the family compound was a joyous occasion. Steph's mother and grandmother were there to meet their shuttle and talked excitedly about the upcoming wedding. Steph was thrilled when both of the women who were the most important in her life were anxious to include Lia in their wedding plans.

Although she'd badgered her mother about what she would be wearing for her wedding, she was told it was something extremely appropriate.

More important than wedding preparations was reconnecting with Krissy. With her work in DC and Krissy's at the compound in Peru, they'd only connected through teleconference for the past three years.

That evening, Krissy's shuttle arrived from Peru. Although Steph wanted to be the first to greet her friend, she opted to spend the evening with Nicky and Lia.

"To what do we owe this unexpected joy of your presence?" Nicky teased. "I thought you would be spending this night catching up with Krissy."

"I am anxious to see her, but so is her family. It's been a long time since she's been home. We will have our time together on Friday before our wedding. I won't be able to be with you before the wedding, so it will give us time to renew our friendship. She is going to be my maid of honor, after all."

"I'm happy for your restraint, as I do love having you in my company. We haven't talked about going on a honeymoon. I have been reading about wedding practices on Earth and have learned about taking your new wife on a wedding trip."

Tears sprung to Steph's eyes. "I don't expect anything like that. In this day and age, it's an archaic practice. We will both be so busy starting the new business, we won't have time for…"

"Of course, we will. I don't plan to be starting work until the finishing touches are put on the test kitchen. I have been making arrangements with Alex and the day after our wedding, we will be leaving for Peru. I am anxious to see the wonders attributed to our ancient ancestors."

Steph was thrilled. This was something she'd wanted to show Nicky ever since she first met him. With the excitement of the new restaurant, she had no idea there would be any time for them to get away to be alone once they were married.

"Oh, Nicky, this is exactly what I have wanted since we first met. There was never enough time for us to get away and allow me to show you where the people from Plantas first returned to this planet."

"I will take that as a yes. Perhaps we can take this evening to do some packing to ready ourselves for this momentous trip we are about to take."

"I'd like to help you with your packing," Lia said. "My son has made a good decision. I disagree with you about it being an archaic practice. Even on Nalo, newly mated couples take time to get away from everything and everyone, to get to know each other better. As I recall, your father and I went to a lovely resort on the far side of the planet. It was close to where I grew up and I felt completely at home there. We had a wonderful time together and repeated that trip every five years. With the pressures of being first the Crown Prince and then King, he needed our time away."

~ * ~

The day before the wedding dawned early and, reluctantly, Steph left the house that would soon belong to her and Nicky to go to her parent's home where she would stay until the time of the wedding the next day.

Krissy was waiting for her when she arrived. It was so good to be with her best friend, if only for a short while.

"Are you getting excited?" Krissy asked.

"Excited, frightened, thrilled, take your choice. Last night, Nicky told me we will be going to Peru the day after the wedding. I thought the practice of a honeymoon disappeared years ago. I guess I was wrong."

"I have to admit," Krissy said, "I've known about it for several weeks. Alex called me so I could make all of the arrangements for the best accommodations. As the first descendant of those of our people who went to Nalo, to come to Earth, Alex thought he should be treated as a visiting dignitary. With my connections with the Visitor's Center, I was able to get everything arranged."

"Oh, Krissy, what would I do without you? Are you excited to see what our mothers have come up with for us to wear tomorrow?"

"I am, but at the same time, I'm not. My mother let the cat out of the bag last night. I think you will be thrilled. Let's go down to the salon and see what they have in store for us."

~ * ~

Nicky and his mother were being treated like royalty, which of course they were, but it was unexpected. They were on Earth, not back on Nalo. Here they were just like everyone else. It was true, his ancestors were refugees who had escaped Plantas and landed on Nalo, but that was many generations ago. Now he was nothing more than a former diplomat from Nalo.

"Are you getting acclimated?" Alex asked, breaking into his thoughts.

"I am, but I never expected…"

"You have to realize that the people in this complex are all related to those who came from Plantas. In other words, you are family. I've studied the history of our people and considering what your ancestors went through, it's a miracle you are even here. Add to the fact your mother was a queen on Nalo and you a prince, you're special."

Nicky shook his head. "I've never felt special in my entire life. Back on Nalo I was the spare heir. When my brother took over the monarchy, he was more than ready to have me disappear. Being sent here was his way of getting rid of me. I'd be a little harder to kill than my father."

"What does that mean?"

"My father was a very agile man, even though he was getting older. I've never bought the story of how he tripped on the stairs and hit his head. It didn't make sense then and it still doesn't make sense now. As much as I hate to admit it, I believe my twin brother pushed him down the stairs so he could ascend to the throne sooner rather than later."

"Whew, that's a lot to digest."

"It certainly is. Of course, I can't prove anything, but I know my mother shares my suspicions."

Alex shook his head, as though he could hardly believe what his soon-to-be brother-in-law was telling him. "I almost forgot. My father sent me to get you so you can see what you will be wearing for the wedding."

"I thought I'd wear the tuxedo I bought for state dinners when I was in Washington."

"Hardly. The folks have been planning this wedding ever since Steph first met you. They want it to be special. Back when our people first came here, our ancestor Nina married Rand Jacobson. At that time, it was a traditional wedding. Rand asked her family to plan it without telling her. Imagine her surprise when he came back to Peru from one of his diplomatic missions and he'd planned a secret wedding."

"What does this have to do with what I'm going to wear tomorrow?"

"You wouldn't know, not growing up here, but that first wedding is well documented through photographs and videos that were taken at the time. Your wedding attire is an exact replica of the robe that was worn by Rand on that auspicious day."

Nicky thought about what Alex was telling him. He also thought about his mother saying she'd had something made especially for the wedding. At the time she told him of her plans, he wondered how she would fit in with the modern-day descendants of the refugees from Plantas. Now he realized he should have never questioned her motives.

~ * ~

On the morning of the wedding, Steph and Krissy dressed in the wedding robes that were reminiscent of the pictures she'd seen of the wedding between Nina and Rand.

"Everything is perfect," she said, as her mother fussed with her hair.

"I was afraid you would be disappointed about not wearing a traditional wedding gown like the girls here on Earth wear."

Steph shook her head. "At first, I was, but the history behind these robes is one hundred times better than a traditional Earth wedding dress. I feel like a princess."

"You forget, you will be a princess, once you marry Nicky. His mother is a queen, and if Nicky had been born first, he would have been king."

"Oh, Mother, you seem to forget, Nicky wasn't born first and if he had been, we would have never met."

Her comment brought laughter from not only her mother but from Lia as well.

"You are so right, Steph," Lia said. "Nicky is much happier living here on Earth than he ever was on Nalo. I'm afraid his twin brother has made his life a living hell. To be truthful, I'm just as pleased to be here as he is. I fear his life would have been cut short had he remained on Nalo."

Steph knew what her soon-to-be mother-in-law was alluding to. She and Nicky had often talked about his suspicions regarding his father's untimely death. How could anyone be so cruel as to kill their own father?

~ * ~

Nicky waited nervously for the wedding to begin. Alex stood by his side and would act as his best man. It seemed strange to see his friend dressed in ceremonial robes. He knew Alex would be more comfortable in jeans and a t-shirt or dressed in a suit ready to rock the corporate world.

Even he felt a bit uncomfortable. Over the past almost four years he'd become accustomed to dressing like the men on Earth. After leaving Nalo, he thought he would never be wearing the traditional robes again.

Before he left Nalo, most of the younger generation had adopted the pants and shirts everyone saw while watching the videos and other transmissions for both Earth and Seros.

"Just think, in less than an hour you will be a married man. Will that make my sister a princess?"

"Hardly. I don't even think of myself as a prince or my mother as queen. We are no different than anyone else here on Earth. To be truthful, I'd like to forget that part of my history."

"I thought that would be your answer. You're okay in my book. I know you love my sister and your position with our new company will be the icing on the cake. You don't have to be a prince to satisfy her. Just be who you are."

Music floated into the room where Nicky waited for the wedding to begin. He recognized the song as one that had been played at Miro's mating service. It made him wonder how his mother had arranged that.

"I know the music," he said.

"I'm surprised to hear you say that. It's traditional music from our ancestors who came here from Plantas. I know that's what my folks have told me, but I had my doubts. Now I can see the truth in it."

Together, Nicky and Alex went into the reception hall where the wedding was going to take place. As soon as they entered, the music changed and Krissy walked down the aisle. She was a vision wearing the traditional robe, but nothing could compare to when he saw Steph. She looked like a true princess, or perhaps an angel, like the ones the priests talked about when they spoke of the angels from the One God.

In the future, if anyone asked him what vows he'd spoken, he would be hard pressed to give them an answer. Thankfully, they were vows couples had been saying since the beginning of time. All he knew was once they were spoken, Steph would be his wife for the rest of their lives.

Chapter Twenty-Four

Steph and Nicky were the perfect couple. Within the next five years they were living in their home in the complex, close to where the training center for the chefs who worked in the chain of restaurants were schooled in the perfection of each recipe. They'd also brought two children into the world. Rand was their oldest and named for his great-great grandfather, while Shelly was named for Steph's grandmother on her father's side.

~ * ~

"Can you believe I have been on Earth for twenty-five years?" Lia asked.

Her question came as a surprise to Nicky. "I know how long it has been as that is how long Steph and I have been married. Is there a reason you are bringing this up now?"

"Among my people, the citizens of Nalo, for hundreds of generations, it is well known that when a person is ready to die, they know it is coming. I am telling you this because when I die, I want my ashes returned to Nalo. This is where I was born and where I want my ashes to rest, even though my spirit will be with the One God. Will you promise me that I will be returned to rest with my ancestors and your father?"

"This is something I have not thought of before. I have always considered this our true home. I do understand your request and when the time comes, in the far-off future, I will honor your wishes."

Lia thanked her son profusely and returned to her cottage.

Her request shook him to the core. He had never harbored thoughts of returning to Nalo for any reason whatsoever. Since leaving the diplomatic corps, he maintained little if no communications with his brother. How would he be greeted when he returned with his mother's ashes?

Knowing he had to seek the counsel of his family, he called Rand and Shelly to ask them to come to share the evening meal with their parents. When he told Steph of his invitation, he did not tell her the reason for this family meeting.

By the time everyone was assembled, Nicky was more distressed than when he spoke with his mother.

"I have called you here tonight because I think it is time you know the entire history of our family."

"What are you talking about, Dad?" Rand asked.

"Your mother has always known the entire story, but I had hoped to spare you and your sister from knowing all the details. You know your grandmother, as well as I, came from Nalo. What we have never talked about is what our roles on Nalo were. Your grandmother was the first queen of Nalo who had no blood relations to the refugees from Plantas. Your grandfather loved her more than life itself. When they had their first child, it was twins, my brother Miro and myself. We were both princes, but Miro was the Crown Prince and destined to be king. He also chose a mate from someone without the blood of Plantas flowing through her veins."

"Are you telling us you are royalty?" Shelly asked, her expression one of shock.

"Yes, I am. I suffered greatly because of my relationship to my brother. Since he was the oldest, he was destined to be the King of Nalo. I was little more than the spare heir. I knew I would never achieve the role of king and for that I was thankful. When my father died unexpectedly, Miro ascended to the throne. He was more than happy to send me to Earth as the ambassador from Nalo and I was pleased to no longer be subservient to him.

"When I met your mother, I put everything I left in Nalo behind me. I never wanted to return. Now your grandmother has told me she knows the time is near for her to die. She has asked that I return her ashes to Nalo and I have agreed. I think it is time we all went to Nalo to honor the woman who gave me life and who has been my champion for my entire life."

"Are you saying we will be returning to Nalo and leaving Earth?" Steph questioned.

"I am saying we will be taking a holiday. It will last for about a year and when it is over, we will return to Earth. I have no desire to stay there any longer than is necessary."

"I, too, have had several conversations with your mother. In them she has expressed her regret that Miro has no heir. She is worried what will become of the monarchy. Does this bother you as well?"

Nicky took a deep breath. He hadn't given his brother's plight a lot of thought.

"Does that mean Rand could become king of Nalo?"

"The One God has plans for us all, but I pray he will not allow such a thing to happen. I have no fond memories of growing up, not only in the palace, but also in the shadow of my brother. I have a feeling he has not been the kind of king our father, grandfather and great-grandfather were."

~ * ~

The trip to Nalo came sooner than anyone ever expected it to. On the third morning after Nicky disclosed the past that he'd kept so well hidden, Shelly crossed the compound to take her morning meal with her grandmother. Ever since she'd gone away to college, whenever she was home, she spent her morning with Lia before leaving for her job with the company. While her brother trained to be a chef, like their father, she took more practical business courses while in college. She much preferred the way things ran than in the hands-on experience of cooking.

To her surprise, the cottage was still locked up for the night. Taking the key her grandmother gave her for emergencies, she slipped it into the lock and opened the door. Once inside, she noticed the coffee hadn't been started for the day.

Cautiously, she went through the house, calling her grandmother's name. When she reached the bedroom, she saw her grandmother still in bed. She reached out to wake Lia only to realize her skin was cold to the touch.

Tears rolled down her cheeks. She knew enough about life to realize her grandmother was no longer with them. For the first time, she wished she could telepathically communicate with her family, as her ancestors once did. Instinctively, she reached for her communicator and pushed number two to be immediately connected with her father.

"Shelly, is something wrong?"

Choking back her tears, she finally managed to tell her father what she'd found when she came to the cottage this morning.

"Call your mother and brother. I will be there as soon as I can and will let the rest of the family know what has happened."

Unable to stay in the cottage with the shell of her grandmother's body, Shelly went out to the patio before placing calls to her mother and brother. It seemed like an eternity before everyone arrived at the cottage. Along with her immediate family, her Uncle Alex as well as her Aunt Krissy were soon with her.

She was glad Alex and Krissy were there for her mother. They'd married a year after her parent's wedding and they all remained close.

Her mother was immediately comforted by her brother and sister-in-law. It was Rand who consoled Shelly, while her father was the stalwart one. He took charge of everything, including calling the funeral director in Santa Fe.

~ * ~

The entire community came to pay their last respects to the woman who had come into their midst from the stars.

The hardest part of the grieving process was placing the vision call to Miro.

"I am surprised to hear from you, brother. Are you in need of financial aid from the monarchy?"

Nicky bit back the bitter words he wanted to speak to his brother. "I am doing well on my own, Miro. What I have called for is to inform you that our mother has died. She has requested that I bring her ashes back to Nalo so she can rest there with our father and those of her family."

"I thought she would have come to her senses and leave that backwater planet. Of course, you can bring her ashes back to Nalo for her final rest. Since you are bringing her back where she belongs, will you be bringing your family with you? Mother told me you have a wife and two children."

"They are hardly children anymore. Rand is twenty-four and has joined me in the business as one of our top chefs. Shelly, on the other hand, is twenty-two. She has just graduated from the University of New Mexico and has joined the corporate staff at our headquarters. We have arranged to take a year off from our duties to make the journey to Nalo. I was wondering if you could have the cottage readied for us. It has four bedrooms and will be the perfect place for us to stay."

"Why not utilize one of the apartments in the palace? No one is using them, especially now that Bria has left me."

Nicky was shocked. "When did she leave you?"

"Not long after Mother left for Earth. She lost yet another baby and went back to where she was working when we first met."

"Have you taken another wife?"

"No. I have never divorced her because the priests have told me I will not be free to marry again until she dies. Considering she is healthy as a horse, as you people on Earth like to say, I won't ever be free of her."

Nicky ached for his brother. Not only did he have to go through life with the realization he had no heir to the throne, he was also attached to the wife who no longer loved him. In no way could Nicky understand being in such a situation. He praised the One God that he and Steph had a strong marriage and two beautiful children to carry on his legacy.

~ * ~

It took about a month for the space shuttle from Earth to Nalo to be booked for the entire family. Shelly was excited about making the trip, especially since her Aunt Krissy and Uncle Alex were making the trip with them. They wanted to take their kids with them, but considering both of them were studying abroad for the entire year, it would just be the two of them who would be going.

After taking the flight from Santa Fe to Washington, DC, they waited nervously at the shuttle port for their flight to be called.

"I can't believe we're finally going to go to Nalo," Shelly commented,

"I pray you won't be disappointed. Nalo is very different from Earth. I worry about the state of the planet under the control of my brother."

"You worry far too much Nicky," Alex said. "Your mother and I engaged in many talks and she assured me things at home were going well."

Shelly knew her uncle was trying to put her father at ease, but she also knew what her grandmother had disclosed to her after her father told them about his past. Lia was very concerned about the way her older son was running the planet. Even though this information had come to Shelly only recently, she worried about what they would find once they arrived on Nalo.

To everyone's surprise, the space shuttle that arrived to take them on their journey carried the royal crest of Nalo.

"I can't believe it," Nicky gasped. "Miro sent his personal shuttle to pick us up. The last time I saw this in use was when Mother immigrated here to be with us. Of course, I came on the royal craft when I first arrived as well. This one is much more advanced than what we had back then."

As soon as they boarded the shuttle, the captain greeted them. "It is a pleasure to have you as our guests on this flight to Nalo, Your Royal Highness. Please accept my condolences on the loss of your mother." The man glanced at the urn Nicky carried, containing the last remains of his mother.

Shelly could tell her father was embarrassed by the greeting, and responded to the captain. "Thank you, sir. My father is overwhelmed, as he has not been addressed so formally in many years. I know you will make our flight a pleasurable one even under theses unfortunate conditions."

Once they were assigned to their quarters for the flight, Nicky expressed his gratitude to his daughter. "I think you have taken the wrong path in life. It is evident you are not only my daughter but the great-great-granddaughter of Rand Jacobson. You are a born diplomat."

Shelly blushed at her father's compliment. It wasn't the first time she'd heard such a comment. When she started working for the company, prior to her graduation from the University, her Uncle Alex told her once she graduated, he wanted her to be the head of customer relations because of the way she handled problems that were posed to her.

Maybe they are right. I have a feeling I might enjoy working within the diplomatic corps. It would be a good way for me to utilize some of the courses I took while I was at the University.

~ * ~

The flight from Earth to Nalo was relatively a smooth one. Some of the time warps and wormhole jumps were a bit rocky. Luckily, the discomfort was over within a reasonable amount of time. The speed with which they traversed the universe was surprising. Especially so considering they'd all read in the history books about the length of time and the turbulence their ancestors experienced.

About an hour before they were ready to land, the captain made an announcement telling them to get their personal belongings together.

"Are you nervous about returning to Nalo?" Steph asked.

"I'm not as nervous about returning to Nalo as I am about seeing my brother in almost thirty years. We certainly didn't part on the best of terms. To be truthful, we never enjoyed so much as a friendship. Growing up, he never let me forget that one day he would be king and I would be his subject. From the first day of our life there was no love between the two of us. Had it not been for my grandmother, my childhood would have been extremely lonely."

"I am so sorry to hear this, Dad," Shelly said. "Despite your relationship with your brother, I applaud you for the life you have lived. You were a successful diplomat and an esteemed partner in the family business. You have nothing to worry about. I'm certain you have exceeded your brother in all of your accomplishments."

Nicky leaned across the aisle and gave his daughter a hug. She always knew the correct words to say to settle an uncomfortable situation.

~ * ~

Shelly and Rand were both anxious to see the planet where their father and grandmother grew up, but tactfully allowed their parents, as well as their aunt and uncle, to leave the shuttle ahead of them.

As they watched, a military guard approached them, calling their father "Your Royal Highness." Had they not been given such a greeting, Shelly would have worried for their safety. She'd never heard of any shuttle being greeted by military forces.

As soon as she stepped from the shuttle, an officer approached her. "You must be Her Royal Highness, Princess Shelly."

Turning to Rand, the officer made the same greeting, also calling him by name.

"We have been sent by King Miro to give you a personal escort to the palace. Once there, you will each be assigned your own personal bodyguard."

Shelly knew her expression was one of surprise and it was mirrored on her father's face.

"Is there a problem on Nalo that would warrant personal bodyguards for those in our party?" Nicky asked.

"No, Prince Nicos. It is King Miro's wish that his family be treated with the upmost respect and protection."

Shelly wished she could read her father's thoughts. She too thought it was strange to have a military escort, but perhaps she was used to the freedom she enjoyed on Earth.

Three hovercrafts waited for them once they cleared customs. They were assured their luggage would be delivered to the palace and they were not to concern themselves with it.

Her parents were escorted to the first hovercraft and took off with their bodyguards. Alex and Krissy were in the next craft, leaving Rand and Shelly to take the third. She wondered if they were separated for any particular reason and worried that she might not see the rest of her family again.

If the stories she'd heard from her father about his twin brother were true, it frightened her more than she wanted to admit.

The flight to the palace took only a matter of minutes and once they landed everyone in their party was reunited.

~ * ~

Miro waited in the reception hall to see his twin brother. He knew he would have no problem in recognizing Nicos. Even with the poor quality of the vision calls, they still looked so much alike, one could take the place of the other with no one being the wiser.

The captain of the royal guard announced the arrival of Nicos and his party. Miro was overtaken with emotion at the thought of being once again in the presence of the brother he had teased throughout their growing-up years.

As soon as the visitors entered the reception hall, Miro focused on Nicos. Had he not known they were but only minutes apart in age he would have thought Nicos was much younger. His hair wasn't streaked with the same silver strands in Miro's dark hair. He also didn't carry the worry lines across his forehead and around his eyes.

"Brother," Miro said, coming to greet Nicos with a hug. "I have been so anxious to have you return to Nalo."

"You know I wouldn't have returned had Mother not made me promise to bring her ashes back to rest in her beloved Nalo."

"I understand. Our relationship hasn't been the loving one it should have been. Had I known the trials and tribulations of being king, I would have stepped aside and allowed you to rule in our father's stead."

"As I recall, you always coveted the throne. I am sad to think it was not everything you hoped it would be. That said, it is good to be home. It has been a long journey. I am anxious to get to the cottage and relax before we have any formal engagements. I am hoping tomorrow we can both lay our mother's remains to rest alongside our father."

"Of course. Please allow me to offer you a welcoming luncheon before you go to the cottage. I know the food on the shuttle is far from desirable. I have ordered all of your favorites to be prepared to welcome you home."

Nicos was uneasy about staying at the palace any longer than necessary, but would not dishonor his brother by not accepting his generous invitation.

"Allow me to introduce you to my family. This is my wife, Stephanie, our son Rand, and our daughter Shelly."

Steph and Shelly both curtsied as Lia had shown them many times before her passing. Rand bowed his head slightly and held out his right hand in the acceptable greeting on Earth.

"My brother has, indeed, a handsome son as well as a beautiful mate and daughter."

He bowed slightly at the women and took Rand's hand.

"This is my brother-in-law and sister-in-law, Alex and Krissy Jacobson. Alex and I are partners in the restaurant business that we own."

"Restaurant? Of course, I remember now. Somehow, I expected more from you. I know you were not happy as the ambassador. To be truthful, I thought perhaps you would become homeless and penniless. Had that have been the case, I expected you to come home to Nalo with your tail between your legs."

Miro paused to see if his taunt would bring forth an angry response from his brother. Over the years, he'd found he missed teasing the 'Spare Heir' about anything and everything he knew would rile his younger brother.

"You must know, it wasn't happiness that prompted me to do

something other than work at the embassy. To be truthful, I was bored out of my mind. I thought I would enjoy the diplomatic corps more than I did. One of my loves has always been gourmet cooking, so when Alex suggested the restaurant, I knew it was something I would enjoy. As a trained chef, I now train other chefs. Rand also shares my love of cooking and, when I retire, he will be able to step into my position with Interplanetary Cuisine. It has been a good move for me. As you can see, I hardly have my tail between my legs, nor am I coming home penniless. The restaurant has been a very good investment for all of us."

"You have changed, brother. I remember a time when such a taunt would have ended in a physical altercation between the two of us. I pray the palace chef's offering will be pleasing to your more refined Earthly pallet."

~ * ~

Miro led the way from the reception area to the private dining room where a lavish luncheon waited for them to be seated before they were served.

"I was worried there for a minute," Alex whispered to Nicky. "I thought perhaps your brother planned to have us killed and served up for his dinner."

Under his breath, Nicky laughed. "My brother is a lot of things, but in no way is he a cannibal. When we were growing up, his taunts were a daily thing and usually ended up with me losing my temper. I've finally matured enough to not allow him to get under my skin. It took several severe punishments from my father to get me to understand physical violence would get me nowhere. Thankfully, I was more interested in books and learning than my brother and excelled over him both in school and in the military. I think the final straw to his ego was when I gave up the position of Ambassador."

Their conversation ended when they entered the private dining room. While Nicky was accustomed to the opulence of the room, he knew his family was awed by it. The long table was laid with the gold-trimmed china and tiranium flatware. There were three crystal goblets at each place, one for water, one for wine and the third for an after-dinner cordial.

"This is very impressive," Steph said, complimenting her brother-in-law. "I am certain this will be one luncheon I will remember for the rest of my life."

"Why, thank you, Princess Stephanie," Miro replied.

Nicky knew the title stunned his wife.

"Why would you call me that?"

"Because you are more than my sister-under-the-law. Since you and Nicos are mated, that make you royalty, even if my brother no longer embraces the title to which he was born."

He looked around the table. "It is the same for you, Prince Rand and Princess Shelly. Since I have no heirs, you are second and third in line to ascend to the throne. When I die, perhaps one of you will assume my position and run the planet, as it has been run for several generations by members of our family."

Nicky watched the expressions on the faces of his children. This was something he hadn't thought of before, and now it seemed like an unthinkable thing to even mention, but it was only logical. If his brother were to die, there would be no one to ascend to the throne.

The impact of the statement brought a look of astonishment to Rand's face, but the look on Shelly's face was one of excitement. Was it possible his daughter had aspirations of becoming royalty?

~ * ~

Shelly was in awe of everything in the palace. It exceeded every story her grandmother ever told her about her life as queen of Nalo and living in these luxurious accommodations.

Hearing her uncle call her Princess and indicate she was third in line to rule the planet of Nalo came as a complete shock. Although her father told them he was a prince, she never thought of herself as a princess.

She decided since she was on Nalo, she was going to learn as much about the monarchy as was possible. With the information gleaned from her grandmother, she knew the cottage where they would be staying had one of the most extensive libraries chronicling the history of not only Nalo, but also the refugees who came from Plantas to become the ruling family for the planet.

The foods they were served, while exotic, she recognized from the restaurant they referred to as the family business. It was evident the recipes from Nalo were ones her father learned how to prepare prior to coming to Earth as the official ambassador.

"My compliments to the chef," Nicky said, shattering Shelly's internal ramblings. "It's too bad he has a permanent position here in the palace. I would be tempted to try and recruit him to come to back to Earth with us and open his own restaurant within our chain."

Miro laughed at his brother's proposition. "I'm afraid you wouldn't be able to convince him. You do remember Alb, don't you? He has been the chef here since before our father died. I'm afraid he is too old for such a journey, to say nothing of the challenge of making a new life for himself on a strange planet."

Shelly watched her father intently. She knew he blamed his brother for the death of their father. The mention of King Kratan seemed to hit a raw nerve deep within her father's calm appearance.

~ * ~

"Just how did our mother die?" Miro asked. "I pray she didn't meet with an unfortunate accident in the same way as our father."

Nicky knew his brother's accusation had to do with the way his mention of their father affected him.

"Mother came to me, a few days before her passing, and told me of her wishes to have her remains brought back to Nalo for her final resting place. On the morning after her passing, Shelly went to visit her grandmother. They always ate breakfast together. Recently, Shelly had taken over the cooking, while Mother made the coffee. When Shelly arrived, she knew something was amiss. Thankfully, she had a key to

Mother's house. She let herself in and found Mother had passed peacefully in her sleep. I am certain she knew her time to be among the living was coming to an end. She was ready to be reunited with not only our father but also with those loved ones who have passed over from life to death."

Miro nodded his head, but Nicky could see there was no remorse or sorrow hearing of the way his mother's life came to an end.

"It must be a relief not to have to take care of her any longer."

Before Nicky could answer Miro's hateful comment, Steph found her voice. "I loved your mother as much as I love my mother. They were the best of friends and I couldn't have asked for a better mother-in-law if I'd had to pick her for myself. There was not one individual who ever met her who didn't love her. Lia's death was mourned extensively within our community, as well as by every staff member of Interplanetary Cuisine. To even hint that anyone would have wanted to cause her harm is a gross injustice."

Miro got to his feet and applauded her. "Well said, Stephanie. I am pleased to see my brother has chosen a mate who is his equal in every way. It is no wonder you have been blessed with two such outstanding children. Your presence here on Nalo will be a great boon to our people."

Chapter Twenty-Five

The opulence of the palace was replaced by the simplicity of the cottage, where her father had perfected his skills as a chef, and where her grandmother and great-grandmother had both gone to escape the palace, they'd called home for so many years.

Shelly immediately saw the charm of this cottage. Of course, by Earth standards it would have been called a mansion, having four bedrooms as well as a gourmet kitchen. In comparison to the palace, she could see why her uncle made such negative comments about it.

"How could you leave a place like this, Dad?" she asked. "It's a perfect home."

"Perfect, yes, but leaving was easy because it put me many lightyears away from my twin brother. I've made no secret of the fact we were not the best of friends. It was not of my doing, but Miro was so hungry for power he was pleased to find a way get rid of me."

Shelly nodded. She'd seen the animosity between her father and uncle firsthand during the time they spent at the palace. For two brothers, twins, to be so hostile against one another was something she would never understand.

While the others went off to explore the remainder of the house, Shelly left the group. The library pulled her like a magnet. Here were the books that contained the history of her people. They were not only the history of the planet Nalo, but also that of Plantas.

From her grandmother, she'd learned how many of the volumes of history books had been brought from Plantas by those in the first ship, the only one to land on Nalo.

She found the books she was looking for. They were almost hidden on the upper most shelf of the bookcase, against the north wall of the room. Even with her height of six foot seven, she couldn't reach it and was pleased to find a rolling ladder.

Climbing to the top of the ladder, she pulled one of the old books from its resting place. Although she was certain the house was cleaned on a weekly basis, it was evident no one had touched this book for many years. Dust covered the tops of the pages and made her sneeze.

Once she removed the dust and opened its cover, she was transported back many generations to a planet that no longer existed. The fact she could easily read the words made her bless the ancestors who insisted all descendants of those who came from Plantas should have the translator chip imbedded at birth. From everything she'd learned, the technology to reproduce the chip had been included on every ship that left the doomed planet so long ago.

All her life she'd heard the oral history of her people. In no way could they even begin to compare to the stories written and stored within the pages of the books contained in this library.

It didn't take long for the exhaustion from their trip, as well as the royal reception at the palace to overcome her. With sleep came dreams.

"You are where you belong," her grandmother Lia said.

"I feel at home, but what about my life on Earth, my parents, friends and my brother?"

"They will miss you, but during your stay on Nalo, they will realize this is your destiny."

Another woman entered the dream.

"You are as beautiful as you have appeared in my visions. I am your great-grandmother, Felda. I was the second queen of Nalo. You have royal blood in your veins, even though your father doesn't want to acknowledge it. Read the books in this library and prepare yourself for your destiny."

~ * ~

"Where is Shelly?" Steph asked, once they finished the tour of the house and the grounds.

"She said she didn't want to join us," Nicky replied. "She has such a lust for history, I'm certain she's engrossed in those old books."

"Have you read them?"

"Only because my grandmother insisted that I read them. Miro, on the other hand, was more interested in being with our father and preparing to take over the throne than he was in the history of our people. It's a shame because our grandfather was an astute student of the history of both Nalo and Plantas. I fear we may lose our daughter to the lure of Nalo. She is third in line for the throne and so like both her grandmother and great-grandmother, it frightens me. I'm surprised I didn't realize it until we arrived here. There is something about this planet that is intoxicating."

"Would you want to stay?"

Nicky took her in his arms and kissed her. "I don't know. Even if I have no inclination to ever take the throne, I would consider retiring here. It would all depend on what you want. We could easily retire in Peru, or any other place around the globe where settlements of the refugees from Plantas have been established. Whatever decision we make, it will not be made today. For now, I would like to rest until it is time for dinner."

Steph agreed. She was tired and needed not only rest and nourishment but also time to entertain the proposition her husband just put to her.

~ * ~

Shelly's dream ended, taking her into a deeper sleep. The overstuffed chair afforded her the comfort to slumber peacefully.

Someone touched her arm and she opened her eyes. Beside her stood her grandmother, as well as the great-grandmother she saw in her dream.

"Are you real?" she asked, hardly able to believe her eyes.

"The One God has granted us the ability to appear to you," Felda began. "You need our guidance and assurance that Nalo will be very important in your future."

"How can that be? I have a life on Earth. That is where my friends and family are, and…"

"Yes, you have a life on Earth, but you also have a life here. Your father came to Earth as an ambassador from Nalo. Even though Nalo opened an embassy on Earth, the same hasn't happened here. You have the education to become the liaison needed between the two planets. Consider your options. In reality, you are third in line to become the ruler of Nalo. Miro will not live forever and perhaps it's best if you acclimate yourself to this planet and the needs of the people who depend on the monarchy to help them through their daily lives."

There was another touch to her arm, sending her back into a deeper sleep.

~ * ~

"We were worried about you," Steph said when Shelly joined them for dinner.

"I was so excited to read the books, I couldn't resist going to the library. I did fall asleep though."

Shelly pondered the dream she had as well as the apparitions she saw. It was possible it was yet another dream, but it all seemed so real. Someone had touched her arm, not once but twice.

"It's this house," her father said. "There is so much history here. Are you enjoying the books you found in the library?"

"Very much so. I agree about this house. The library with all the history books it contains is fascinating. While I was there, I fell asleep and had the strangest dreams."

Her father nodded his head in agreement. "Am I correct to say you were dreaming of your grandmother and great-grandmother?"

"How did you know?"

"They both came to me in a dream. They are convinced you have the ability to take over the throne when the time comes."

"I don't know if I'm worthy. I have my education and my position with the company, but I know nothing about diplomacy and running a planet."

"We have only just arrived on Nalo. As planned, we will be here for a year. Take that time and learn everything you can. It is possible you will find something here you cannot find back home."

~ * ~

Nicky ached for his daughter. It was possible she was weighing up all the information. It was also possible she could be the heir to the throne that Miro needed. It was something they would have to talk about.

As thoughts about Miro crossed his mind, he wondered if the One God withheld children from him and Bria because of what Miro did to gain the title of King of Nalo.

The ringing of the bell announcing a visitor broke Nicky's train of thought. He knew he should have answered the door, but he heard Alex greeting whoever it was at the door.

"Your highness, what a pleasure to see you again," Alex said.

Hearing his brother was the visitor who came to the cottage surprised Nicky. If he could believe what his mother told him, Miro never lowered himself to visit her while she lived there.

"Is my brother here?" Miro asked.

"Yes, I am," Nicky said as he walked into the foyer. "To what do we owe for the honor you are bestowing upon us?"

"I thought we needed more time together. We never made plans for the disposition of Mother's ashes. I was also hoping you would be preparing one of your gourmet meals. I gave Alb the night off. After the fabulous meal he prepared for your arrival, I thought he deserved it."

"Well, then, you are in luck. I was just assessing the contents of the pantry and refrigerators. It won't be equal to what Alb prepares, but I have found since going to Earth I have developed simpler tastes."

Nicky saw the questions forming in the eyes of his family. They, like him, were wondering what this surprise visit from the King of Nalo would mean.

"You have a wonderful family, Nicos," Miro commented. "I envy you the love you have found and the children you have fathered."

"What about Bria? I thought you loved her."

"I did, too. She wanted the title of queen as well as all the things my money could provide her with. After losing so many babies, she decided she liked her position at the resort much better than her lot as queen. I have to admit, I was not saddened to see her leave the palace. She was far below me socially as well as…well, I think you know what I mean. She came from a lower class than us and her manners were not well suited for the palace."

Nicky thought he was going to be sick. How could his brother be such a bigot? Bria had been his choice. At the time he'd questioned it, but after seeing her, he understood. She was a very beautiful woman with a figure most women would kill for. Miro always was a sucker for a woman with a big bosom. It was a shame she did not have the intelligence to go along with her beauty.

"I am sorry to hear that she wasn't everything you thought she would be. At this stage in your life, are you looking for another woman to take her place who can give you children?"

"I'm beginning to think the problem with having children lay with me rather than her, since I have heard she has found a new mate and they have a child. They weren't officially able to mate, but it didn't bother her. She got the child that she always wanted and was able to keep the money that comes from the monarchy on a monthly basis. Her recompense for being mated to me for so many years without producing a child."

"Is there a chance the child could have belonged to you.?"

"Hardly. She was gone from the palace for almost a year before she told me of the man she met and the child she was carrying. There was no talk of divorce and that was that. At least she has the one thing I was unable to give her."

While they talked, Nicky made his way to the kitchen in order to begin preparing their dinner. He'd planned on making a lighter fare since they'd eaten such a large luncheon at the palace. Earlier, he'd found some meat and broth in the refrigerator and started simmering a soup made with the broth, meat and several fresh vegetables.

"We are planning to have a light dinner," Nicky said. "With having a large midday meal, I didn't think we needed anything heavy tonight."

Miro patted his ample belly. "I eat too many heavy meals, as you call them. The soup you are preparing smells delicious. It reminds me of the meals our mother made before she became queen."

Nicky nodded. "Speaking of our mother, do you know where we should scatter her ashes?"

"Father's ashes were scattered in Mother's garden. It was where they both seemed to enjoy being whenever they were able to have a few quiet minutes together. I think that would be the ideal place for them to rest eternally."

Chapter Twenty-Six

The entire family gathered in the flower garden. A priest from the church attended the gathering and said the appropriate words to lay the ashes of the former queen to rest.

Shelly loved the pomp and circumstance surrounding the blessing of the soul of her beloved grandmother. She knew the words weren't necessary for her grandmother to rest in peace. Her soul was already with the One God and those who left life before her. How often had she talked about the day when she would again see her beloved Kratan as well as her parents and brother? Now they were together for eternity and were watching over those left behind.

Across the garden, she saw a young man. While he didn't stand with the family, he was, indeed, attending the ceremony. She knew there were several servants from the palace as well as many residents of Capitol City who came to pay their last respects to the woman who had once been their queen.

With the ceremony completed, her father greeted several old friends and palace servants, while her mother, Uncle Alex, Aunt Krissy, and Rand stayed to themselves. She walked through the beautifully manicured garden, taking in its splendor.

"I'm told you are Princess Shelly."

She turned at the words spoken from behind her. To her surprise the young man she saw earlier was standing right behind her.

"I am, but I'm not accustomed to being called 'Princess.' I'm just Shelly, but you have me at a disadvantage. Who are you?"

"I should have introduced myself. I am Zoran and my Aunt Mira was your grandfather's sister. I know we aren't related by blood, but…"

Shelly laughed. "On Earth, I'd say we are kissin' cousins. We're related by circumstances, if not by blood. I'm pleased to meet you, Zoran. On Earth, people would probably shorten your name to Zor. My given name is Michelle, but no one has ever called me that. My parents have called me Shelly all my life."

"Zor? I like it. Would you do me the honor of eating the luncheon with me? As an invited guest, I would much prefer eating with someone my age than being stuck with my parents and those of the older generation."

"I know what you mean. I would like to eat luncheon with you. Perhaps you would like to meet my brother, Rand. We are in the minority on this adventure. We're definitely not interested in the same things my parents and aunt and uncle are."

"I prayed that would be your answer. I'm anxious to meet your brother and be able to show you the things of interest to the younger generation."

Before she could answer, Rand joined them. "Mom sent me to see what you are doing. We are ready to go in for the luncheon."

"I was just thinking the same thing. By the way, this is my new friend, Zor. He's a kissin' cousin of ours. His aunt was our grandfather's sister."

"It's good to meet you," Rand said, holding out his hand. "Does that mean you're associated with the hovercraft factory I've been hearing about?"

"Guilty as charged. I'm the Administrative Vice President. My cousin runs the place and as far as I'm concerned, he can have the headaches that go along with the title. You'll like him. At least you will when you get to meet him. Since my presence isn't always necessary at the plant, I was the one designated to come to today's ceremony to represent the family."

Together they made their way into the formal dining room where many tables were set with the finest linens, crystal, china and tableware Shelly ever saw. Her mother motioned her over to where she and Shelly's father were seated.

"I saw you talking with that nice young man," Steph said. "Will you and your brother be joining us or will you be keeping company with your new friend?"

"Mother, Father, this is Zor. His aunt was Grandfather's sister."

Nicky got to his feet. "My brother pointed you out to me. Your proper name is Zoran, if I'm not mistaken."

"You are right, sir. Princess Shelly says we're kissin' cousins."

Everyone laughed at the ease with which he picked up the slang from the planet Earth.

"There is no need for you to be so formal, Zor," Nicky said. "When I left Nalo, so long ago, I left behind the title of Prince Nicos. My friends call me Nicky."

"Thank you, Nicky. It would please me if you would allow me to share this luncheon with both Shelly and Rand."

Shelly tried hard not to laugh at how formally Zor addressed her father. Of course, on Nalo, he was known to all as Prince Nicos. He deserved the formality his former title afforded him. It was just alien to her. On Earth her father and mother were simply Nicky and Steph. While they were on Nalo, she would have to get used to the title her father was born to.

Although the luncheon they were served right after their arrival was elegant, it couldn't compare to the food Alb prepared for this special day. Some of the dishes were familiar ones her father and brother prepared for the restaurants; others were exotic and totally different from anything she'd ever eaten before.

"I'm impressed with this meal," Zor commented. "I've never been a guest at the palace before. As far as I can remember, King Miro has never hosted an event for the people. I'm told his marriage to Queen Bria was quite the affair, but that was long before I was born,"

"I know very little about my uncle, even though he and my father are identical twins. They've been separated for over thirty years. From what I can see, they have very little in common. As for the title of 'Prince,' it no longer fits him, just like I am unaccustomed to the title of 'Princess'."

Zor laughed at what she said. "I know little about our king. He is a very private person. What I do know is that he doesn't run the planet with the gentle hand his father had. At least, that's what my father says. He longs for the days of your grandfather's reign, but things cannot be changed and must be accepted for what they are."

Although Shelly wondered what Zor meant about her uncle's reign as king, she let the statement drop. She would be on Nalo for a year and that would give her time to come to her own conclusions about the monarchy of Nalo.

~ * ~

Once the invited guests left the palace, Nicky stayed behind to confer with his brother. It was the first time the two of them had been together alone in far too many years.

"I've heard some disturbing things today," Nicky said.

"Disturbing? Who would say such things?"

"It matters not who, Miro. I have heard you are not the beloved king our father was. People say you rule with an iron hand and do not have the respect of your subjects. It saddens me because those of our family who ruled before have always had the love of the people. What have you done to lose that love and trust?"

"You don't know how stiff-necked these people are. I have had to increase taxes and..."

"And nothing, Miro. Taxing the people is not the answer. Our father ran this planet without alienating the people. I have a feeling if I were to look into your finances, I would see you are getting rich off those who once loved our father. You cannot take your riches with you when you die. What good will it do you if you are not held in high esteem by your subjects?"

"You don't know what I had to endure to take the throne."

"I know more than you think I do. Mother and I have both voiced suspicions that Father's death was not the accident it was thought to be. He was not a feeble old man who was unable to maneuver the stairs of the palace. I would not accuse you publicly, but you have always been hungry for the prestige and honor of being the King of Nalo."

Nicky watched his brother's expression as he heard the accusation that had laid dormant for almost thirty years.

"I-I…"

"You don't have to admit it or deny it for my sake. I have my own opinions and you have your version of what you perceive as the truth. For appearances, this will not be discussed again during our stay. As far as anyone on Nalo is concerned, we are pleased to be in each other's company after so many years. I thank you for the ceremony and reception you have provided for our mother today. If you need me for anything, you know where you can find me."

Nicky turned and left his brother alone in the throne room. In his opinion, this room belonged to his father, not the brother who committed a cardinal sin to gain power.

~ * ~

"What the hell happened after we left, Nicky?" Alex asked as soon as Nicky arrived at the cottage.

"I don't think you want to know. I actually accused my brother of murdering my father. I didn't use those words, but I made myself perfectly clear. He neither confirmed nor denied the accusations. He didn't have to. I could tell the truth by the look on his face. He was horrified to think the secret he's been keeping is no secret whatsoever."

"Do you think you are safe to remain here? I know we were planning to stay for a year, but do you not fear for your life?"

Nicky laughed. "You don't know my brother as well as I do. If any harm were to come to me, we would not be the only ones to question it. By hurting me, he would be hurting the other half of him. We may not be close, but we were formed from one egg that split in two. I still have friends on Nalo. Many of them have already contacted me in the hopes I have come back to take the throne from my brother. It is the last thing I want, but there are only three heirs to the throne. I am first in line, followed by Rand and Shelly. Miro knows this as well as I do. He needs an heir, and if I'm not mistaken, I know who it will be."

"Who?" Alex questioned.

"You know I have no desire to rule, and neither does Rand, but Shelly is another thing altogether. She has the intelligence and the people skills to handle the job. She doesn't think she does, but by the time we are ready to return to Earth, she will come to the same conclusion. I plan to ask my brother to open an embassy from Earth to Nalo and put her in charge. She is like your ancestor, Rand Jacobson. She is a born leader and the sooner she realizes it, the better off we will all be."

Chapter Twenty-Seven

Zor and Shelly spent almost every day together. When he was working, she explored on her own, but the evenings belonged to the two of them. They went to many gourmet restaurants and clubs where the young people of Nalo gathered to socialize.

Little by little, she was falling in love with Nalo. This was where she wanted to live and work. She and her father spoke several times about her becoming an ambassador. They even contacted the head of Earth's government about allowing it to happen.

The government informed them that, although there had been an ambassador from Nalo on Earth for many years, King Miro had never requested for a delegation to be sent from Earth to Nalo.

"I don't understand this at all," Shelly said. "If Nalo maintains an embassy on Earth why isn't it the same in reverse?"

"My father was working on inviting an ambassador when he died. From what I have learned about my brother's reign here on Nalo, I can understand why the embassy hasn't materialized. At this point, I think he's afraid of dying without an heir. He's even been receptive to the idea of you taking on the position."

"How do you know I can handle this? I haven't had the schooling."

"You have and you don't even realize it. You are much better educated than I was at the time when I became Nalo's Ambassador to Earth. You have the people skills your uncle doesn't have. He can learn a lot from you. As much as it galls me, I have had many meetings with him about this. I think it's time for the two of us to go to him together and learn what he is thinking."

"What about when you all go back to Earth?"

"We've been talking about that. Your mother and I, as well as your aunt and uncle, are at the age where we can retire. We're considering retiring to Nalo. This was my home, and your mother is falling in love with this planet as well. Your brother is also considering staying here. He's made some friends and has been propositioned by one of the high-class restaurants to come to work for them as their head chef."

Shelly was surprised. She'd been so involved in her relationship with Zor, she hadn't given any thoughts to the plans her family was making.

"What about the company?"

"The company is doing very well without us. We are receiving transfers of our profits on a regular basis. As for Alex and Krissy's children, their daughter is working in the province of China with her husband and their son has relocated to Seros to study medicine. In other words, we are all free to follow our own paths. You know I would help you as much as I can, but I doubt you will need my assistance."

Shelly embraced her father. "I've also been considering staying, not just because of the position of Ambassador, but also because of my relationship with Zor. I know you didn't ever think you'd hear me say this, but I have feelings for him. He, too, has ties to those who came from Plantas. When I told him of all the history books I have been reading, he said he took many history courses both in secondary school and university. We seem to be very well matched."

"I have also researched Zor's background. His family is highly respected on Nalo. If you are saying this man could be well suited to be your life mate, I will tell you I would willingly give you my blessing."

~ * ~

The next morning, they arranged a meeting with Miro. Even though Nicky and Shelly arrived on time, they waited for another hour for Miro to join them.

"I'm sorry to have kept you waiting. Something unavoidable came up. Surely you remember when those things happened with Father, Nicos."

Nicky nodded, even though he knew those times were when his parents were in an argument and official duties were temporarily forgotten. He wondered, without a wife, what could have detained his brother. If he wasn't mistaken it was that, perhaps, he'd been engaged with a hired companion. During their youth, he'd always had an interest in the women who sold their bodies. Many times, their father had preached about the sin of having sexual relations with anyone but their life mates. Knowing his brother as well as he did, Nicky knew he hadn't come to the mating bed with no experience. It was also possible Bria was not a virgin when they were mated.

"We know you are a very busy man, Uncle Miro. I am pleased you have been able to take the time to give us an audience. We have been giving a lot of thought to requesting an ambassador to be sent from Earth."

"As am I," Miro replied. "Your father and I have had many conversations about this and we are both wondering if you would be interested in taking on the position."

Shelly nodded. "My father and I spoke of this last night. Since my family has decided to immigrate to Nalo and I have found someone who is special to me, I think it would be best if the ambassador from Earth does not have any such inclinations. I would be honored to take on a position, much like the one my mother held at Nalo's embassy on Earth. I have neither the experience nor the education to take on any other position."

"My daughter is a wise woman," Nicky commented. "I offered her the position and even though I think she is very qualified, I understand her reasoning. Since we will soon be becoming citizens of Nalo, it would be a conflict of interests for her to represent a planet where she is no longer a citizen. With her in the position her mother held when I was the ambassador to Earth, she will be invaluable, not only to the ambassador, but also to you."

Although Nicky and Miro had spoken about the members of

Nicky's family becoming citizens of Nalo, it seemed as though Miro as surprised by what he just heard.

"You make sense. Do you think Earth will be willing to send a suitable Ambassador?"

"You know they have been pushing for this ever since Father set up the embassy on Earth. Considering the amount of time that it will take for the ambassador to get here, it will give you enough time to build the embassy here in Capitol City."

Nicky could almost read his brother's thoughts on what they proposed. For far too many years, Miro had ruled the planet of Nalo as an individual entity when there were so many other planets within the galaxy who would be suitable allies. Hopefully, he could convince his brother to open talks with their counterparts on Seros as well as on Earth.

~ * ~

Shelly was relieved when the tense meeting with her father and uncle was over. By the time they left, she had been given the assignment to find a perfect place within Capitol City for where the Earth Embassy should be built.

Although Miro invited her to take the midday meal with him, she declined, as she had made plans with Zor for the remainder of the day.

"How did the meeting with King Miro go?" Zor asked, once they were seated in one of the small restaurants.

"Better than I expected. I have so much to tell you, I hardly know where to start."

"How about starting at the beginning? We have all afternoon, since I was able to take the rest of the day off."

Shelly relaxed and began by telling Zor about how both her father and uncle thought she should be the ambassador from Earth.

"I think that sounds like a wonderful idea."

"Well, I don't. I pointed out that since I was planning to immigrate to Nalo permanently, it would be a conflict of interests. I did say I would be open to working for the embassy much in the same capacity as my mother worked for the Nalo embassy on Earth when she met my father. They both agreed with me and I've been assigned to find a suitable location for the building of the Earth embassy here in Capitol City."

"I think I could be of help to you on that one," Zor commented. "When we finish eating, I will take you to the property that was purchased by the crown long before King Miro took the throne for the building of Earth's embassy."

Shelly was shocked. "Do you mean there is a property already purchased for this purpose?"

"My father told me all about it. His aunt was the sister of King Kratan. She told us how her brother bought the property when he sat up the embassy for the ambassador from Earth. He was very excited about building Earth's embassy but his tragic death brought an end to everything he planned. Nothing was ever built on that land. It should be pleasing to King Miro that he doesn't have to purchase the property."

She thought about what her father told her, of his suspicions about the death of her grandfather. Even her grandmother questioned 'the accident' that took her husband's life. Having met her uncle, she knew their accusations could be accurate but would never be investigated.

~ * ~

Nicky reluctantly agreed to take the midday meal with his brother. It would do no good to antagonize Miro when he had finally agreed to establish an embassy for an ambassador from Earth. Although he was surprised by his daughter's rejection of the offer to fill that position, he knew her decision was a wise one.

It was only a matter of time before she and Zor became more than just friends, and when that happened, the position of Ambassador would be put in jeopardy. It had been the same between himself and Steph. There had been no way he could have made her his wife while representing Nalo as their ambassador to Earth. It would be the same with Shelly and Zor.

When Nicky returned to the cottage, he was surprised to see both Rand and Alex waiting for him.

"What happened when you met with Uncle Miro?" Rand asked. "Was he receptive to the idea of all of us immigrating to Nalo?"

"I'm pleased to say he was. Technically, only your mother and aunt and uncle will be immigrating. You, Shelly and I hold a dual citizenship. Since this is my home planet, we will be welcomed. As for the others, how could he say no, without looking like the jerk he is?"

"Well, that's a relief," Alex said. "Krissy and I were worried about whether or not we would be welcome to stay here. Since that doesn't seem to be a problem, we have something we want to talk to you about."

Nicky wondered what Alex was talking about. Surely, he wasn't going to tell him that he was planning to return to Earth. Such a decision would be upsetting, not only to himself but also to Steph.

"What do you mean?"

"If we're going to stay here, what's to stop us from opening a restaurant here in Capitol City? Rand and I met with the restaurant owner who wants to hire him as a chef. When we told him about our operation on Earth, he said he would be interested in opening another restaurant as a franchise and hiring Rand as the head chef. Until all the paperwork can be worked out, Rand will be working in his restaurant. What do you think? We're not too old to open a branch headquarters here on Nalo, are we?"

Nicky was astonished by the suggestion Alex just made. "I think the two of you are gluttons for punishment. I thought we were retiring, resting on our laurels."

"That was the original plan, but think of the possibilities. By opening a franchise of Interplanetary Cuisine, we would truly be interplanetary. Once we're established here, we could put our feelers to restaurants on Seros. It's not like we don't have connections there."

"I haven't seen you this excited about anything since we first talked about establishing the original restaurants all those years ago. I think it's an excellent idea. We have the expertise in management, and we know that Rand is a top chef. With all of our credentials, how could this fail?"

"What about Shelly, would she be able to join us?" Rand asked.

"That's something else we have to talk about. Miro wanted her to be the ambassador from Earth, but she declined the offer. She will be working in the same capacity as your mother did when I first came to Earth. She's having lunch with Zor and breaking the news to him. She's hoping he will help her find a suitable location for the embassy to be built."

"I don't see any problem with that," Alex said. "We shouldn't have any problem in recruiting Steph and Krissy to join us in this new venture. It will be just like when we first started out. Even though we're at an age to retire, we can do this."

Epilogue

Time flies and things change. I can't believe we've been on Nalo for over ten years. Within two years of settling here, my father, Nicky, and Uncle Alex, along with my brother, Rand, opened not one but four franchise restaurants to complement the many more of them on Earth.

I worked with the ambassador from Earth for four years before everything completely changed in my life.

Zor and I were married, or mated as they say on Nalo, within a year of my arrival on the planet.

Although he was comfortable with my position, once we had our first child, a daughter named Lia, for my grandmother, we decided it was best if I stayed at home and was a mother to her. Two years later we welcomed our son, Harden, named for Zor's grandfather,

I enjoyed my time as a stay-at-home mom, but then politics invaded our lives. My Uncle Miro experienced a massive heart attack and died. It happened while he was asleep and he wasn't found until the following morning.

It was something we had anticipated, but not for many years in the future. With the monarchy in jeopardy, Zor insisted I should take my rightful place as Queen of Nalo. Considering my experience working in the embassy, I felt I was obligated.

At the time, my father offered me any help I would need in my new capacity and, believe me, I needed all the help I could get.

Taking control of the throne changed so much, not only for me but for Nalo. In the years before his death, I learned Uncle Miro was not the most beloved ruler ever to sit on the throne. Many of his edicts were changed as soon as I was crowned queen.

Although this was something I never thought would happen, I soon learned what it meant to rule the planet fairly. With Zor by my side as king, we made sweeping changes to the monarchy, including reforms to the civil rights programs and upgrades to the medical care afforded to all of our subjects.

Another change that happened was that my cousin Phillip immigrated to Nalo, once he finished his studies on Seros. He became one of my most trusted advisors and head of the healthcare department of the government. With his advanced schooling, he was the logical choice. Luckily, even the more experienced physicians valued his opinion. Considering his training at one of the top medical facilities in the galaxy, it was only logical.

I also opened an embassy for the ambassador from Seros and sent an ambassador to that planet.

All in all, Nalo has become a member of the coalition with Seros and Earth and the future of our planet as well as our people looks brighter than it has since my great grandfather and grandfather ruled as king of Nalo.

About the Author

At the age of fifteen, Sherry Derr-Wille walked into her sophomore English class and fell in love with writing. Her teacher, Earl Brockman, 'The Duke of Earl,' announced that anyone getting an A on the first test could sit in the back of the room and write. Since no one ever told her to stop, she continued to write for over forty years before becoming published in 2003.

Married to her high school sweetheart, Bob, for over fifty years, she calls him a saint for putting up with a crazy writer. Together they raised three children, have nine grandchildren and five great-granddaughters.

Born a country girl, she loves living in a mid-sized city close to the Illinois border with Wisconsin. Being retired gives her time to follow her heart writing along with editing for several private clients and three publishers.

Chapter One

Callie Appleman watched as the last of her belongings were loaded into the U-Haul truck. The house where she'd grown up with her grandparents after her mother was killed in a car accident had sold in less than a week and now, she was embarking on a new adventure.

Like her mother, she was eighteen when she got pregnant with her daughter, Lanie. Also, like her own father, the guy who should have been Lanie's father had disappeared before her birth.

Callie's mother, Karen, finished high school and attended the local vocational school to become an administrative assistant. The wedding plans were in motion when Brent Martin announced he didn't want to go through with the wedding. His parents wanted him to do more with his life than get married at an early age. They moved him out of state, never to be heard of again.

At a time when Karen should have been the happiest, she was devastated, but her parents, Joe and Anna Mae Appleman, told her not to worry about the future. They would support her decisions and help her raise her child.

Callie had been born two weeks early but was extremely healthy. Never in her life had she wished for a two-parent home. She loved her Nana and Poppy. They loved her in return. Even when her mother was killed in a senseless car accident, her grandparents kept her home life on an even keel.

It had been the night of her senior prom when she and her steady boyfriend got carried away and soon learned that in nine months, they would be parents. Like the mysterious Brent, who Callie had never met, Tim Austin announced he wasn't going to be tied down with a wife and a child. He'd been accepted at MIT in Boston and had no intention of playing daddy to some kid who might or might not be his.

Again, Nana and Poppy Appleman stepped up to the plate. They insisted Callie should go to college, even though it would be delayed by a year.

Lanie was born on a cold February night, full term and with the lungs to prove it. The following September, Callie began her studies to become a nurse. It took five years of hard work, but at last she became an RN and was hired at the local hospital. If she thought she was done with studies, her immediate supervisor had different ideas. She encouraged Callie to take night courses in order to one day become a director of nursing.

Even though working days and studying nights was grueling, her grandparents encouraged her every step of the way. It took about two years, but at last the work was done. Callie knew there would be no position waiting for her, but it didn't matter. For the first time since getting pregnant, she was self-supporting.

When she mentioned moving out, it was Poppy who insisted she stay with them and save her money. Her quest for independence was put on the back burner when she came home to find Nana lying on the kitchen floor. The nurse in her took over as she tried to find a pulse. It was soon evident Nana was gone. How could that be? How could she have died alone?

Moments later, Poppy came home from playing Bingo at the Elks Club to the horrific scene of death. From that day on, Callie could see Poppy's health slowly deteriorating.

A year after Nana's passing, Poppy met Callie at the door when she came home from work. Lanie was playing with her friends next door, so they were entirely alone.

"Callie girl, you know I love you and Lanie more than anything else in this world," he began. "It's been a year since your nana went to be with our Lord. I've made all the arrangements and paid for everything for my funeral. I don't want you to be sad. I'm ready to be with my beloved Anna Mae."

Tears flowed down Callie's cheeks at the prospect of not having Poppy in her life anymore. "I know what you're saying, but I will miss you terribly."

"You know, Nana and I will never be far away from you. Our spirits will always be with you. What I want to talk about today is what will happen once I join her. This house is ours free and clear. Several months ago, I put your name on the deed. When the time comes, I want you to sell this old barn and move out of this town. This place is a bear to heat in the winter and without air conditioning it's like a sweat lodge in the summer. As for getting out of Minter, you know what it's like in this small town. Lanie's grandparents on her father's side live just three blocks away and never make an effort to see her. Everyone here knows about your past, present and future. It's time to put your education to use and start a new life. Between what we insisted you save and what you will get for this house, even if you don't have a job right away, you'll be okay."

~ * ~

Callie brought her mind back to the present. She'd kept only a few pieces of her grandparent's furnishings. The rest had been either sold at the estate sale or taken to the local consignment store.

Yesterday she'd signed the papers for the closing on the house and she knew as soon as she pulled away today new people would be living in her childhood home. They told her of the big plans they had for the house. They were going to put in a completely new HVAC system and redecorate the five upstairs bedrooms. They were planning to turn the old Victorian house into a bed and breakfast.

"Oh Callie, I'm so glad we got here before you left."

Callie turned to see Phil and Lillian Austin coming toward her. In the nine years since Lanie's birth they'd come to see her only two times. The first had been on the day she was born and the second was at Lanie's christening.

"You just caught me. My friends, Steven and Marcie Olson, are getting ready to leave with the U-Haul. Lanie and I will be following."

To her surprise, Lanie took one look at her paternal grandparents and turned away, getting into Callie's car.

"Why did she turn away from us?" Lillian asked.

"Why do you think? She knows who you are, but you haven't been in her life. I honestly don't know why you are here now."

"You're being harsh," Phil said. "You know she's our granddaughter and…"

"And nothing. Tim said it all when he walked out on us before Lanie was born. From what I hear, he's doing very well working in the Twin Cities. Never once in the last nine years has he ever sent one cent for Lanie's support."

"That's what we want to talk to you about," Lillian said. "Ever since she was born, we've been putting aside money for her education. There is a sizable amount in the account. We've had a cashier's check made out to you so you can put the money into an account wherever it is you're headed. All we ask is when you're settled, you will let us know where you've deposited the money so we can continue to contribute to it."

Callie didn't know how to reply. These people hadn't seemed to be interested in her daughter and now they were telling her how they'd been putting aside money for her education.

"Thank you. Are you doing this for Tim's other kids?"

"There's no need. We are in their lives and Tim has already started college funds for them. It's not right that he won't acknowledge Lanie. From everything we've seen and heard, she's a fantastic child. We were wrong not to be in her life. Now we don't even know where you're moving."

Callie softened a bit. "I'd rather not tell you where we will be. What I can say is that I've been offered the position of Director of Nursing at a good hospital. To be truthful, I don't have a place to live, but Lanie and I will be able to stay at a motel until we find something we want to buy."

She felt a bit guilty about not telling Tim's parents exactly where she was going. For some reason she didn't want the good people of

Minter, Wisconsin to be able to easily find her.

"How are you going to get along without your grandparents there to take care of Lanie while you work?"

Callie wanted the conversation to end. What did they care? They hadn't been concerned until now, when she and Lanie were going to be moving halfway across the country. "The hospital has a wonderful daycare program for the kids of their employees. Of course, she will be in school during the day and the end of her day will coincide with the end of mine. We'll be just fine. As a matter of fact, Lanie is looking forward to moving. Over the past year she's been bullied because she doesn't have a father like all of the other kids in her class. It was good of you to come and see us off and when I have established an account for this check, I will let you know the account number. If you want to continue contributing that will be appreciated, but don't feel obligated, since we will be so far away."

The expressions on Phil and Lillian's faces told her they were relieved not to have to think about the grandchild they didn't want to acknowledge. The money they put away for Lanie's education was more guilt money than anything else.

She turned her back on the Austins and got into the car. They lived three blocks away and hadn't made any move to get to know their granddaughter until the day they were set to leave for Arizona.

"Why are you crying, Mom?" Lanie asked as they pulled away from the house that had been their home for all of their lives.

"It's hard to leave."

"I don't think that's the reason," Lanie said, sounding wise beyond her nine years of age. "It's because of the Austins, isn't it?"

"What to do you know about them?"

"Jenny Marsden told me her mother said their son, Tim, is my dad. She also said they were embarrassed to have me as their granddaughter, because…"

"Because what?" Callie asked.

"I don't want to say it but it was because you were both so young when you got pregnant. She said it was your fault I didn't have a dad. I told her it was his fault. If he wanted nothing to do with me, then I wanted nothing to do with him. That shut her up, but it didn't stop the other kids from calling you and me nasty names."

Callie ached for her daughter. She knew what the names were; she'd been called a bastard all through school and a slut when she got pregnant with Lanie. Poppy was right, she needed to get out of this town and away from all the people who thought they knew things they shouldn't.

"That's not going to happen again after today. Once we get to Arizona, no one will know anything about our past. The only thing they will know is what we are now and what we will be in the future. Never think you are anything but a cherished daughter and granddaughter. The Austins told me they've been putting money away for your education. I took it for you, even knowing it was guilt money. They promised once I have an account established for you, they will continue to contribute to it. Never feel bad about taking it. If they are willing to finance your education, take it and be grateful to them. When we get to Arizona, I think it would be nice to write them a thank-you note, if for no other reason than to show them you are grateful and know the proper way to do things."

"I will, Mom. Do you think I'll ever meet my dad?"

Callie's tears flowed harder. "I doubt it. He's been back to Minter many times since you were born and I've never heard a word from him. I only heard he was in town from others. He's a very shallow man and we're better off starting our new life without him. If he should ever take the first step, I know you will welcome him into your life and I won't stop you."

Lanie now wiped tears from her eyes. Callie knew she wanted a father in her life, but after the first year of no response from Tim, Callie decided to make the best life possible for her daughter, just like her grandparents did for her.

Other Books by the Author
at
Rogue Phoenix Press

The Return of the Ancients

Nina is devastated when she realizes she must leave Plantas along with the man who is to become her mate, Ragnar, and her best friend, Tarena. When Nina arrives on Earth in Peru at the Nazca plains, she is greeted by a young archaeology student, Rand Jacobson. Even though she is attracted to Rand, she is still grieving the loss of Ragnar.

Ragnar is surprised when, after being greeted as a god on the planet Seros, the military opens fire on his family. After being taken prisoner, he is treated like a lab rat until a scientist, Geni, comes to his rescue. At her estate, he learns the physicians who work with her have saved the lives of his family and friends.

You Again

While attending college at the University of Wisconsin in the 1960s, Carole Martinson fell in love and eloped with Phillip Vanderlin. When his parents realized she was a farmer's daughter and below them socially, they insisted they divorce.

Fast forward to 2019 and Carole is invited to a wedding cruise financed by her granddaughter's fiancé's grandfather. With no knowledge about the groom's family, Carole flies to Florida for the cruise she and her second husband never got to take. Upon her arrival, she immediately recognizes Phillip.

Phillip never forgot his first love. He is thrilled when he realizes the grandmother is the girl he was forced to leave behind so many years ago.

www.ingramcontent.com/pod-product-compliance
Lightning Source LLC
Chambersburg PA
CBHW071501170626
46811CB00007B/2659